The Promise of Ashwood

Isabella March

Contents

Prologue

Ashwood, Hertfordshire, 1794

Eleven-year-old Grace Denham winced as she heard the floorboard creak beneath her foot as she crept down the dimly lit wing of Ashwood House. It was one wing of many, and Grace prayed that the red rug muffled some of the sound.

"Adam!" Grace hissed out into the corridor. "Come out!" she demanded. "This is far from amusing!"

Grace continued to venture down the corridor carefully, holding her breath as she took every step and preparing herself for the sound of footsteps, moving with purpose to scold her for being somewhere that she was not permitted.

Grace felt as though the eyes of the Beresford family portraits that hung on the walls were following her, knowing that she was somewhere that she was not supposed to be. Oh dear, she was going to be in such trouble.

"Adam!" Grace stressed again. This was all his fault. Grace had wanted to stay in the kitchen; after all, that was where she was allowed to be. But Adam had managed to persuade her to venture upstairs to the wing that housed the Beresfords' bedrooms.

It frightened her to think that each one of the ten-foot doorways that she crept past could have been the Duchess' bedroom.

Grace's hips were suddenly seized in a pinching grip, and Grace fell backwards against a taller figure, who promptly burst out laughing as Grace yelped in fright.

Grace wriggled out of his embrace and turned on him, looking up into the hazel eyes of her friend, thirteen-year-old Adam Beresford. He had large eyes that always seemed so bright with happiness, and the remains of his youthful chubby cheeks swelled when he smiled, or deviously grinned. A lone sandy curl fell into his eyes and he shook it away.

"I am dreadfully sorry," he lied, looking down on her, "but you are far too easy to tease." Adam had grown about six inches over the summer, and now stood a head and a half over Grace.

"It is always you who teases me. I wonder why I put up with it," Grace huffed. "One of these days it will be me who manages to frighten you!" Grace declared with determination.

Adam's face, which had been round with his smile, suddenly fell, and Grace realised exactly why. The moment the words had left her lips, she knew that they were sharing the same thought.

"I wish I did not have to leave you," he whispered quietly.

Adam's mother and father had announced only a few weeks ago that Adam was to leave Ashwood that very September to attend Eton College. He was thirteen now, and his parents were determined that Adam begin his proper education befitting of a young man of his station.

"I want to go to our school," hissed Adam impatiently.

Their school was simply the village school, taught by the vicar in a classroom adjacent to the church. Adam, and his two younger siblings, Jack and Susanna, both attended.

Adam's father insisted that his children be socialised. His mother, on the other hand, wanted a governess for them. Adam detested the idea and loved going to school in the village.

The school was where he and Grace had met several years ago, and they had been the closest of friends ever since.

In fact, Grace could not recall a day in the past few years in which she had not seen Adam. They were inseparable, almost.

"Adam, you cannot go to school here," Grace said regretfully.

"Why not? You are," Adam pointed out.

"It's a village school, silly, and I am a village girl," Grace countered. "Mama says boys like you go to school faraway to become gentlemen."

Adam hissed exasperatedly. "That's what my mama says, too. I need to become a gentleman," he said distastefully. "I need to give up my childish ways and grow up." He spat a raspberry. "What exactly about me is childish?"

Grace giggled. "Blowing raspberries for a start," she teased.

Adam smirked. "I still wish I did not have to go," he said again, the sadness in his voice ever increasing. "Mama won't even let me come back on holidays. She says gentlemen holiday in London."

Grace had not realised that. She had thought he might be back at Christmas, that they might only be parted for a few months before he returned from school. "What?" she gasped. "What do you mean you aren't coming home for holidays?"

Adam's expression grew more sour. "I begged her, I promise I begged her," he swore angrily. "I don't know what it is that she hates about me being here, but she is determined for me to be away from here until I become a gentleman and get married." He shuddered.

Adam and Grace suddenly turned when they both heard nearing footsteps and hushed voices echo down the long corridor. Grace gasped, and Adam thought quickly as he grabbed Grace's hand and dragged her behind one of the thick, red velvet drapes.

The drapes were still drawn, this wing of the house having not yet been opened, and so Adam and Grace were concealed in the little window space. They could have easily sat up on the window ledge, but Adam hugged Grace tightly, not leaving even an inch between them. Grace huddled into his chest, closing her eyes and praying that if it was Adam's mother approaching, that she did not discover Grace in a place where she was explicitly not allowed.

"I cannot believe this, Cecily," hissed Peregrine Beresford, the Duke of Ashwood, and Adam's father. "You want to give up this house? My family's home?"

"Of course not, Perry," snapped Duchess Cecily Beresford, Adam's ever so elegant mother.

Grace had never heard the Duke and Duchess of Ashwood referred to as anything but. It seemed so strange to hear their Christian names. Grace was not at all certain that she had been aware of them before today.

"I merely want to shut the house for a few years and relocate to the London house. Don't you think it would be better for the children?" she urged. "The culture, the society in London is simply far greater than what we have at our doorstep in Ashwood."

Grace felt Adam stiffen as they listened.

Much to her panic, the duke and duchess seemed to pause near them as their quarrel grew.

"I agreed to send the boy away," huffed Peregrine. "I know he needs his education, and God knows that boy needs to grow up ... but I don't like London, and I never have."

"Perry, this is not about you," Cecily said condescendingly. "This is about the children. Who are our immediate connections in this village? The closest friends I would ever consider inviting to dine with us are thirty miles away." Cecily sighed exasperatedly. "If you need an example of what exactly an Ashwood connection is like then you need look no further than little Grace Denham."

Grace's eyes snapped open as she heard her name, and once again she felt Adam grow tense.

"The boy can have friends," Peregrine sneered.

"Oh, come now, Perry. Surely you are not so dense!" growled Cecily. "I put up with his little friend when they were young. It was ... sweet even. But he is not a child anymore, and neither will she be in a short while," Cecily retorted. "One only has to see how Adam dotes upon her. She has her hooks in Adam already!"

Peregrine laughed. "She is but a child!"

"She is a pretty-ish sort of girl who will no doubt grow up into a pretty-ish sort of woman, and her acquaintance with Adam will only become more dangerous. He is headstrong and stubborn as it is. He will not think twice about his responsibilities with Grace under his nose and filling his head with thoughts of her all the time!"

Their argument was quickly becoming too much for Grace to understand. She didn't know what they were talking about. She had no idea what it was to have her hooks in something. She did not even own a fishing line! But what she could tell from their tone was that the duchess disliked Grace immensely, but then Grace's own mother had been telling her that for years.

Adam's hold on Grace did not loosen one bit as they listened to his parents argue.

"Oh, really, Cecily," the duke complained condescendingly. "I really do think you are overstating it a little bit. Adam is still young, and he does not understand the way of things yet. He will learn, and when he does, we will ensure that he is married to the right sort of lady."

Cecily sucked in a sharp breath. "And I agree," she said stiffly. "He does need to learn what is expected of him, but I guarantee that no suitable bride will make her way here while he is still besotted with that girl. We need to sever this connection, and the time is now. He is young enough to forget her, Peregrine."

Their words kept flying over Grace's head as she continued to struggle to understand what they were saying. Now his mother was complaining about Adam, it seemed. But why? Adam was the kindest, sweetest, albeit terribly playful, boy she had ever known. What complaint could she possibly have?

The duke sighed, resigning now. "And you would have us all go?" he asked her. "Jack and Susanna also?"

"Yes," confirmed Cecily. "Jack shall have a tutor and Susanna shall have a governess, and Jack will join Adam at Eton when he is old enough. Susanna shall be finished ..."

"Susanna is only seven," Peregrine remarked. "You want to be in London that long?"

"Peregrine," Cecily attempted tenderly. "When we return here, our sons shall be gentlemen, and our daughter shall be a finished lady. They will be prizes for any noble family." Chuckling, she added, "And Grace Denham will be married to a ... a butcher or someone, and Adam will never trouble himself with thoughts of her again."

"If I am to have any peace, make the arrangements," Peregrine finally agreed.

Grace heard them part, the duke walking one way, and the duchess the other. Both she and Adam stood motionless until they could not hear the sounds of footsteps anymore.

Adam's grip loosened, but he did not release Grace, only giving her room enough to look up at him. She saw an unfamiliar intensity in her eyes. He looked angry and upset, and it hurt her to see him this way.

"I didn't understand what they were saying," whispered Grace, "but I did hear that they do not like me." Not that the revelation was a surprise.

"I hate my mother," hissed Adam.

"Don't say that!" scolded Grace. "It is a sin to disrespect your parents."

"I don't care," snapped Adam. "What she said was horrid and I do not forgive her for it." He exhaled sharply. "She thinks I could forget you! Bah!" he sneered. "I could never forget you," he said with determination, his hands moving from her waist to cup her face.

Grace's eyes widened at his close proximity as Adam seemed to study her face.

"She imagines I will marry someone different. How angry she will be when I tell her every day that I am away that the only girl I would ever marry is you, Grace."

Grace thought her friend defiant, that he would deliberately anger his mother to spite her. "You mustn't tell tall tales," she scolded. "If you do, then surely your mother will prevent you from coming back to Ashwood."

Adam's eyes narrowed and his eyebrows furrowed. "I am not lying, Grace," he said earnestly. "I will only ever want to marry you. I know it."

Grace stared into Adam's eyes, searching for any falsehood. She could see the sincerity there, and it stirred a fluttering in her stomach that made her fearful but terribly happy at the idea of always having Adam with her. "If you're teasing me, I will hate you forever," Grace whispered.

Adam smiled, his eyes lighting up at they did, and his cheeks swelling as they always had. "I'm not teasing you," he promised. "I'm being perfectly serious. Why would I want to marry anyone else?"

Grace jumped up, suddenly wrapping her arms around Adam's neck and letting her feet dangle beneath her. Adam cuddled her to his chest as he chuckled. Though he wasn't strong enough to hold her for long, and they soon fell to the ground, still concealed in the space behind the drapes.

Adam fell backward and Grace lay atop his chest, their noses only inches apart.

"You are my Grace," Adam murmured, almost inaudibly, as he reached up to tuck a fallen strand of her charcoal coloured hair behind her ear. "How beautiful you are."

Grace could feel the thundering of Adam's heart, and she was certain her own pulse matched his.

"Will you marry me then, Grace?" Adam asked her, his voice louder now. His eyes had not left hers as he awaited her answer.

"We can't get married," Grace mumbled. "We are too young."

"Will you marry me when we're old enough?" Adam pressed.

"But you're leaving Ashwood," protested Grace, the thought returning to her mind. "You're leaving here. What if you do not come back?"

Adam pursed his lips, a determined flash in his hazel eyes. "Of course, I am coming back. You're here, Grace."

Grace loved hearing the conviction in his voice. "Why would you want to marry me?"

Adam's eyes narrowed. "Because I love you, of course," he said bluntly, as though it was obvious.

Grace gasped, and sat upright, quickly climbing to her feet and clapping her hands over her mouth. Adam followed suit, standing up, still very close to her, but frowning.

"What?" he demanded to know. "Why would I ask you to marry me if I didn't love you? Don't you love me?"

Grace had never really thought about love. If she did think about it, she would think of her parents. They loved each other, she thought. Her father always kissed her mother when he came home. They laughed together and spoke secrets to each other.

Adam was her best friend. He always had been. He was the one she told her secrets to. She laughed with him more than anyone. And dear God would she miss him when he went away. "Maybe I do," Grace confessed.

Her admission put the brightest smile on Adam's face, and he immediately went to the small, gold ring that he wore on his little finger. He had only recently begun wearing it. It had been a gift from his parents upon his enrolment at Eton.

"I will give you a girl's ring when I have my own money," promised Adam. "But I want you to keep this for me," he insisted, placing the ring in the palm of Grace's hand and closing her fingers around it. "I'm coming back for you, Grace, I promise. And when I do, I am going to marry you."

Feelings of joy and excitement coursed through Grace, which was a stark contrast to the despair she had only been experiencing just minutes earlier. Grace gripped Adam's ring tightly.

"I have an idea," said Adam suddenly. "Jack."

"What about Jack?" wondered Grace. Why had his thoughts suddenly gone to his younger brother?

"Jack is going to be a clergyman when he grows up," Adam said excitedly. "Mother insists. He could marry us now."

"What? Will we be married properly if Jack says the words that the vicar says?" Grace asked him excitedly.

Adam grinned. "I don't know, but it means that I will have a wife in Ashwood who I will return for one day." Adam seized Grace's hand and his kissed it, sending all the blood rushing to Grace's cheeks. "I promise, I promise that I will come back and be your husband properly when I am a man," he swore. "Will you marry me, Grace? Please?"

"And when you come back, I will be your wife?" A smile appeared on Grace's lips at the idea of being with Adam always.

Adam nodded.

"Then yes," she nodded, "I will marry you."

Adam beamed, wasting no time in surprising Grace with her first kiss. He lifted her off the floor in excitement as he pressed his lips firmly to hers, smiling even wider as he pulled away.

"Promise you'll write to me," Grace insisted. "Every week. And I will write you every week, too."

"I will write to you every week, if you promise that you will wait for me," he bargained seriously.

"I will wait for you," promised Grace.

Adam took her hand again and dragged her out from behind the curtain. "Come on," he urged, "let's go and find Jack." And they ran off together in search of Adam's eleven-year-old brother.

Chapter 1

Ashwood, Hertfordshire, 1806

12 Years Later

"Thank you for coming all this way, Doctor Carlton," Grace Denham said again as she walked him to her family's front door.

Doctor Carlton's practice was in London, and a thirty-mile distance was no easy journey. However, the only doctor near the Hertfordshire village of Ashwood charged about a month's wages for a house call.

Doctor Carlton had a merciful reputation, and he thankfully had only charged Grace a small fee for her mother's care.

"I am only sorry I could not do more to help," replied Doctor Carlton regretfully. "Your mother must stay in bed and rest that leg. She is not to walk on it. Not for two months at least. I shall return then to check on her. Are you to care for her?"

Grace shook her head. "No. My younger sister, Claire, whom you met upstairs. She is to stay home and tend Mama.

I would ordinarily be at my employer's this minute ... but alas ..."

Doctor Carlton held up his hand. "Not to worry. I am certain your sister is more than up to the task. You have my address in London. Please do not hesitate to write." Placing his hat atop his greying tight curls, the doctor bowed his head. "Good day, Miss Denham."

"Good day, Doctor," replied Grace with a small smile, and she closed the door. Exhaling, she leaned against the timber frame, and her eyes ran over the room before her.

The mending was piling up. The laundry had not been done. The breakfast dishes were still dirty. Bread had not been made. And those were only the downstairs chores. Upstairs were bedrooms full of dusting work and laundry that had not been attended to.

Grace's seventeen-year-old sister, Claire, usually tended to the house, and had done so on her own since their middle sister Kate had married a year earlier. But Claire's time had been greatly occupied by their mother, and the household chores had not been a priority.

Grace quickly returned to her mother's bedroom upstairs, where Claire was propping her broken leg up with a pillow.

Mrs Ellen Denham smiled at her eldest child as she entered the room and held her hand out for Grace. Grace sat down on the edge of the bed and put her hand in her mother's.

Mrs Denham was a lovely lady, with a rounded face and figure and a kind constitution. She had aged in her face, and her dark hair had greyed, in the last five years since Mr Denham had passed away.

When her father died, both Grace and Mrs Denham had found employment as housemaids with the wealthy Slickson family; a landed family in a neighbouring village. It was where they had remained employed until Mrs Denham had taken a fall down a flight of stairs and had snapped a bone in her lower leg.

Were it not for Doctor Carlton, her leg might have been removed.

But without their mother's income, Grace's would not be enough to live on. Her meagre wage would not feed her mother, and her three siblings still at home. Her fifteen-year-old brother, Peter, hardly made a wage as a blacksmith's apprentice, and were it not be for Jim Ellis being their brother-in-law, and Kate's husband, they would not have been able to afford him that.

Jem was the youngest, at twelve years old, and much like Grace at that age, he was much too concerned with being a child, and Grace did not have the heart to ask him to give that up.

Which meant that it was up to her, as the oldest, to support the family. She had resigned her position in the Slickson household and had taken her reference to a place that she had once swore that she would never go again.

"Doctor Carlton says you must rest for at least two months, Mama," Grace reiterated.

"Oh, dear," worried Mrs Denham. "Two months? How on earth will we manage? Jem will have to go to work. He won't be able to go back to school in a few weeks when the summer ends."

"Mama, please do not trouble yourself," Claire urged. "All will be well. Grace always manages to look after us." Claire looked up at her elder sister with her confident, blue eyes.

Grace, Kate, and Claire Denham were all very similar in appearance. The girls all had thick, dark hair, and blue eyes, though Grace's did have a strange shade of violet in the iris, making them appear more the colour of cornflowers. It had been said once to her, and Grace had never forgotten the comparison. They three were not remarkable in height, and all stood just over five feet tall, but they were remarkable in bond, especially after their poor father had died.

"In fact, Mama, I am inquiring about a new position this very day," Grace added, pasting a positive smile on her face.

Mrs Denham frowned. "A new position. Where?"

Grace gulped. "Ashwood House." Just thinking about that great house sent a shiver down Grace's spine. She had not crossed the threshold since she was a girl of eleven, and even then, she was only allowed to play in the kitchens.

Mrs Denham looked as Grace felt. Claire, whom already knew of Grace's plans, offered her sister an expression of support. "Oh, no, Grace," insisted Mrs Denham. "Really, must you? After what he said –"

"Mama!" cried Grace, interrupting her. "Really, I do not want to dwell on the past. It was childish, and any thoughts surrounding it must be considered so as well. We are in need of a better wage, and the Beresfords' pay their housemaids more than the Slicksons' do." Grace huffed. "They are not even going to be there anyway," she murmured. They hadn't returned to Ashwood in years.

Mrs Denham closed her mouth and nodded. "Well, I am sorry for you, Grace," she said sincerely. "But I am grateful for you, also." She squeezed Grace's hand. "I am glad they are not here. I never liked that woman, duchess or not," she said determinedly. "Always walking about as though there was a dirty smell under her nose."

It seemed wrong, really, to be speaking of a great lady like the Duchess of Ashwood so, even if Grace found herself quietly agreeing with her mother. But if she hoped to work in the Duchess' household, she would need to keep such thoughts to herself.

"I must go, Mama. Mrs Hayes is expecting me at three o'clock," said Grace, eyeing the little clock on the mantle. It would take her a good half hour to make the walk to the great Beresford estate, and she would need to leave very soon.

"Ah, well there you have a decent woman," Mrs Denham said decidedly. "At least she will be kind to you. I have never heard an uncivil word leave her lips."

Grace did agree whole heartedly. While she was not a close acquaintance of Mrs Hayes; obviously as their ages were so different, Mrs Hayes was nothing but a kind and decent woman. She was the housekeeper at the Beresford estate, but when Grace had known her more intimately, she had been Miss Hayes, the nanny to the three Beresford children.

The family so valued her they kept her on long after the children were grown.

Grace kissed her mother's forehead, and Claire scurried around the bed to walk out with her sister.

"How are you feeling?" Claire asked worriedly.

Grace offered her sister a reassuring smile. "I am well," she promised her. "I am going to be a housemaid and that is all. I think you forget I am three and twenty years old, Claire. I'm not a child, and I have quite forgotten anything unpleasant from years past."

Twelve years might have passed since Grace had been in view of the grand Ashwood House, but she still felt every bit a girl of eleven as the nerves coursed through her veins.

The baroque style stately house towered over in comparison to anything else within a mile radius. It was impossibly large and ostentatious, and any passer-by would know just how rich the family who owned it had to be.

Well, the Beresfords were a well-known wealthy British family, even if they hadn't been in residence in well over a decade.

Grace did have happy memories here as well, despite the knots that were currently in her stomach. And perhaps these memories were a reason why she had also endeavoured to avoid travelling near Ashwood House.

If she listened closely enough, she was certain to hear the Duchess crying out at her for putting her dirty hands on the wallpaper. She could hear another voice, too. One that she liked to push out of her mind.

Grace forced herself to think of her poor mama, her sister, and her brothers. If she did not secure a higher paying position, they would starve. She was an adult now, and any troubles or woes were long behind her.

Grace did not walk in the main gate. It was not proper. Instead, she walked around to the side gate, another mile, what felt like, to the entrance that vendors and servants used. It was the entrance that she had always used as a child, as it led directly to the kitchens.

The kitchen was the only part of the house where she had been permitted. It was strange to think that she hadn't made this journey in so long, and yet it felt like second nature to find her way.

Grace walked through the secluded courtyard, often used by footmen who smoked tobacco. Or at least, it had been historically. Taking a deep breath, she walked confidently up to the kitchen door and knocked, hoping that she was not late.

The door was opened by a servant she did not recognise. She was young, perhaps nineteen or twenty, and dressed as a scullery maid. "Yes?" she prompted, frowning.

"Good afternoon," greeted Grace. "My name is Grace Denham. I believe Mrs Hayes is expecting me."

The door was opened wider for her, and Grace stepped into a virtually unchanged kitchen. It was exactly as she remembered, although perhaps a little smaller. Though, she had grown a little since she was a girl.

Large, wood stoves lined the far wall, suitable for preparing elaborate feasts for aristocracy. A wide timber work bench filled the middle of the kitchen, filled with bowls and tureens of fruits and vegetables. The smells of the dinner that was being prepared made Grace's mouth water.

There were servants everywhere. Of course, the Ashwood estate employed many. It took dozens of hands to keep such a house in perfect condition. Beside the kitchen was a dining room, with one long timber table positioned in the centre of the room.

There were a handful of servants seated at the table, some with cups of tea, others with piles of mending in front of them. Servants carried baskets filled with laundry. Footmen carried unused silver for polishing.

This was certainly livelier than the Slickson household. Grace had only been one of four maids, one being her mother. Though well-off, the Slickson's wealth could not compare.

And then Grace saw a face she recognised. Mrs Hayes. She was perhaps five and forty years old, with a still youthful air about her, even if the lines in her skin betrayed her age. She was dressed in black, in direct contrast to the housemaids.

It was not usual that a nanny would be retained by a family when the children were grown. Ordinarily, Miss Hayes would have moved onto another family. What it must like to be so valued, Grace wondered.

But she was the housekeeper now, and so was called Mrs Hayes, and she greeted Grace with a kind, knowing smile. "Miss Denham," she said cheerfully. "Welcome. May I call you Grace? All of the housemaids are referred to thus."

"Of course," Grace nodded. Mrs Hayes could call her whatever she liked so long as Grace secured employment.

Mrs Hayes led Grace into the housekeeper's room off the kitchen. It was a small office with a window, a few comfortable chairs and a desk. On it, there was a half-drunk cup of tea beside some letters.

Grace was invited to sit down in the chair before the desk, and Mrs Hayes sat down in what would be her usual spot.

Mrs Hayes shuffled through some of her papers on her desk before she pulled out the reference letter that Grace had mailed her.

Mrs Slickson's housekeeper had been very generous in her reference and had understood the predicament that the Denhams were in when Grace had resigned her position.

"Thank you for providing me with your reference, Grace," said Mrs Hayes sincerely. "I can see that you were very valued by the Slicksons. A hardworking and loyal employee." She smiled, before looking up. "I hear your mother was hurt recently. How does she fare?" Mrs Hayes inquired.

"Oh, I thank you for asking, Mrs Hayes," said Grace gratefully. "She has broken her leg. The doctor came to see her earlier, and she must rest for at least two months."

"Well, I wish her a speedy recovery," she offered thoughtfully.

"Thank you." Grace smiled.

"Can you tell me a little about your experience with Mrs Slickson?" prompted Mrs Hayes.

"Yes," nodded Grace. "In recent months, Mrs Slickson began to request personal attendance from me. I gained considerable experience in hair, the mending of valuable garments, dressing ..." Lord, if Grace could somehow manage to become a lady's maid someday, her family's situation would be just that little bit better.

"Excellent, that is a very valuable skill to have," commended Mrs Hayes, before her expression changed. "You are much changed from when I knew you last, Grace," observed Mrs Hayes. "Of course, you were but a child, though all I can see when I hear your name is you and Adam ... pardon me, Lord Adam running about and getting underfoot, giggling away as you got up to mischief."

It was the first time in a long time ... a very long time that Grace had heard his name spoken out loud. Her family never mentioned him. They had long stopped talking about him years ago. And Grace had long stopped crying over him.

But that didn't mean that the moment his name was spoken that she was not reminded of every wonderful thing that had happened between them up until he had gone away to school. Adam had been the most important person in her life once.

The moment Grace realised such fond thoughts were entering her mind, she pushed them aside, almost aggressively, with thoughts of sensibility as she reminded herself as to why she was there.

"I hope that any of my ... our ... childish antics, will not dissuade you from giving me a chance, Mrs Hayes," Grace said, her begging tone nearly evident.

Mrs Hayes chuckled. "Oh, no," she assured her. "You only made me think of him, of them all," she said, referring to the Beresford children, "when they were young."

She missed them, Grace surmised. Of course, she would. Mrs Hayes had raised them.

"But alas, the season of longing is nearly over," continued Mrs Hayes, though Grace was a little unsure of what she meant. "Forgive me, I am a little distracted today by some rather good news." She exhaled and placed her hands over one another on the desk. "I know you will be an excellent addition to the Ashwood household, Grace. I would like for you to begin tomorrow morning. Take this afternoon and tonight to pack your belongings. Can you be here by six o'clock sharp?"

The nerves that Grace felt were quickly replaced by an overwhelming sensation of relief. Just knowing that her family were going to be alright was enough to make her put up with just about anything.

"Yes, of course," confirmed Grace. "Thank you, Mrs Hayes. I do sincerely appreciate this opportunity." Grace felt like bowing out of gratefulness, but she managed to make it out of Mrs Hayes' sitting room and out into the courtyard with a little decorum.

She inhaled in a deep breath, sucking in the good smells and fresh air of the last days of summer. Everything would be alright. There was no reason to be nervous or ... anything other than happy at what had happened.

Ashwood House was different now. She was different.

Grace set off home, ready to tell her mother and Claire the good news.

Chapter 2

Grace shared a bedroom with Claire, and Kate had slept in with them, too, before she had married Jim Ellis. So many years of being in such close proximity to each other had ensured that the sisters were in each other's confidence.

So much so that Claire was watching Grace carefully as she filled an old carpet bag with every possession that she owned, which wasn't very much.

Mrs Denham knew what had happened, of course, but Claire and Kate were the ones who cuddled Grace as she cried herself to sleep for weeks, months.

"Really, Claire, I wish you would not hover so!" cried Grace as she folded her church dress. "This is a good thing! I will be earning twice what I made working for the Slicksons. You will have food in your belly. Besides, are you just upset that you no longer have an excuse to call so that you might get a peek at Arthur Slickson?" Grace teased. It was a little joke within their family that Claire fancied the Slickson heir, Arthur. Grace thought him a little self-centred, but he was traditionally handsome, and the type of man to set Claire's heart alight.

Claire blushed immediately. "Hush!" she scolded bashfully. "Besides, I am not hovering," retorted Claire. "What if he comes back for a visit?"

"He won't," said Grace sharply. "That was made perfectly clear." Sighing, she added, "Will you go and start dinner? Peter will be home soon, as will Jem, and they will be starving. I need to finish packing."

Claire reluctantly nodded and she left their bedroom, and Grace felt a pang of guilt for being short with her sister. She knew Claire was only looking out for her best interest. Just as Grace would if their roles were reversed.

Grace went to the armoire and pulled open her drawer. There were three, and the first drawer had always belonged to her. In it, she kept books, ribbons ... and treasures. She pulled open a stack of letters, fixed together with a white ribbon. On it was a little golden signet ring. The ring that had been gifted to her in promise so many years ago.

It was silly, really, to feel a hurt from a promise made by a child. Grace didn't feel it as keenly as she once did. Time had helped. But never once could she have born the thought of parting with these letters, with the ring given in good faith to her by Adam.

When he had gone away, he had kept his promise. He had written for a little while. In his letters he had complained about his teachers, his classmates, and his parents, blaming them for sending him away. He claimed to miss her and to love her.

As it came time to mark a year since Adam had gone away, and the Beresfords had left Ashwood House, Grace had received a letter from Adam. The last letter he would send.

Grace untied the ribbon, carefully unthreading the ring, and slipping it onto her thumb loosely so that she would not lose it as she selected the letter on top. She unfolded it, and saw it was dated September '96.

Grace, it began.

Just Grace. Every other letter was addressed to his dear Grace, or his beloved Grace, but this letter was just plain Grace. She could remember reading it and knowing just from the way it was addressed that something was wrong.

I am sorry that this message must be relayed through letter, and I could not tell you in person. I must end our understanding.

What we agreed can never be, and you must know why.

I have grown up this year, and I cannot fool myself any longer. I cannot pretend that I can do whatever I like. I have been forced to face who I am, and that is the heir to one of the richest titles in England. Who I marry, and who I concern myself with, must be carefully considered.

As much as our friendship has meant to me, it must cease. We cannot be friends, or anything else, as it is not proper. You must understand that we are cut from two very different pieces of cloth.

This will be my last letter. I will not write to you again, and I must hereby consider you a stranger, just as you must consider me a stranger.

I wish you good health.

Sincerely,

A.B

Grace felt a sudden frog in her throat, startled at how his words could still affect her. She could still see where the ink had run from where she had cried over this letter.

Oh, how this had killed her heart when she was a girl. Each word had been like a knife, stabbing her over and over as the letter went on.

He had changed. But what had she expected? Adam made a promise to her that he could not very well keep, even if he'd wanted to. Grace hadn't known what his true duty was when she had known him, and she doubted that Adam even knew. It was only had she had grown up into an adult that she realised the vast wealth of the Beresfords, and Adam was heir to it all.

He was destined for greatness and would surely have a bride who would equal it.

"Enough," she told herself, though she had told herself this many time over the years. She would not even be seeing Adam, so she did not know why she was forcing herself to relive these memories. Grace didn't know where he was, but he certainly was not going to be at Ashwood House.

Grace finished packing, including the letters, and the ring, reluctantly, and brought her bag down the stairs to place it at the door, ready for her to leave in the morning.

Claire had made stew, and it smelled divine. It was boiling on the stove with Claire tending to it diligently. Her brothers,

Peter and Jem, her sister, Kate, and her husband, Jim Ellis, were all seated around the table, conversing jovially.

The moment Kate saw Grace, she jumped up from her chair, racing over to give her a hug. Kate looked wonderful, a little flushed, but well. She looked to be wearing a new lavender dress, with a silver pin at the collar. Her good husband was talented at forging such trinkets. It was how he had won over Kate in the first place.

"You are bound for the lion's den!" she hissed under her breath, her blue eyes flaring.

"Hush," retorted Grace. "I am a servant in a house is all," she said dismissively. "Really," she insisted, knowing that Kate's mind was exactly where Claire's had been. "The wage is good, and there is nothing to fret about." She took her sister's hand and led her back to the table. "How was your day, Jim? Peter?" prompted Grace, cheerfully changing the subject.

Jim Ellis was a tall man, wide with animal strength, and looked quite the giant next to Kate. Or perhaps, it was Kate that looked like the elf beside him. His skin always seemed to be tinged a little darker thanks to the soot that never fully seemed to wash away. He looked like brute, but he was kind and soft, and very tender in his affection for Kate.

If it were not for him taking on Peter as his blacksmith's apprentice, the Denhams would simply never have been able to afford it.

"Nothing out of the ordinary," replied Jim. "A few wheels. Peter shoed a horse by himself."

Peter Denham was fifteen, and the physical labour was already showing in what were once skinny, lanky limbs. He smiled proudly. "It was nothing," he said dismissively, though Grace knew he was proud to have ownership over tasks.

"It doesn't sound like it. I certainly would have no idea how to shoe a horse," enthused Grace. "And what did you get up to today, Jemmy?" she asked her twelve-year-old brother.

Jem's hair was always scruffy, his knees were always scraped, and his clothes were always covered in grass stains, and that was exactly how Mrs Denham, and indeed Grace, wanted him to be.

"I went fishing," he replied, "but I didn't catch anything. Then my friends and I went swimming in the pond, before we climbed trees this afternoon."

"Swimming?" remarked Grace. "You are quite mad. I am sure the pond is freezing."

"Oh, it is," confirmed Jem with a wicked grin. "The first one to get out has to sit in the front row when we go back to school. It wasn't me, of course," he assured her proudly.

Claire served them their supper, before taking a bowl up to their mother, and Grace committed herself to enjoying her last meal with her family for a while.

Everything was going to be alright. It simply had to be.

"I am furious!" seethed Cecily Beresford, for about the nineteenth time that morning. "Utterly and completely humiliated!"

Her ire on this particular day was aimed at Adam's younger brother, Jack. Jack had had quite a night, it seemed, and had spent the remainder of it in a London gaol cell. He had been collected quietly by his father before dawn that morning, and a fine paid, along with generous compensation to ensure that nothing reached the papers.

Jack sat in the carriage opposite his mother, his head leaning back with a handkerchief over his eyes as he suffered a headache from all the alcohol that he had indulged in.

Adam's nineteen-year-old sister, Susanna, sat in between her two brothers, with Adam on the other side, sitting opposite his father, Peregrine.

Adam did feel keenly for his brother, and perhaps would have been more sympathetic were this a rare occurrence. It was rarer that Jack was not finding someway or another into trouble. He had a knack for recklessness and impulsivity, and often defied their parents on purpose.

Adam could hardly remember a time that his parents had meant for Jack to become a clergyman. Jack was about the farthest thing there was to a clergyman.

But that didn't mean that Adam did not try and look out for him. With their mother the sort of woman she was, it was important that he looked out for both of his siblings. It was a responsibility that he took pride in.

"Mother," said Adam firmly. "Leave him be."

"Yes, Cecily, we have had enough of this for now," agreed Peregrine. "I want to enjoy today."

"Five hundred pounds worth of damage!" hissed Cecily to Peregrine. "And two unspeakable women."

"Mother," snapped Adam. Susanna did not need to be hearing such things.

Adam's parents were seated apart, or as apart as two could be in a carriage. They were not particularly close or loving, nor had they ever been. But they seemed to quarrel most over their children, and what they believed was best, without consultation, of course.

Adam did agree with his father, however. He wanted to enjoy this day, too. They were finally going home. After twelve long years.

Adam had completed his studies at Eton and Cambridge, as had Jack. It was only now that Susanna was finished that Cecily conceded that it was time to return to Ashwood House.

He still remembered his childhood home in vivid detail. Every memory he had was precious, innocent, and good. He had been his happiest when he had lived at Ashwood, and Adam sincerely hoped to regain some of that now that he was returning.

Adam had most definitely grown up while away at school. He had to. Someone had to be the one to get Jack out of trouble. He had matured, most definitely, and his view of the world wasn't as simple as it once had been.

Adam had also known considerable pain, and that had practically forced him to leave his fanciful, childish ways behind him. He was smart, savvy, and quick. He worked closely with his father on school holidays, learning all that he could.

And in the three years since the completion of his studies, he had grown up romantically as well. His mother treated the London Season as though it were a mission and was cunning in the way that she operated a ballroom. It was she who had orchestrated the introduction between himself and his new fiancée, Lady Sarah Ashley. Sarah was an heiress with twenty thousand pounds, and boasted a connection to Earl Ashley, her father, and the wealthy Fitzmartin family through her mother.

Cecily had not found fault with Adam in the three weeks since he had proposed. Poor Jack had borne the brunt since. Adam was certain his antics the night before were as a result of Cecily's incessant need to be criticising something.

Adam knew that his decision to propose was the right one. It was the done practice. Thousands of marriages had been society matches, just as his would be. As the heir to his father, he would be the Duke of Ashwood one day, and it was his responsibility to marry advantageously.

Love was not particularly important nowadays anyway. One only had to look at his mother and father to be sure of that. While he once might have thought he had found it, Adam now knew he was wrong, and had been entirely foolish.

"I hardly remember Ashwood," remarked Susanna, in as cheerful voice as she could muster.

"And whose fault is that?" grumbled Peregrine.

Adam rolled his eyes and looked out the window, squeezing his sister's hand to let her know that he knew she was only trying to break the tension in the carriage. They could not arrive soon enough. Adam needed a break from his parents, as did Jack.

The wilderness of Hertfordshire was a welcome sight after so long in London. It was so good to see natural clusters of trees again. There would definitely be many good rides to be had, and the thought of being gone for a whole day on the ride was ridiculously tempting.

He kept his eyes firmly fixed on the landscape, finding a memory attached to nearly every distinctive tree and boulder that they passed. He had spent much of his childhood outdoors, running about, chasing her.

It had, of course, crossed his mind that he might encounter her upon his return to Ashwood. But it had been a long time since their acquaintance had been ended, severed, utterly annihilated. Adam was entirely unsure of what he would do or say should he ever see her.

It was hard not to imagine her now as the memories played over in his head. She would be twenty-three. He knew her birthday. Was she married? He didn't know. Would she have children? Was she happy?

Even though it had been so many years since he had last known her, for a very long time, Grace Denham had been at the centre of Adam's existence. Whatever their encounter, should there even be one, Adam was determined to be indifferent.

They were no longer children.

The final few miles felt like hours as his mother continued to grumble on about her grievances over Jack's behaviour the night before. But the road that led to Ashwood House could not be mistaken, and the enormous, pearl white house soon came into view.

Peregrine, too, managed a smile as he peered out the window and took in the great estate.

The gates were already open, and the carriage took them down the long drive that was lined with perfectly groomed hedges. They were earlier than expected, and so the household were not all waiting for them outside the house.

They had been due to return in a week, but Cecily had hurried them out of London in a rush after Jack was collected from the gaol.

"I will organise baths for everyone," Cecily decided. "Jack, you stink of whiskey. You are then to go to bed immediately."

Jack let out a loud groan.

The carriage pulled to a stop, and Adam heard the footmen jump down as they prepared the step and opened the door. Adam and Peregrine climbed out first, and they assisted Susanna and Cecily out. Jack reluctantly stumbled out of the carriage last. Cecily was quick to start barking orders as Adam looked up at the house properly, a smile quickly teasing the corner of his lips.

"Come on," Adam urged his brother and his sister to follow him. "Let us go and surprise Miss Hayes."

The mention of their childhood nanny brought out exactly the enthusiasm that Adam had wanted to see in Jack and Susanna, and the three siblings took off in a run towards the side of the house, ignoring the protests of their mother behind them.

Chapter 3

Grace arrived, worldly possessions in tow, ten minutes before six the next morning. While the village slept, the house was awake, with the servants all sitting down to breakfast before they commenced their daily responsibilities.

Grace knew of several of the servants. They all attended the same church and frequented the odd public assembly. She had even danced with a few of the footmen on occasion. Despite all being servants, there was a certain stature afforded to one who worked in the great Ashwood estate.

Mrs Hayes introduced Grace briefly to the household over their bowls of porridge, before taking her into the butler's study. It was a similar size and layout to Mrs Hayes' sitting room, and an older, bespectacled man sat in a leather chair, his nose buried in that morning's newspaper.

"Good morning, Mr Cole," greeted Mrs Hayes cheerfully.

The newspaper crinkled as Mr Cole looked over it. He offered Mrs Hayes a polite smile before setting his newspaper down on his desk. He was dressed immaculately, as only the butler of Ashwood House would be.

Mr Cole had been the butler of Ashwood for eons. Grace could remember him scolding her and Adam for running about downstairs when they were children. She almost shivered noticeably as another memory unwittingly bubbled to the forefront of her mind.

"Allow me to formally introduce Grace Denham," said Mrs Hayes. "Grace is replacing Frances Rivers."

Grace could remember hearing Frances Rivers' name being read out in church during the marriage banns.

"Welcome to you, Grace," replied Mr Cole courteously, though not in a way that he recognised her as Mrs Hayes did. His light blue eyes returned to the housekeeper. "You are to begin making arrangements?" he checked.

Mrs Hayes nodded. "Yes," she confirmed. "When will you alert the house?"

"I am waiting on a confirmation. I do not want to be mistaken and have the news spread falsely," Mr Cole said coyly.

Grace knew the tone. This was not a conversation for her ears, and she respectfully vacated the room, waiting out into the hallway, returning to her bags. As much as she knew it was none of her business, she could not help but feel curious about the subject. What exactly was the house to learn, and when would they learn it?

Mrs Hayes emerged moments later and said nothing, and Grace knew better than to ask. She motioned for Grace to follow her, before leading her to a narrow staircase.

My, it had been a long time since she had been up and down these staircases. Grace knew they ran all through the internal walls of Ashwood House. Purposefully hidden behind concealed doors to allow the servants to slip in and out without being noticed by the fine, fancy figures who graced the halls.

Mrs Hayes did not show her age at all as she led Grace up a number of staircases to the third storey of the house. What might have once been a large attic, or a roof cavity, was converted into two dozen little bedrooms. The hallway was long and narrow, illuminated only by lamps; there were no windows. The hallway was cut in two, a door separating one half from another.

"The housemaids, kitchen and scullery maids, cook, and I, sleep through here," explained Mrs Hayes. "Only Mrs Reynolds, the cook, and I, have keys to this door." Mrs Hayes produced a set of keys from her pocket and unlocked the door, leading Grace through to an identical hallway filled with bedrooms for the female servants.

Mrs Hayes found the room that she was looking for on the right and opened the door inward. This room had a little window, facing east, and the light from the sunrise had begun to stream into the small room. There were two little beds, neatly made, as well as two identical sets of drawers. A mirror, basin, and writing desk completed the simple furnishings.

A dark uniform was folded on one of the beds, alongside a white apron and cap.

"This will be your bed," Mrs Hayes motioned to the bed with the clothing. "And those are you drawers. You share this room with Ruby Trickett, though she is already downstairs." She took a breath and smiled. "I admire what you do for your family, Grace," she complimented. "It must not be easy with your mother so indisposed. I hope you will come to me if you do need any help."

"Thank you," said Grace gratefully, "again, for everything," she emphasised.

Mrs Hayes nodded to the uniform on the bed. "I will leave you to dress. Then I will direct you to your morning responsibilities."

Grace was shown the quickest routes to get to certain rooms in the house via the servants' staircases. Despite having played in the house years ago, it was still difficult for her to get her bearings, and the tour did help.

Most of the rooms were shut, with large sheets draped over the ornate furnishings because the Beresfords were not at home to use them. But today, Mrs Hayes was pulling down the sheer lace curtains that hung behind the drapes at every window and laundering them.

It was Grace's task then, owing to the fact she had small and nimble hands and experience in mending expensive fabrics, to comb over every inch and mend any tears, snags or pulls in the expensive curtains. There was a smell about the curtains, one that often lingered when a room had been shut up for a long period. She supposed they were lucky that the curtains had not been destroyed by mothballs.

As time consuming and fiddly as the task was, Grace settled in, grateful for the work, and knowing that every shilling she was earning would be feeding her mother and siblings well.

The curtains from the drawing, dining, library, sitting and parlour rooms were all folded on the servants' dining table, while Grace sat with the first one in her hands. She was not sure what time it was, but Mrs Reynolds and the kitchen maids were starting on the midday meal.

A redheaded maid sat down on the bench seat beside Grace. She had large, green eyes and a handful of freckles across her nose. Smiling, she said, "Mrs Hayes asked me to come and assist you. I am Ruby Trickett."

Grace realised that this was the Ruby who would be sharing her room. "Grace Denham," she introduced herself. "It's lovely to meet you."

Ruby nodded in reciprocation. "You don't happen to have any idea why we are suddenly mending curtains, do you?" she asked curiously as she picked up the other end of the curtain that Grace was inspecting, beginning to look for imperfections.

"No," replied Grace.

Ruby found a pull nearly immediately and fetched a needle and thread from the sewing kit to begin fixing it. "Where were you working before coming to Ashwood?" Ruby wondered aloud.

"I worked for the Slickson family," replied Grace. "Do you know them?"

Ruby grinned. "Of course," she enthused. "Dear me, is not Arthur Slickson terribly handsome?" she asked, a slight blush to her cheeks.

Grace wagered that Ruby would get on well with her sister, Claire. They both seemed to appreciate the handsome Arthur Slickson. Although Claire was much too shy to admit it. Not that Grace exactly approved, no matter how rich he was. Vanity was not something Grace enjoyed in a man's character.

"He is not ugly," Grace allowed, to which Ruby laughed.

Grace settled into the task well, chatting to Ruby nonchalantly and finding that she enjoyed her light-hearted conversation. She seemed an easy person to get to know, and Ruby liked to talk about a lot of different light topics and did not like to delve into the droll. Ruby was twenty, and from a small village ten miles away. Her aunt was a housekeeper for the Earl of Greenwich and had recommended her to Mrs Hayes six months earlier.

As they sewed, Grace noticed Mrs Hayes enter the kitchen a little while later, speaking quietly to Mrs Reynolds as she prepared luncheon.

"You stitch so neatly," complimented Ruby. "You would not even know that there had been a tear."

Grace's attention returned to the hole that she had just repaired, admiring it with a small smile. She supposed she did mend rather well. "I have four younger siblings," she replied. "Mending, altering, hemming, mending again, was all a part of growing up."

No sooner had she finished that sentence, the kitchen door burst open, and Grace jumped with such a fright that she pricked her finger suddenly with her needle. A bead of blood dripped from the tip of her index finger as her head, and the head of every other person in the room, turned towards the commotion at the door.

Three people, two men and a woman, entered the kitchen with searching eyes. The first person through the door was a young woman, an impossibly pretty, young woman, with two perfect blonde curls framing her face below a rose-coloured bonnet. Her spencer coat was the same shade of pink as her bonnet, and it went over a fine white gown.

The first man into the kitchen was young as well, with a handsome, albeit tired looking, face. He was a head taller than the woman and sported a lean torso. His brown hair looked unkempt, as though it hadn't been comped, and his coat and breeched, while rich looking, appeared slept in.

The second man was as handsome, if not more so, than the first. He looked the oldest of the three and was slightly taller than his male companion. He was just as lean, and dressed just as richly, though his attire was neat and uncrumpled. His shoulders were broad, and his jaw was strong and mature. His hair was lighter than the other man's, having a slight curl to it, and it was combed out of his eyes. His eyes, Grace could see from where she was, were hazel, and in them she could see the boy she once knew.

But he wasn't a boy anymore. He was a man, and he was here.

Grace was frozen to the bench seat she was sitting on as she stared at him. Adam was here, after twelve years! On the day she had begun working at Ashwood, it had to be some cruel trick of fate.

But Adam didn't see her. His smile was for Mrs Hayes, and Grace's heart flipped in her chest as she saw it. It was almost like her heart missed it and would not listen to her head. He might've grown up, but him smile still looked the same. His cheeks still swelled, and the smile reached his large eyes.

"Miss Hayes!" cried Susanna Beresford, her arms extending out to her childhood nanny.

In Grace's shock, she had not seen the look of pure adulation on the face of Mrs Hayes. She cried out in delight as happy tears began to fall down her rosy cheeks as she received Susanna. She hugged her tightly and kissed her cheek. "Oh, my girl!" she cried. "You are a lady!" She gasped as she looked up, and she reached her Jack.

Grace watched as Jack nearly fell into his nanny, bending his head to her shoulder as he hugged her, Susanna shifting so that he had room. From what she could see of Jack in that moment, he needed that affection.

"Oh, my darling, Jack!" gushed Mrs Hayes, as she all but petted his head, just like she would have if he were a child, before her eyes settled on Adam. "Both of you boys have grown into such handsome young men. I can scarcely believe it!"

"You have not changed at all, Miss Hayes," Adam assured her, and Grace sucked in a silent gasp as she heard his adult voice for the first time.

He had still sounded like a boy when she had last spoken to him, but now he sounded like a man, with a deep, confident, calm voice. It was enough to send what felt like the thirty-seventh shiver down her spine.

When Jack released Mrs Hayes, Adam leaned down and kissed her on the cheek, before hugging her as his siblings had. Mrs Hayes stood up on her toes as she cupped the back of his head, just like a mother would when she cradled her child.

"I was not expecting you today! Not that this isn't the best of surprises!" remarked Mrs Hayes and she pulled away and stood before the three Beresford siblings.

"We came home early," replied Adam. "I hope it will not be too much of an inconvenience to open the house."

"Oh, no!" dismissed Mrs Hayes. "I will have the maids – oh!" she cried, and Grace knew exactly where her mind had gone.

No. There was no way she was ready to face the man who had once been her friend, her ...

How could she anyway? He had made it quite clear a long time ago the difference between themselves, and Grace was sitting there as definitive proof that he was right. She somehow found the strength to rise from her seat, jumping over the bench and diving into the laundry, hiding from where Adam would be looking in mere moments.

"Oh, you will want to see ..." Mrs Hayes stopped abruptly when she realised that Grace was no longer sitting at the dining table mending curtains. "Where did she go?" she wondered. "Oh, never mind. Come on now, you three had best get upstairs and changed and I will arrange for the house to be opened. How glad I am to have you three home."

Chapter 4

"What on earth is the matter with you?" hissed Ruby in a terribly bemused tone.

Only once Adam and his siblings had left the kitchen with Mrs Hayes did Grace emerge from the laundry, stepping tentatively as she did. Her heart was still thundering in her chest, and she felt the need to rub her eyes, to pinch her arm, just to make sure that she was truly awake.

Grace was certain that her cheeks were flushed. "I thought I saw a bee," she murmured. "I don't like them."

"Inside?" scoffed Ruby. But she didn't dwell on the subject for long. There were much more pressing matters as she raced over to the kitchen maids with a wicked grin on her face. "Gentlemen!" she squealed, though hushed.

The two kitchen maids looked just as starstruck and excited at the fact that Adam and Jack had only just been through. If they had come from afar, it was highly likely that many of the servants would have never encountered the Beresford family before.

Grace would certainly never advertise that she had known them once. She didn't really know them now, and as a servant, it was not her place to engage in any sort of familiarity.

And then the contents of Adam's letter hit her again, right in the stomach, taking the wind out of her. Lord, how easy it was to think of him as merely Adam. He was not Adam, nor would she ever address him as such.

He was Lord Beresford, the heir to the dukedom, and everything that she was standing on.

"That's quite enough from the lot of you!" cried Mrs Reynolds, clapping her hands to grab their attention. "Honestly, if the reverend heard such frivolity, he would rap you three over the knuckles with a cane. Now, we have suddenly a meal to prepare for His Grace, so Elsie, Eve, move it!" She waved on the kitchen maids and they quickly returned to their chores.

Bells started to ring, and Grace could remember Adam telling her once that the ropes in each room were connected to the bells downstairs, alerting Mr Cole their need for a servant. The family were well and truly returned, and Grace was quite certain she was going to have a coronary.

When great, rich families like the Beresfords returned to their homes after extended absences, the household were expected to greet them in a receiving line outside the house. As they had returned early, Mr Cole had ordered every footman, housemaid, kitchen maid, gardener and groom to form a receiving line in the entry hall instead.

Adam was going to see her. There was no way around it, and Grace was at quite a loss of what to do. She was not so much worried about what he would do. She truly expected nothing from him. He had grown into exactly what his parents had wanted him to be; a gentleman. She was afraid for herself. Grace didn't want to feel hurt again. She had spent so much of the last decade convincing herself that what was done was done, and it couldn't affect her. She certainly didn't want to cry in front of him.

There was a part of her, a large part, really, that felt ashamed. Grace stubbornly didn't want Adam to be right about their positions. Cut from two very different pieces of cloth, he had called them. She remembered his words exactly, as though they were burned into her memory. How literal his words would be when he looked upon her in the dress of his servant.

And there was another part, this one smaller, that was battling to come to the surface, to convince Grace to walk right over to her former friend, and to punch his perfectly manly jaw. Only a cruel person would hurt someone they were supposed to love, and he had made her a promise. She never thought that Adam would be one to break his word.

Grace stood in a straight line of maids, between Ruby and Elsie, a sea of black and white. She kept her chin down and hoped that as he had changed in appearance, she had, too, and would not be so easily recognised.

The only room that had been properly opened before Mr Cole had ordered for the assembly had been the drawing room, and the duke and duchess emerged together.

Grace felt a pull in the pit of her stomach as she laid eyes on the duchess. She had always been a very glamorous woman, and a day of travelling had not changed that. Twelve years might have passed, but she still appeared as youthful as porcelain, draped in diamonds and rubies, and dressed in a high waisted red satin gown that looked to be the epitome of fashion in town.

The years had not been as kind to the duke as they had been to his wife. He did look older, his skin a little paler and weathered. He was still dressed exceptionally well, and he greeted the onlooking servants with a respectful nod, whereas the duchess seemed to wear only a sneer, as though there was a foul smell in the air.

The sound of feet descending the stairs caught Grace's attention, but she quickly caught herself and brought her eyes back down. Out of the corner of her eye, she saw Adam, Jack and Susanna join their parents in fresh attire. Mr Cole stepped out before them and bowed his head. The rest of the household followed suit, and Grace dropped in a curtsey.

"Cole, it is very good to see you, old man," Peregrine Beresford greeted his butler with an old familiarity.

"We are so very pleased to see you are returned, Your Grace," replied Mr Cole. "I hope the journey was swift and uneventful."

"Yes, well," murmured Cecily Beresford distastefully, as though she was most seriously displeased about something. Though, as Grace had never encountered her otherwise, perhaps this was what she was always like.

Mrs Hayes stepped forward next, motioned to come by Mr Cole, and she was received by boththe duke and duchess. Cecily even smiled, and Grace thought her face might crack.

For such a reaction, the duchess must have really liked Mrs Hayes.

"Mrs Hayes, how do you do?" asked Peregrine eagerly as Mrs Hayes curtseyed.

"I am well," she replied earnestly, "and I am very glad to see you all back at Ashwood after so long."

"I thank you all for gathering here to welcome us," Peregrine raised his voice to speak to the hall. "My family and I are very glad to return to our home, and I am grateful to see it in such condition. Maintaining such a house is no easy feat, and you all have my thanks."

"I trust that as much care as is necessary to open the house will be taken regardless of our unexpected arrival," added Cecily, ice in her voice.

Grace suspected then that the duchess' mood, even if she had always seemed put out, was connected to their early return. She wondered if it had anything to do with Jack ... he had seemed sloppily dressed and dreadfully tired. Like he had been drinking. That's what a lot of men in the village looked like when they fell out of the tavern.

He clearly was not a member of the clergy, though when she had last seen him, he had been marrying Grace and Adam.

Adam and Grace used the servants' staircase to go down to the library, no running the risk of encountering his mother or his father. Jack could always be found in the library, his nose buried in a book.

They found Jack on one of the settees, lying on his back with his legs in the air, leaning against the back of the sofa.

He held his book up in front of his face but craned his neck to see who had entered the library.

He looked relieved when he saw Adam and Grace. He righted himself, sitting up on the settee and abandoning his book beside him.

Jack had the same hazel eyes as Adam, but darker hair. He was dressed only in breeches and a shirt and would be considered utterly disgraceful by his mother if she saw him.

Grace often noticed that Adam's mother scolded Jack quite a lot. Jack could be silly and naughty, especially in church, and the duchess never seemed very fond of him.

Her own mother had called Jack "the spare", though Grace was not entirely sure what it meant.

Jack grinned when he saw Grace, appreciating the breaking of rules, but it turned into a smirk when he saw Adam holding Grace's hand. "Mustn't let Mother catch you," he teased.

Grace looked to Adam.

"Never mind her," Adam said dismissively. "I need your help, Jack. Would you marry us?"

Jack looked completely dumbfounded. "What? Are you mad?"

"Just say the words," Adam insisted. "You're going to be a clergyman; don't you know them?"

"But you have to be grown up!" Jack insisted. "I am just a boy and Grace is the same age as me ... you are not grown up, Adam. You are only two years older than me!"

Adam released Grace's hand and placed his hands on his younger brother's shoulders. "Please?" he asked again, softly. "You know I'm going away to school. I want to marry Grace now and I'll do it again when I am grown up. You know how much I love her. You like to tease me about it."

Grace's mouth dropped open.

Jack smirked again. "Well, I suppose I do know some of the words."

"What are you doing?"

All three of them turned towards the door to see seven-year-old Susanna Beresford standing there, clutching the arm of her doll. She had a pink ribbon in her hair, one that matched the sash on her otherwise white day dress.

"Nothing. Go away, Susanna," instructed Adam.

Susanna did not obey her brother. "Can I join in?" she asked as she trotted over to them, her blonde curls bouncing.

Grace worried that if they did not allow Susanna to stay, she would run off to tell her mother, and the duchess would find out that Grace was somewhere she was not supposed to be.

"Adam is going to marry Grace," Jack informed her, his wicked grin returning.

Susanna gasped in pure delight. "A wedding?" she exclaimed. "Can I be your bridesmaid, please?" she begged Grace, dropping to her knees and seizing the hem of Grace's dress.

Grace looked up at Adam, and even he could not help but smile at his younger sister. Grace knew that Adam loved his younger siblings, the same as Grace loved hers. One day, they would all be family properly. After all, Adam had promised to come back.

Jack cleared his throat. "Please take your lady's hand," he instructed, deepening his voice.

Adam chuckled and took Grace's hand in his.

"Dearly beloved, we are gathered here today to join this boy and this girl in holy macaroni."

Susanna was no longer wearing her bonnet, and Grace could see through her eyelashes that she wore her hair in a beautiful, twisted knot with curls, with a few fresh flowers pinned throughout. She looked the epitome of a young debutante. Grace wondered if she even remembered begging to be her bridesmaid when she was little.

"They are much grown since many of you may have seen them, but please allow me to introduce my children. Lord Beresford," he gestured to Adam, who smiled politely as he nodded to the servants.

Grace dared to look at him, but he was not looking in her direction. She noticed his eyes returned quickly to his brother. Jack looked rather green, and Adam's concern was on him.

"Lord Jack Beresford." Peregrine's tone tired a little as he gestured to his middle son.

Grace almost thought her suspicions about a problem with Jack were confirmed.

"And Lady Susanna Beresford."

Susanna beamed, shuffling on her feet as she nodded to several people in greeting.

"Thank you again for gathering to greet us. I am sure you all have many things to do, so please, you are dismissed." Peregrine waved at them.

Grace did not need to be told twice. By some miracle, Adam had not seen her, and she was not going to wait around any longer in case he did manage to look in her direction. She, Ruby, and a few other servants were responsible for opening the ladies parlour, and so she sped off in that direction, leaving her thundering heart behind her.

Chapter 5

Adam felt badly for not appearing more polite when being received by the servants, but he was quite certain Jack was on the verge of fainting. He had been sick in his chamber pot only moments before. He threw up nothing but whiskey, and Adam was certain his stomach was the better for it.

Once the servants had dispersed, Adam brought his brother back upstairs to what had been Jack's childhood bedroom. It was still quite how he left it, with shelves and shelves of books lining nearly every wall. Jack loved to read, and when he wasn't getting himself into trouble, he often became quite the moody reader.

Adam saw his brother into bed, lying him on his side to ensure that he did not choke on his own sick should he vomit again. He brought the chamber pot and its liquid contents over to the side of the bed next to Jack, holding his breath as he did so.

Jack was asleep in seconds, exhaustion overcoming him, and gentle snores began to escape his mouth. Adam did feel keenly for Jack, equal to the amount that his brother frustrated him.

Jack was the insurance, the spare son in case anything ever happened to Adam. His parents had treated him as such for so long that Jack had cottoned on eventually. He was always second best, and Adam often felt immense guilt because of it. Adam was meant to be the gentleman, the heir, and Jack was to wait in the wings, just in case. Second sons were bound for the church or the military as they would have no money of their own.

When Jack grew old enough to understand his options, his position in life, and their parents' views, he rebelled, as any headstrong teenager would do. Adam and Jack were very similar in that respect. They both thought with their hearts and not their heads. They often made decisions based on feeling rather than sense.

But Adam never pushed the boundaries as much as Jack did. Jack drank, he got into fights, he spent his nights occupied by countless women, and it had come to a head last night when he had found himself arrested. Adam had pieces of the story, but it seemed Jack had been in a compromising position with a pair of sisters, and they were discovered by one of their husbands. A fight had ensued, and a great deal of damage had been caused.

Adam knew that his parents would throw money at the problem, but he quietly hoped that a return to their childhood home would be good for Jack to find some purpose. He had a good education, a clever head on his shoulders, and he was a decent man when sober. Adam hoped he might even find a nice, respectable girl to help him settle down.

Adam left Jack's bedroom door open. He wanted to hear if he spluttered or threw up again. He thought about ringing for Mrs Hayes, but then decided against it. Mrs Hayes was the housekeeper now, and not their nanny. It was not her responsibility to keep Jack alive anymore.

Angrily, Adam cursed his mother. Cecily had never been the type of mother to sit at her child's bedside and worry.

Adam's bedroom was next to Jack's, and he purposefully left his own door open as well. His trunk had been brought up by the footmen, who had placed it beside the old one at the end of his bed.

Like Jack's, his own bedroom had not changed either. The bed, the tables, the lamps, the desk, the sofas ... it was all exactly how he remembered it, and he felt a sense of peace in returning. He went to his childhood trunk and opened both of the latches, lifting the lid up.

Nostalgia filled him as his eyes settled on his tin soldiers, his train set, his jacks, his chess set – what was that?

Adam's eyes found a piece of paper tucked down the back, and the moment he saw it, he remembered exactly what it was, and the exact moment he had put it there. He pulled it out and unfolded it, viewing the marriage certificate that Jack had forged, spelling mistakes and all, and he and Grace had excitedly signed all those years ago.

Lord, Adam had been in love with her. As much in love as a thirteen-year-old boy was capable of. A tight pain, like the feeling of a needle prick, began to startle his chest as such a specific, happy memory came to the forefront of his brain.

His head turned towards his window, and Adam found himself walking over to look out at the view. While he could only see the Ashwood gardens, the village was out there, not at all far by carriage. Was she there? Did she remember him? Could she see him in her memories just as clearly as he could see her?

Was she married?

Adam couldn't even comprehend the thought, let alone entertain it. He wouldn't allow himself to. It had been too many years ...

Before he knew it, Adam was opening his other trunk, the one filled with his clothing, his books, his stationery, and his letters. They had made a promise once, one of a few on that day, Adam thought bitterly, but one of them had been to write to each other, and Grace had kept that promise for a while.

She had written to him for a year. And eleven years after the fact, Adam had never been able to part with her letters. She had used different terms of endearment to address him each time she wrote, and all the way at school, knowing that Grace thought of him as her darling, or her sweetheart, it had helped to ease the loneliness he felt in being so far from her.

She wrote him diligently until her last letter had arrived. Why he wanted to subject himself to her words again, Adam had no idea, but he couldn't help himself as he opened the letter. The minute his eyes fell on the single name Adam, he felt like he was fourteen again, experiencing heartbreak for the very first time.

He wasn't her darling or her sweetheart anymore. It was just Adam.

Adam,

I am sorry to have to write this in a letter, but I must.

I don't want to write to you anymore. I am tired of it and I have realised how silly I have been this whole year. I have wasted my summer writing to you instead of spending time with people who are here and that seems ridiculous. You have your own life, and I am going to start mine without having an obligation to you.

I enjoyed being your friend when we were children, but it is time to grow up. You have your entire life ahead of you, and I no longer want to be in any part of it.

This will be my last letter. Please do not write to me again. I will not open it, nor answer it. I am moving on from you, and I suggest you do the same.

Grace

To say that Adam had been devastated had been an understatement. He had not expected such a letter from Grace, such a complete change in what their plans had been. Adam had been completely serious in his promise. He had fully intended to finish his education and return for her. He would have written her faithfully for years, for as long as it took to come back for her.

But his attachment had clearly been deeper than hers, and Adam had long resigned himself to that fact. He had spent a long time with a broken heart, and a long time learning to be alright, and to grow up just as she had told him to.

Adam had grown up. He had completed his education and had entered into society seamlessly, as any heir to one of the richest titles in Britain would. That part was his mother's forte, as was her engineering the eventual engagement between himself and Lady Sarah Ashley.

Adam was twenty-five now, and these matters were not supposed romantic.

"Adam, I am writing to Lady Ashley. Would you like me to enclose a note for Lady Sarah?" Cecily had appeared at Adam's door, and her eyes fell on his state disapprovingly. "What on earth are you doing? Ring the bell for a servant, Adam, honestly." She shook her head.

Adam ignored his mother's scolding, and honestly thought about her question. Did he want to enclose a note for Sarah? The girl was his fiancée. They had been engaged a few weeks now. He had left abruptly. He ought to say something, but what? Was it awful that he didn't have anything in particular to say?

"Well?" prompted Cecily.

"No, Mother," murmured Adam.

"I'll write something for you," Cecily decided. "An apology on behalf of your idiotbrother," she seethed. "I am inviting the Earl and Lady Ashley, and of course,Lady Sarah, to stay for the winter. We need society in this village. It will give you and Sarah time to get better acquainted and we might start to make plans for a spring wedding. What do you say?"

Her question at the end of her speech was merely a formality. Cecily did not care one bit what Adam had to say. She would do what she pleased. But Adam did think it would be a good idea to better get to know Lady Sarah. They did get on. She was amiable, and indeed, very pretty. But Adam did want to like her. He would sooner sentence himself to a madhouse then to have a marriage as affectionate as his parent's.

Peregrine and Cecily Beresford were about as agreeable as syphilis.

"Mother, it would not kill you to nicer to Jack," Adam said, changing the subject.

Cecily's eyes narrowed. "Watch your mouth," she snapped. "He was coddled too much as a child anyway. All three of you were. I would never have dared behave in the way that he does. And neither would your father. He won't be getting a kind word from me until he cleans up his act." With that, she turned on her heel and stalked off down the hallway.

Adam shook his head and swore under his breath as he began to put the letters into his old trunk, safely with their silly marriage certificate. He knew he ought to throw them into the fire, to be rid of them, but he couldn't. He had long resigned to the fact that he would rather have a few happy memories than none at all.

Adam's mind wandered to thoughts of the village again, knowing that at this very moment, she could well be wandering the street, going about her day. She wouldn't know that he was returned. What would she say? Adam stopped himself then. What would he say to her?

He was determined to be indifferent, but that did not stop the curiosity from bubbling to the surface. What did she look like now? Who was she now?

Would Grace know Adam if she saw him again?

It was almost like fate itself that pulled him from his bedroom, down the stairs and out into the grounds of Ashwood. Horses were among his father's favourite pastimes, and so he kept a myriad of fine stallions and mares in the Ashwood stable.

With the help of the groom, Adam chose a fast chestnut coloured stallion and saddled him, before setting off towards the village. As he rode, his mind raced with the possibilities of what he might find. None of which helped him to find the right thing to say to her that did not start with him shouting at her for breaking her word. Logically, Adam knew that he couldn't hold it against her. Grace had only been a girl, but their friendship, he was certain, had meant something to her.

Adam seemed to subconsciously find her house. He hadn't even really thought of where he was going, but he had found his way there all the same. It had tired over the years, weathered without repair. There were shingles missing and window frames that were rotting. A window upstairs was open, and Adam knew someone was home.

Adam had not dismounted and was about two hundred yards from the front door. As he stared at it, it opened, and a young, dark haired woman emerged.

Adam's breath caught so quickly in his throat that he nearly choked. Her long, charcoal coloured hair was down, wavy, and reached her hips. She was pale, and slender, and quite pretty. He couldn't quite make out her features from where he was, but it had to be her. God was taunting him with her standing there.

Grace started off down the street with a basket under her arm. Like a fool, Adam nudged his horse forward as he followed her. Grace walked to the next street over, and Adam kept up with her. She made her way past numerous little shops flogging their goods and was heading towards a forge. It was on the end of the street, pumping smoke up into the air.

What business did she have at a forge?

As Adam approached, slowing his horse down, he could see a large, burly man beating his hammer against an anvil repeatedly. He was assisted by a young man, a boy of about fourteen or fifteen. Grace entered the forge, and the blacksmith stopped his work immediately. His face softened when his eyes settled on her, and he received Grace into his arms.

Adam fell off of his horse.

Nursing what would be some nasty bruises, Adam was nearly sick himself as he watched the blacksmith kiss Grace softly. Oh God, he had contemplated the thought of her being married, but seeing it cut him to his core.

"Adam?"

Adam heard his name being called and his head snapped around to find a pair of concerned blue eyes.

"Are you alright?"

They were so familiar, but not the same shade of cornflower blue that could be found in the eyes of the woman over there kissing her husband.

Her hair was dark, and her skin was pale, and she looked so similar to Grace it was startling, but it wasn't her. It had to be her sister.

"Kate?" Adam recalled as he quickly climbed to his feet, brushing the dust off of his breeches.

She shook her head. "No, I am Claire," she corrected. "Kate is over there with her husband." Claire pointed to the forge, and Adam's head spun so quickly he nearly gave himself whiplash.

Kate was looking at both Adam and Claire, allowing him to get a better look at her face. Like Claire, he could now see the differences. They were very alike, but she wasn't Grace, and a guilty feeling of relief washed through him.

"What are you doing here?" Claire asked. "Where did you get back?"

"About an hour ago," Adam said breathlessly. Lord, had he only made it an hour before he had gone riding into town. "Please, where is Grace?"

Claire looked up at him with a completely confused expression on her face. "Why, Ashwood House, of course," she replied, frowning.

It was now Adam's turn to be confused. "What on earth are you talking about?" he demanded to know.

Chapter 6

"You two, come with me."

Grace and Ruby were beckoned by a maid dressed all in black, the dress of a lady's maid. Grace did not know her name, but she knew that the woman worked for the duchess.

She was perhaps forty or so, with a stern, no-nonsense air about her, and a hard, cold stare.

The two girls had just finished attending to the opening of the ladies parlour. The furniture had been uncovered and plumped, the fire laid, and every surface dusted twice.

"I am Miss Naismith, maid to Her Grace," the lady's maid introduced herself, leading Grace and Ruby out of the hallway and into the internal staircase with ease and experience. Grace did not recognise her, but then she did not imagine that she would have taken much notice of the duchess' lady's maid when she was a child.

"I am Ruby Trickett," Ruby replied, keeping up with Miss Naismith's quick pace up the stairs.

"Grace Denham," added Grace.

Miss Naismith paused for the briefest of seconds upon hearing Grace's name, before continuing on her path. "You are both to change the duchess' linens, quickly and quietly."

Grace tried to ignore the feeling of dread that bubbled in her stomach at the idea of being in such close proximity to the duchess. Really, she was sure that she had nothing to worry about. Grace was certain that the duchess would have forgotten all about her, not that she ever paid much attention to Grace in the first place. The duchess did not seem like the type of woman who conversed with her housemaids anyway.

They emerged from the internal staircase and out into the once familiar hallway that housed the great bedrooms belonging to the Beresfords. Grace struggled to compose herself as she walked past the pictures of the historical painted faces that once frightened her. They passed window after window, until they came to the very place where ...

... where she had felt love for the very first time. Lord, it seemed a lifetime ago now that she had been running about with Adam. How much had changed.

Miss Naismith opened the door to the duchess' bedroom and led Grace and Ruby inside. Considering the richness of Ashwood House, it ought not to have been a surprise at the grandeur of the duchess' bedroom. But it was.

Central to the far wall was an enormously imposing white bed, with gold detail on the frame. A red velvet canopy hung from the ceiling and draped down around it, the curtains fixed to the posts with a thick, golden rope. The rest of the furnishings were just as rich and luxurious, namely a white marble fireplace with a golden fire poker set. Grace wondered if they were real. Lord, if they were, such an ostentatious item could feed the whole village for a year!

Grace recovered from her amazement quickly and was thankful to see that the duchess was not in her bedroom. She and Ruby quickly set to work in stripping the bed of its linens. They looked and smelled clean, and Grace wondered at the necessity, but she then supposed that rich people could have whatever they wanted.

"I've never been in here before," Ruby whispered to Grace as she pulled the pillows from their slips.

Grace could see that Ruby was just as amazed as she was. Miss Naismith then left them, closing the door behind her.

Together, they folded the duvet and left it on the trunk so that she could remove the sheets from the mattress. The sheets themselves felt divine to the touch, and Grace could not bear to gather them up in a crumpled pile for laundering. She folded them as well, and together with Ruby, they went to make their way out of the bedroom.

But the door was opened again before they could leave, and Grace came face to face with Cecily Beresford. Her hazel eyes were searching, and they settled on Grace almost instantly. Grace's heart stopped. Cecily's eyes flicked to Ruby, and a slight frown creased her forehead.

"Get out," she demanded rudely.

Ruby did not need to be asked twice. She all but ran from the bedroom, leaving Cecily standing between Grace and the door. Cecily pulled gently on the door behind her and it swung close with a slight squeak of the hinges before it latched.

"It can't be little Grace Denham, can it?" she remarked.

Grace hoped the duchess did not mean to refer to her as it. "I am Grace Denham, Your Grace," she said politely, respectfully, curtseying to the duchess as her station deserved.

Lord, whatever happened, Grace could not afford to anger the duchess. She needed her position at Ashwood House. If she was sacked, then her family would certainly starve. Her mother, Claire, Peter and Jem entirely depended on her keeping her job.

"My goodness," remarked Cecily, pursing her lips as she appraised Grace shamelessly, her eyes floating over Grace from the top of her head, to the tips of her toes. "You have grown up."

That tended to happen to children, thought Grace before she chastised herself. "I have," she said instead, as pleasantly as she could manage. "Are you well, Your Grace?" she asked politely.

She duchess responded with a facetious, teasing sort of laugh. "Oh, child, you shall not address me with questions. We are not acquainted," she said mockingly, and Grace clamped her lips shut, feeling embarrassed. "What are you doing in my house?" Her tone changed to one of short temper. She was demanding an answer from Grace.

"I work here," replied Grace, thinking her gown and apron explanation enough.

The duchess' eyes narrowed. "Mind your tongue!" scolded Cecily sharply.

Grace gasped. "Forgive me, I meant no offense," she pleaded, though entirely unsure what for. She needed to remember what her mother had always told her when she was a child. The duchess had never liked her, and Grace needed to endeavour to be as perfectly pleasant as she could muster.

"Why are you working in my house?" asked the duchess firmly.

"I have been a housemaid for five years, Your Grace, ever since my father passed away. My mother recently took a nasty fall and broke her leg. I am here to support my family, Your Grace." She prayed that the duchess could sympathise.

Cecily did seem to sense Grace's sincerity and desperation. Her shoulders, which had been quite tense, relaxed a little and she seemed to click her tongue as she thought. "Well, it seems you have the perfect motivation to be on your best behaviour then," she mused.

"I beg your pardon?"

"I know my son severed all ties with you years ago," said Cecily, so casually it felt like a slap across the face. She seemed pleased when her words made Grace flinch. "But you will have absolutely no reason to speak to Lord Beresford. There will be no repeat of any childish antics. I shall have no reason to dismiss you if you behave just as a housemaid should. You are not to be seen or heard. My son need not even know you are here. Am I quite understood?" The duchess took a step towards her, standing several inches taller than Grace.

Grace nervously nodded, feeling as though she was once again a little girl getting into trouble for running amok with Adam.

"Run along now, and back to work. It seems your dear mama is depending on you," Cecily urged, waving Grace off.

Grace nodded, before quickly darting back to the bed to collect the linens. She quickly curtseyed to the duchess before leaving the bedroom, finding Ruby waiting for her in the hallway. Ruby immediately took some of the laundry to ease Grace's load as she stared at her expectantly.

"Well?" she prompted. "What on earth was that all about?"

"The duchess just had some very specific instructions on how she wants her linens to be pressed," lied Grace quietly

Ruby scoffed. "Please!" she exclaimed, but Grace was tight-lipped and would not reveal any other information.

As they came to the end of the hallway to where the concealed doorway was situated, they both heard a loud bang as the front door in the entry foyer below burst open. Curiosity got the better of both of them as she quickly peered out to see what the matter was.

A small gasp escaped her lips as she saw Adam stumble inside, looking quite out of breath, sweaty, and searching. Grace jumped away from view, and quickly pulled open the door, ushering Ruby through. "Come on," she urged. "The duchess expects these linens to be cleaned."

The moment they reached the kitchen, a delicious aroma filled Grace's nose. As the servants had spent a good few hours opening the house, their luncheon had been delayed, and it seemed like a hearty soup was to be enjoyed by all. At least, she hoped that the stew was for them and not for the Beresfords.

Her stomach instinctively grumbled. Mr Cole was already seated at the head of the dining table, and many of the servants had begun to gather for their meal.

Mrs Hayes smiled at Grace and then Ruby as she emerged from her sitting room. "You girls go and pop those in the laundry and then come and have something to eat," she instructed, motioning them along.

As Grace and Ruby put the linens down on the large workbench in the laundry, she heard a deep, male voice call to Mrs Hayes in the dining room.

"Miss Hayes ... Mrs Hayes," he corrected himself, and Grace paled. She couldn't be sure he was looking for her, but then she couldn't be sure he wasn't looking for her, either. Whatever Adam's reason for being downstairs, Grace was determined that she would not be seen.

"Go on then," Grace told Ruby. "I'll put these in the water. Won't you save me a seat?"

"Alright." Ruby nodded and skipped out of the laundry.

The minute she was gone, Grace fled the laundry in the opposite direction. Lord, it couldn't be this soon after the duchess' warning, could it? She darted up the back staircase, taking the narrow steps two at a time. Where she was going, she had no idea. Grace heard footsteps behind her. When she looked over the railing to the floor below, she could see Adam starting upwards.

"Grace?" he called out.

Christ!

Her mind immediately filled with memories from her childhood of when Adam would chase her about this house. Only now it wasn't a game. She increased her pace, running all the way up to the third floor where the servants' bedrooms were located. Grace's heart was absolutely thundering, and there was no way that enough air was making its way into her lungs with how shallow her breaths were. Grace sprinted up the hallway, past the bedrooms of the male servants, and eyed the door that separated them from the bedrooms of the female servants.

Sanctuary! She would hide in her bedroom. He would surely not know which it was.

Grace reached for the doorhandle desperately, and her heart stopped when she realised it was locked. She suddenly remembered that it was kept locked, and only Mrs Hayes and Mrs Reynolds had keys to this door.

She spun around, facing back down the hallway, feeling quite like a cornered deer in the woods. She immediately went to the first bedroom on her right, having no idea which servant it belonged to, and hissed under her breath when she found it to be locked as well.

Grace did not have time to try another door. She was no longer alone in the corridor. She had been cornered by a man who was once her very best friend, her sweetheart.

His hazel eyes were fixed on her as his broad shoulders rode and fell quickly as he breathed hard. "Grace," he rasped, with a single shake of his head.

Chapter 7

She had run from him. Adam was certain of it. She had scurried up the stairs as quickly as her legs would carry her in an effort to get away from him. Somewhere inside, Adam knew that this behaviour meant that she really did want nothing to do with him. She must have had nothing to say to him.

Her letter had been quite enough.

But Adam's heart was ruling his head in that moment, and he needed to speak to her. Surely, she could not be so callous as to not even want to greet her old friend. They had been friends once.

Adam saw her back first. She was facing a closed door, trying to turn the handle, and appearing frustrated that it would not open. He first noticed that she had not grown very tall. Like her sisters, she was quite small in stature. She wore a plain, dark navy dress with a white apron tied around her waist. He could not see her hair for it was tucked underneath a white cap. Was it as long and wavy as Kate's? Adam immediately wanted to see it down.

She turned, not seeing him standing there, sucking in heavy breaths, and reached for the first door on her right, and found it, too, was locked. Once again, Adam was hit with the realisation that she was truly trying to hide from him.

But his thoughts were quite quickly eclipsed by the very fact that he was truly seeing her for the first time in twelve years. Lord, he had always thought her a pretty girl. Impossibly pretty. He would frequently get into trouble at school for staring at her and missing the answers when the vicar would call upon him.

He would be grateful in years to come that he had this opportunity to look on her again. Grace had grown into a truly beautiful, young woman. Her face was soft, and heart-shaped, with a lovely flush to her cheeks from the three flights of stairs she had just climbed. Her large, corn-flower blue eyes found him the hallway, widening with shock. Adam wished he were closer. Her eyes used to look violet in low light and he wanted to know if that was still true.

Cornflower blue was still his favourite colour, even after all this time.

Her pink lips parted, and he heard her gasp. A few tendrils of her charcoal coloured hair had fallen out from under her cap, and they were framing her face perfectly.

"Grace," he said, his voice hoarse from panting. Adam suddenly realised that it was the first time in many years that he had said her name aloud.

And yet she said nothing. Not words escaped her parted lips, not even his name. She stared at him, half in shock, half in ... well, he honestly couldn't tell. Adam dared to take a few steps towards her.

Grace seemed to instinctively press herself up against the door, trying to move as far away from him as she possibly could. Adam could not pretend that he had not seen that, and he ceased his approach. Why was she so anxious to be away from him? Ought not he be the one to want to keep his distance?

His anger, his hurt, and his questions kept being pushed aside by his pure elation to be seeing her again. Adam was so glad to know her, to have a chance to know her. No matter what he had been through, what she had put him through, here he stood, ready to throw himself into the deep.

"How ... how are you?" he asked, nerves shaking his voice a little.

Grace shifted nervously on her feet; her hands pressed against the door behind her. "Well," was all she could muster in reply. Her eyes dropped, and Adam felt the urge to demand she looked at him, just so that he could see her eyes.

But her answer vexed him. Well. Was that all she could say? Was that all he deserved?

Grace focussed her stare at the ground in front of him, her shoulders rolling forward in a way that closed herself off. There was a sudden coldness to her, which was a word that he never would have used to describe the Grace he had known.

She truly did mean every word in that letter, and nothing had changed, not even after all this time. What he had been expecting, Adam really didn't know. But he couldn't stop himself from wanting to just speak to her again.

But this was the result. What had he done to deserve this?

"I am well, too. Thank you for asking," he said facetiously, and without thinking.

She looked up again, her eyes flashing to his as they narrowed. There was anger there, fire, and he could see something in her. She was holding her tongue, but she felt something. If it was anything other than an apology, he couldn't understand it.

Grace took a deep breath, then, and she calmed herself, composed herself, regaining the focussed coldness of a moment ago. Adam didn't like this about her. It annoyed him, really, that she had the nerve to be this way.

"Footmen see to the gentlemen," Grace then murmured. "You should have no need to speak with me. I am but a housemaid, so I am of no consequence to you."

Adam felt so shocked at her words that he needed to take a step back, feeling as though she had pushed him herself. "Really?" he repeated, his voice little more than a gasp. "I never imagined you to be a rude person, Grace. How things have changed." His teeth clenched.

"Rude?" retorted Grace, with as much resentment in her voice that he had ever heard. But she said nothing further. Once again, she swallowed her tongue and regained her composure, seemingly determined not to answer for herself.

Adam realised Grace would not apologise. She would not right the wrong she did him, and he was a damned fool to be standing in front of her, waiting for her to make it right. She wasn't his friend, and she certainly was not anything more than that.

What came next, Adam was not proud of. He did not like that he had been so determined to injure her in that moment, but it was as if he could not control his own tongue. "I am engaged," he said, in such a spiteful tone that he never knew he had. "Won't you congratulate me?" It was utterly ungentlemanlike, but he simply couldn't help it.

The blood drained from Grace's cheeks as shock spread across her face as she heard the news. She, again, said nothing, but the damage was done, and somehow, in some deep, horrid part of Adam that resented Grace Denham enormously, it made him feel better.

Adam turned on his heel and left her there, fuming as he walked. Lord, he was furious with her, and he knew that he would be angry at his own behaviour in time. But today was not that day.

Adam descended to the second floor and emerged out into the hallway that housed the family's bedrooms. After checking on Jack to make sure that he was still sleeping soundly, Adam knocked on Susanna's door, entering after he heard her soft greeting.

Susanna's bedroom was in disarray. Every possession that she owned seemed out on the floor as she organised what to put away in her trunk. The wardrobe doors were open and there was clothing everywhere. Some of the dresses Adam could remember Susanna wearing when she was a child.

"Why don't you ring for a maid to help you with this?" Adam asked her, before immediately chastising himself. What if Susanna followed his advice and Grace was sent to assist? He would certainly be making himself scarce.

"I haven't seen most of my things since I was seven," replied Susanna. "I am actually quite enjoying myself," she mused with a smile. She then looked up at Adam and her expression changed.

Adam realised he must not have had a very neutral look on his face.

"Adam, what is it?" she asked, concerned. She abandoned the gown that she was holding and stepped over the obstacles on her floor to reach him. She placed a comforting hand on his forearm.

Adam was very protective of his younger siblings. Naturally, as Susanna's elder brother, Adam would always watch over her, but he felt it necessary to ensure that Susanna was protected from many of the consequences of being a woman in her position. They need only look at their parent for the result of a marriage of convenience.

At nineteen, she was still divinely innocent, but she was not oblivious.

"Grace is here," Adam said simply, his voice annoyingly thick.

Susanna's green eyes fell with knowing and concern. There had been a time when Susanna had been desperate for Grace's approval. She would have done anything to be

Grace's friend, and Adam had found her terribly annoying. Selfishly, he had wanted Grace for himself. As she had grown, Susanna had perceptively understood Adam's motivations during those times.

"Did she come to see you?" Susanna asked softly.

Adam exhaled sharply. "No," he replied. "She is a house-maid." And she had done the exact opposite of coming to see him. She had run from him. The thought made his blood boil. "She has nothing to say to me. Not even an apology."

Susanna knew everything, as did Jack. Adam had not been a pleasant person to be around for a while after Grace's letter had arrived. Susanna, at the time, had been disappointed that she would not be a proper bridesmaid, as only a little girl could be. As she had matured, she had been more tender, and cleverly never mentioned Grace again.

"Will you be alright, Adam?" she asked him quietly.

Adam managed a small smile for his sister. "Of course, I will be," he assured her. He was determined that he would never be so affected by Grace Denham again.

Adam might have walked right up to Grace and slapped her across the face. At least, that was what it had felt like once he had informed her of his engagement before stalking off away from her.

Grace was certainthat his confession of such a fact in that way was a deliberate attempt to wound her, and, by God, he had succeeded. A silent sob had escaped her chest in that moment as she had crumpled to the floor, the moment he was out of view.

What had she done to deserve such a reception? After all this time, and after everything he had put her through, that was how Adam had chosen to renew their acquaintance? But, she thought, there would be no acquaintance. That would be their only encounter, she was determined. The first and last meeting was done, and she would keep her promise to the Duchess. Adam was aware of her presence, though that was not her fault, but she would certainly be keeping her distance. And truthfully, after such a display, Grace had no desire to speak with Adam Beresford again.

That Sunday, Grace visited her mother, but told her nothing of meeting with Adam again. Mrs Denham was very worried for Grace as the news of the Beresfords returning to Ashwood had reached her.

"I do not see them, Mama," Grace said, which was truthful. The footmen served the family. The housemaids were kept out of sight.

Mrs Denham shook her head angrily. "Oh, if I were but going with you today, I would have something to say to that boy for treating my daughter so ill, I assure you!"

"Mama," calmed Grace, "really, we were children," she dismissed, perfectly convincing. "There need not be any more to it than that. Mrs Hayes is seeing to it that I am valued and perfectly busy at Ashwood House. I have little time to dwell on anything other than my duties."

Mrs Denham settled and tapped Grace's hand affectionately. "You are such a good girl, Grace," she said, her voice thickening. "Off you go." She shooed her. "You do not want to be late."

Grace leaned over and kissed her mother's forehead before leaving her bedroom. "Peter!" she called. "Jemmy! Are you ready?" Grace's younger brother's both emerged from their bedroom dressed in their Sunday best, Peter quickly helping to adjust young Jem's collar.

"I do not see why we should have to go if Mama cannot go," complained Jem.

Grace's eyes narrowed as she smirked. The sun was out. Her twelve-year-old brother would far rather run about with his friends than sit for an hour and listen to a sermon. "Hush," she scolded, before combing his unkempt dark hair through with her fingers.

Claire was dressed in her best gown as well, dark hair up, and bonnet atop her head. The four siblings went down the stairs one by one and out the door, calling their farewells to their mother.

Every one of their neighbours was out and about on their way to the church for the morning service. The church was in the centre of the village, a gorgeous stone building with a tall belltower that rang out as it beckoned the flock.

Kate and Jim were already seated when they arrived, and Grace filed her siblings in the pew. Claire seemed to linger, looking around as subtly as she could manage for someone, whom Grace knew to be Arthur Slickson. He was seated beside Grace's old mistress, Mrs Slickson, and not paying any attention to Claire. Grace ushered her down, before taking a seat herself on the end. The church was quickly filling, and Grace smiled to several of the servants from Ashwood House that she now thought of as friendly acquaintances, if not her friends. Ruby was sitting with a few of the other housemaids in her Sunday best, and she waved kindly at Grace.

The hum of friendly conversation in the church silenced as one final party joined the congregation. Grace, as did everyone else, turned her head back to see who had joined them.

The duke walked down the aisle, the duchess on his arm. He looked perfectly indifferent, but she walked with her nose in their air, as though she were trying to appear taller than those she passed. Behind them was Adam, with Lady Susanna on his arm. Susanna had a kind smile on her sweet face as she passed the congregation, and Adam seemed to admire this in his sister. No sooner had Grace willed herself to look down, Adam's eyes found her for the briefest of moments.

But he looked away a moment later and passed her without a second glance. Grace swallowed loudly.

Jack walked behind his family, looking as though he wished he were anywhere else. Despite looking as though he didn't want to be there, he was dressed decidedly better than the last time Grace had seen him. He indeed looked handsome when sober, and not ill with drink.

The Beresfords took their places in the front, elevated box, that had stood empty for twelve years, looking as though they had never left. Grace didn't even realise that she was looking over at them before Claire took her hand in comfort.

Grace smiled at her sister, and squeezed her hand, forcing herself to concentrate as the vicar took his place at the altar.

Chapter 8

In the weeks that passed, the leaves began to change, and the last rays of summer began to fade away. Winter was inevitable, and there was a chill in the air already alerting every resident of Ashwood that it was coming.

With the coming cold season came confirmation that Adam's fiancée, Lady Sarah Ashley, and her mother, Lady Ashley, would be coming to stay at Ashwood House come early November.

Receiving this news after several weeks of actively avoiding a certain housemaid gave Adam purpose. He couldn't change what Grace had done, and she was certainly not going out of her way to mend any of the hurt between them, and so he needed to continue to move forward with his life.

Lady Sarah was a sweet girl, and the match pleased his parents. Anything that eased their displeasure was a good decision. It had taken Adam a long time, many, many years, in fact, to really understand his position in life. He was the heir to a vast fortune, an enormously rich estate, and a title that came with an immeasurable level of respect and honour. Not only was it his birthright, but it was his responsibilityto take pride in his future. With such an inheritance came the livelihoods of every family who lived upon his land.

"Well, that is the best news I have had all week," Cecily declared over breakfast, having stolen the note from Sarah out of Adam's hands, reading over the words excitedly. "Finally," she scoffed, "some society. But then," she continued, eyeing Jack, who was sitting at the other end of the table, his nose in a book as he absently crushed the remainder of his hard-boiled eggshell with the back of his spoon. "Did not we need some good news this week?"

Adam rolled his eyes. Susanna, who was sitting beside Cecily at the dining table, peered over their mother's shoulder at the letter. Her expression was neutral, if not reserved.

"Do not be coy, Mother," murmured Jack distastefully, not looking up from his book.

Adam pursed his lips as he looked upon his troubled younger brother with concern. Their father had officially written to the bishop this week, suspending all future plans for Jack's joining the church. Of course, it was long known within their household that Jack had no intention of writing sermons for the rest of his life, but it had not been set in stone until this week.

Jack was not meant to give sermons, nor was he ready to practise a Godly existence. Despite having made this decision, Adam was not entirely sure what else Jack coulddo with his life. He was a twenty-three-year-old young man who had never received a kind word from his parents. He was lost, and Adam knew that no matter what he said or did, Jack always felt like he didn't belong.

Now he would certainly need a rich wife to support him. He would need a good woman, the sort of woman to help him, to give him a purpose and a place where he felt valued and needed. He hoped those women would be one and the same.

Cecily hissed under her breath. "Do not test my patience, Jack," she snapped. "Were it not for the shame of having such a son out in society embarrassing us, I would not have you under my roof."

"That's quite enough, Mother," Adam said curtly, almost wincing on Jack's behalf, but Jack had already left the table, slamming the dining room door behind him. Adam glared across the table. "Has it ever crossed your mind that perhaps he might strive to the occasion if you but praised him once?" he demanded to know.

Cecily's eyes narrowed. "Do not you start," she hissed. "It is not yet ten in the morning." She shook the letter in her hand. "It is supposed to be a good day. There is to be a wedding, and a most agreeable match. I will not have your brother spoiling it because he cannot be controlled."

Adam looked to his father for some sense, but Peregrine had all but left the table, despite being physically present. His nose was deep in the newspaper, and his face was hidden. Despite not having a loving union, Peregrine never went against his wife. It was much too tiresome on his aging constitution.

Susanna looked quite upset at the aftermath of the conversation. Adam stood up abruptly, muttering that he needed air under his breath, before leaving the dining room in search of Jack.

This house, despite having a hundred rooms, could feel suffocating sometimes, and Adam had forgotten that after so many years of being away. A sudden crash and the sound of smashed glass made Adam head toward the library. As soon as he opened the door, the smell of whiskey stung his nose.

The rosewood bureau, where their father's collection of Scottish whiskeys resided beside his reading chair, was opened, and Jack was leaning back against one of the stocked bookshelves with his eyes closed, the broken bottle at his feet. The amber liquid was soaking into the rug.

"Are you hurt?" Adam asked him. "Did you cut yourself?"

Jack opened his eyes and shook his head. "No," he replied. "I threw the damned thing. Don't worry, I've rung the bell for a maid. I wasn't planning on leaving the glass."

Adam didn't have time to dwell on the fact a maid would be coming. The chance it would be her was small. "You know Mother was out of line," he appealed to his brother. "You know what she's like."

"This place is a bloody prison," Jack cursed. "She doesn't want me here, and I don't want to be here. If I were in the city, I could at least go and get –" losing the word, he concluded with, "– lost."

"I want you here, and Susanna wants you here," Adam retorted. "I know you won't abandon her."

Jack shot Adam a glance. "I don't know what to do."

Adam knew that his brother's words had many meanings. Jack really didn't know what to do, and Adam didn't have the answers. How could he when Adam, himself, really hadn't ever made such a decision himself? Adam's life was planned for him. Who he was meant to be was written the moment he was born.

"You will always belong here, I hope you know that, Jack. I will never abandon you. When I inherit, I promise things will be different," Adam swore.

They were interrupted by a knock on the door, and two maids entered the library. The first, a redhaired housemaid that Adam did not recognise. The second, a housemaid who looked as though she would have rather been anywhere else. Her eyes were on the ground as she allowed the red-haired girl to speak for her.

"Begging your pardon, milords, but you rang?" she said respectfully, curtseying. Grace, too, curtseyed.

Adam didn't know why, but the action angered him. The very fact that she wouldn't look at him angered him, and he didn't want to feel angry when he was concentrating on his brother. She certainly didn't volunteer to come upstairs; Adam would wager the house on that fact. She had been forced to attend them.

"Yes," said Jack, "I'm sorry, but my temper got the best of me. I've made a mess of the rug." Jack stepped away from the glass, but caught some under his boot, making a painful crunching sound. "I'll tidy the glass," he uttered shamefully. "Might you get something to clean the floor?"

"Yes, of course, milord," said the first maid.

The very moment Jack knelt down to pick up the glass, his swore in the presence of the women, cutting himself. Blood began to stream down his hand as he clutched it to his chest. His face bore more than pain from a cut, and Adam felt momentarily helpless.

Grace, however, was not so. "Won't you go and some vinegar and cloth to clean the carpet?" she urged the redhead. "I will help milord." The maid nodded and left the library as Grace raced over to Jack's side, carefully kneeling where there was not glass as she produced a handkerchief from her pocket. She took Jack's hand without hesitation and placed the handkerchief on his palm, closing her hand around his into a fist. "Hold it nice and tight," she instructed. "When it stops bleeding, I will check it for glass and then stitch it should the cut be deep enough."

"Are you a nurse, miss?" asked Jack, bashfully for his clumsiness.

"No," replied Grace. "Only I have four younger siblings, all of whom have needed tending to at one point or another."

She smiled briefly, and Adam, who had been unwittingly staring as the situation unfolded, nearly choked on the breath he had inhaled. Jack looked up as Adam spluttered, before looking on the face of the maid who had helped him for the first time. Immediately, Jack stopped, peering at her as he pieced together exactly who she was.

"You ... you aren't little Grace Denham, are you?" he asked in disbelief.

Grace's cheeks reddened. "I may not have grown very much, but we are the same age, milord," she replied.

Jack looked up at Adam as he exclaimed with surprise. "Adam, did you know it was Grace?"

In the weeks that had passed, only Susanna knew of Grace's presence within the household. Adam was not even sure his parents were aware. His mother didn't concern herself with the servants. They were Mrs Hayes' responsibility.

All lightness left Grace's face after her brief interaction with Jack as the attention turned to Adam. She would not smile at Adam. She would not even look at him, not really.

When Adam didn't respond, Jack abandoned that avenue of conversation as his eyes flicked back to Grace. "What are you doing here, Grace?" he asked curiously. "Or should it be Miss Denham?" he asked suddenly, realising that indeed twelve years had passed, and they were no longer childhood friends.

"I am a housemaid," replied Grace, "so it is proper that you know me by my Christian name."

"But whyare you a housemaid," pressed Jack, and Adam felt his own curiosity rise.

Adam didn't intervene, and Grace was obligated to answer the question asked of her by one of her masters. She immediately busied her hands, carefully collecting the glass from the bottle and piling it to the side.

"My ... my father died ... five years ago," she admitted quietly. "Did you hear?"

Adam knew that question was for him, and he felt guilt as he shook his head. No, he hadn't heard that Mr Denham had passed away. What would he have done had he known at the time, Adam wondered. But immediately, that explained so much. Without her father's income, it would be up to the children to earn a living in order to support their mother. Adam knew Grace had brothers, but they were, indeed, several years younger.

"I am sorry to hear that," Adam said softly, and he meant that with all sincerity. Mr Denham had been a good man, and Adam had admired him as a boy. He had always liked how Mr Denham played with his children, laughed with them, and Grace had always glad when he arrived home.

But as deeply as he sympathised, it didn't change anything. She had thrown everything away long before her father had died, and she would not atone for it now. She had not even attempted to.

"How are the rest of your family?" asked Jack.

One of her sisters was married. Kate, Adam recalled. The sister that he had mistaken for Grace weeks ago. He was still bruised from falling off of his horse.

"Well, I thank you," Grace replied. "My mother took a fall, but she is healing and in good spirits. My sister, Kate, is married to Mr Ellis, the blacksmith in the village. Claire, my youngest sister if you remember, looks after our mother. My brothers are both in good health, young and spirited." Despite her mother's injury, she spoke with a sweet fondness in her voice when she talked of her family.

Adam was thankful when the red-haired maid returned with a tray full of clothes and a bowl of water, or vinegar, from the smell of it. As she knelt down beside Grace, Grace opened Jack's hand and gently removed the handkerchief to look at the cut.

The blood had stopped, and a clean cut could be seen on the edge of his palm. Inspecting it closely, Grace decided, "It won't need stitches. It should heal quite nicely. Here." Picking up one of the cloths from the tray, she tore it in half to make a bandage. Grace then wrapped it around Jack's palm, before fixing it with a knot.

"Come along, Jack," urged Adam. "We are in the way."

Jack left the library with Adam, and despite his cut, and the events in the dining room, he seemed in remarkably better spirits.

"Did you know Grace was here?" Jack asked him once they were out in the hall.

"Yes," admitted Adam, saying nothing further.

"Why didn't you say anything?" Jack pressed. "Are you glad to see her?" His eyes suddenly widened as a thought occurred to him. "What are you going to do about Lady Sarah?"

Adam frowned. "What do you mean 'what am I going to do about Lady Sarah'?" he scoffed, conveniently avoiding Jack's first two questions.

"Well, how are you going to tell her that you already have a wife?" Jack mused. "And that she lives under your very roof."

Adam punched his brother in the shoulder, irritated that his own predicament brought Jack the amusement that he had so been lacking these last few weeks. "Don't say such things," Adam snapped. "Grace saw to it herself that our understanding was severed. The very idea is irrelevant now."

Chapter 9

Grace performed her duties as diligently as she possibly could in the weeks since the Beresfords had returned home, all the while under the constant scrutiny of the duchess' maid, Miss Naismith.

The duchess didn't trust Grace, which was something that she couldn't quite understand. She had only but look to her son to see that he had become exactly the sort of gentleman that she had wanted him to be. He was educated, refined, engaged, and entirely without desire to rekindle any sort of attachment that he and Grace had once shared.

Did the duchess could not have known about the letter that Adam had sent Grace, or else she would not have bothered with her spy.

Grace kept up her end of the bargain and took everything that she earned home to her family each week. It would still be a while before her mother would be mobile, and until then, Grace would be on her best behaviour.

She had succeeded in avoiding Adam until that very day when she and Ruby had been summoned to the library. Revealing the loss of her father and stealing a glance up at Adam in that moment proved to her that he hadn't known, and for a moment she could see his genuine sadness for her.

Even if their childhood dreams and promises were lost, her friend was still inside of him. Part of her, a large part, longed to know him again.

"There has to be more that you are not telling me," insisted Ruby that night.

They both were sitting up in their beds. Grace was brushing through her hair, ready to fix it into a braid to sleep in. "I grew up in this village," replied Grace dismissively. "As did many people. We went to the church school for a time as children. Yes, we knew each other, but it has been many years since then."

Ruby huffed impatiently. "I just find it hard to believe that someone like you could be known to two lords like that," Ruby remarked. "It would be like someone likeme being known to two lords."

Grace knew that Ruby had not meant any offense in her statement, but she wholly understood what she meant. It was not usual that someone of her rank could boast a connection like the one she had. Not that she would ever boast.

"Things are different when you are children," Grace offered. "Children don't see rank or status, titles or fortune. Their blindness to circumstance is what makes childhood innocence, childhood friendship, so beautiful."

Ruby sighed, offering Grace a small, accepting smile. "I suppose you are right," she allowed. "I only wish some of my childhood friends had grown up to have thousands of pounds and an estate this size."

"Oh, hush," shushed Grace. She quickly plaited her hair and threw it over her shoulder, before blowing out the candle between them.

Near the end of September, Grace had managed another several weeks without seeing Adam. It was getting easier being within Ashwood House, and Miss Naismith had eased her constant watch. Grace's routine was a boring one, and the lady's maid could see day after day that Grace was not diverting from it.

Her mother's healing was coming along, and the doctor was due to visit in October to check on her.

On the morning of the twenty-ninth of September, as the servants were sitting down to breakfast, the three Beresfords entered the kitchen bearing gifts. Adam, Jack and Susanna made their way cheerfully over to Mrs Hayes, before presenting her with the gifts before the entire household.

"Happy birthday, Mrs Hayes," Adam said tenderly, his sentiments echoed by Jack and Susanna.

Mrs Hayes looked truly touched, and the rest of the household began to wish her a happy birthday as well.

"Happy birthday, Mrs Hayes," added Grace, smiling over at the kind woman. Adam's eyes flashed to Grace's when he heard her voice, but he didn't smile. Instead, he stared at her coldly for a brief moment before turning his attention back to the woman who had been his mother figure as a child.

This small interaction, however, was noticed by Mrs Hayes, and she frowned ever so slightly. "My dears," she said, recovering. "You remembered! Thank you. Thank you all!"

"Of course, we did, Mrs Hayes," Jack assured her, wearing the first smile that Grace had ever seen on his face.

"We hope you like it," added Susanna, motioning to the present.

Mrs Hayes moved her porridge aside and placed the box down on the table. She removed the lid and unwrapped a beautiful silver hairbrush and comb set.

Grace's eyes widened at the extravagance of the present. How beautiful it was!

Mrs Hayes gasped. "Oh, you shouldn't have! It's too much!"

Adam and Jack leaned down either side of Mrs Hayes and kissed her cheeks. She blushed a little as she patted their heads affectionately.

"It's not nearly enough," promised Susanna.

After wishing Mrs Hayes a happy birthday again, the three Beresfords left the kitchen, and the breakfast resumed shortly after. Nobody else seemed to have observed the way that Adam had looked upon Grace, and she was thankful that there were no questions.

Or so she had thought. When the dishes were cleared, and the maids and footman dispersed for their morning duties, Grace was called into Mrs Hayes' sitting room.

The door was closed behind her, and Mrs Hayes set down her birthday gift on the table.

"Perhaps we shall have a special dinner tonight," Grace suggested awkwardly. "Now that we know it is your birthday."

"Oh, no," dismissed Mrs Hayes. "Every one of us has a birthday at some point during the year. I've had enough of them. Those three were too generous." She shook her head at the notion, though Grace could see that Mrs Hayes did genuinely appreciate the thought. "Grace, would you tell me if something has happened between yourself and Lord Beresford?"

Mrs Hayes had noticed the exchange. Grace only hoped her denial was convincing.

"No," she murmured, shaking her head.

Mrs Hayes pursed her lips. "I just find it odd ... you two were so inseparable as children ... Adam, he ... Lord Beresford, forgive me, he talked of little else."

"But that was it," Grace said hurriedly. "We were children. I think many people are forgetting that it has been twelve years since they were last here. If one wanted to remain attached, one would write," she insisted, "and that ... he did not ..." Grace stopped herself, her eyes widening at her sudden outburst of emotion. "Forgive me, please, Mrs Hayes," she begged. "Please, nothing has happened. Lord Beresford is a gentleman now. My only wish is that I am able to go about my duties and carry on with my life."

Mrs Hayes still looked a little confused, but she could see that Grace had little desire to discuss the matter further. "Very well," she allowed. "I am sorry to pry. I really is none of my business and it is a sin to gossip." She then smiled.

"You have done an excellent job since you began at Ashwood House, Grace. You are a diligent worker. Your reference from the Slicksons was entirely factual. I am glad you are here. Would you take the new candles up to the ladies parlour, please?" she asked. "You will find them in the buffet drawers. The duchess complained about the smell of the old candles and so we have ordered new ones."

Grace nodded and left Mrs Haye's room. She immediately went to the buffet, in which all the serving dishes were kept. In the drawers were dozens and dozens of candles. She collected a tray and pulled out the amount that she would need, before she walked to the servant's staircase to rise up into the house.

There would be no one in the ladies parlour at this hour, so she had no qualms with slipping into the hallway and into the room. The duchess' breakfast had been being prepared in the kitchen, which meant that she was still abed, and Lady Susanna would never sit in there by herself.

Grace set the tray down on top of the pianoforte and opened the drapes to let the light of the morning in. The fire had been laid, but was no lit, so without the curtains open, it was entirely dark. Once she could see, the walked around the room and collected the old candle stubs and used the pockets of her apron to hold them.

There was a portrait of the duchess that hung above the fireplace. She looked entirely regal, draped in linens and jewels, captured with a perfectly disagreeable expression on her face. Now that Miss Naismith wasn't following her, it was as though the duchess had begun watch.

Grace jumped when the door to the parlour opened, and she froze, unsure of why considering that she had been told to be in there. She relaxed a little when she saw that the visitor was Susanna, and not someone untoward.

With how hesitantly Susanna was lingering at the door, Grace almost thought that she was waiting for an invitation from her. She frowned, before curtseying.

"Good morning, milady," she greeted softly. "I won't be long, I promise. I am just replacing the candles."

"Oh, please don't rush on my account," begged Susanna, stepping nervously into the room.

Grace found Susanna's behaviour a little odd, but she was not about to question her. She was dressed for the day, looking beautifully elegant in white. Her high-waisted gown was cut in the latest fashion, and her hair was curled and styled in an intricate twist. It was still strange to see Susanna as a lady when she had been but a girl of seven, begging to be allowed to join in with her brothers what felt like moments ago.

"I've wanted to talk to you for a little while, Grace. I saw you come in here alone, and I've been working up the courage to enter," Susanna confessed, and Grace's brows furrowed.

"What on earth do you mean?" Grace placed the tray of candles back down on the pianoforte and walked over to Susanna, careful to keep a distance between them.

Colour filled Susanna's cheeks. "Well, I always admired you so," she admitted. "I know things are terribly different now ... for you, at least," she noted.

Again, Grace frowned. Different?

"No one will tell me," she continued. "I can't really ask about you. To say your name ..." she trailed off. "Would you tell me why you have come to Ashwood?" she wondered.

"Oh," realised Grace. That was no terrible secret. "My mother and I were both employed by Mrs Slickson," explained Grace. "But she took a fall and broke her leg. Forgive me for the crassness of it all, but I earn a better wage here. My father passed away five years ago, and so my family depend on my income."

"You support your family?" remarked Susanna softly. "Did you ever want to get married?"

Grace was a little taken aback by the question, considering it was so personal and she and Susanna really were not acquainted properly. But Susanna was her superior, despite their difference in age. "Marriage is not a possibility for me," she replied quietly. "I cannot in good conscience marry and leave my family. They depend on me. It is my responsibility as the eldest to look after them."

Susanna chewed on her bottom lip momentarily. "Where have I heard that before?" she muttered under her breath. "I am terribly sorry to hear of your father, and your mother. I hope she has a speedy recovery," Susanna willed. "You are kind."

The latter seemed like an observation, and decision even, about Grace's character. Grace felt as though she were truly being appraised again.

"You are kind," Susanna said again. "You are selfless, and you do care about the people you love, don't you?"

Grace really had no idea what Susanna was getting to, but she could honestly nod. "Yes, of course," she confirmed.

"Then why would you ..." Susanna hesitated as she pursed her lips, stopping to think.

"Why would I what?" pressed Grace.

Susanna shook her head. "I am sure he would be angry with me if he knew," she continued, changing the subject. "But I think you are a kind person, Grace. I always did. I always wanted you to like me, I wanted your approval," she admitted bashfully.

Grace suddenly felt quite awkward yet flattered at Susanna's confession. But she could assume that Susanna was talking of Adam's anger, and she longed to be in a position to ask why he would be angry. "I don't know why," Grace replied. "You never needed my approval."

"Grace, I do not have any friends," Susanna revealed, quite vulnerably. "I know that there is a conflict ... but I do not think I could find a better, or more decent, friend than you."

The duchess did not want Grace speaking to Adam. What would she say to this? And yet, her heart hurt for Susanna, who looked to be truly putting herself into Grace's hand. She wanted a friend, which to Grace, seemed like such a simple thing to ask of a person.

"Adam can't know," Susanna insisted. "He is still quite hurt, as you could imagine, though he would never admit it ..." she then gasped and clapped her hand over her mouth. "Oh, do pretend you did not hear that. He would surely see me hanged if he knew I told you that!"

"Milady," Grace said insistently. "I really have no idea what you are talking about." She was obviously talking about Adam, but Grace was completing unsure of whatever hurt Susanna was referring to. When had Adam been the one to experience injury?

"It really does take time to mend wounds, I suppose," Susanna realised. She shook off the thought. "Forgive me, please Grace. I feel really foolish now. I shouldn't have approached you like this ... I just thought it would be nice to have someone kind."

Grace's heart hurt for Susanna, which was a strange feeling indeed. "For what it's worth, I always liked you, milady. When we were younger, I thought of you like one of my sisters. I would love to be your friend."

Susanna beamed and almost skipped a step. "You would?" she checked excitedly.

Whatever the sins of her mother, the sins of her brother, Grace could see an innocence about Susanna. If she could take anything away from having to be in this house, let it be a friend.

Chapter 10

"**I**s your sister happy to be married?" Susanna asked Grace curiously as she received a polishing cloth from Grace.

"Yes, very," replied Grace, nodding.

Grace was sitting in the servants' dining room with around four dozen sets of silverware. As Miss Naismith was safely above stairs practising some new hairstyles on the duchess, Susanna had taken it as her chance to come and visit with Grace again. The duchess' maid would be the only one to relay any information from downstairs. While the other servants would see it as highly odd that Lady Susanna Beresford would assist with household chores, Mrs Hayes was one to set them straight in going about their days.

It helped greatly that Mrs Hayes was so fond of the three Beresfords, and Grace, as well.

Over the last month, Susanna had often taken opportunities to seek Grace out, and Grace had been terribly grateful for it. As much as she might have felt like she was indulging

Susanna in the beginning, she was a dear, sweet young lady, whose company Grace greatly enjoyed. She hadn't realised before now how few friends she really had. Ruby had been the first person that she had befriended outside of her own sisters in years. Counting Susanna as a friend was a real pleasure.

Susanna was curious about many things, and Grace did think that she had a bit of a romanticised view of Grace's life. Susanna saw Grace as independent. A woman of three and twenty, unmarried and earning an income. No matter how many times Grace tried to tell Susanna that they had very differing views of independence, she didn't seem to take notice.

Susanna was still very young in so many ways.

"And did you not mind that your younger sister married before you?" Susanna asked curiously as she picked up a knife and began to polish it.

"Lord, no," rebuked Grace. "I would never condemn my sister's happiness because of the order of our births."

"I am glad she is happy," Susanna said then, a smile on her face. "I remember both Kate and Claire from the school-room. I envied you three a lot. I always wanted a sister."

"You have two wonderful older brothers," Grace murmured softly, her voice breaking unwillingly as she spoke.

"Yes," Susanna agreed. "I do. It still has been a lonely existence for a long time," she admitted. "Both Adam and Jack were away at school for so long. Even now, they like to tuck themselves away."

Grace never liked to inquire, no matter how she might have wished to. If Susanna wanted to speak of specifics, Grace let her, but she never started it.

"Jack hides from Mother," Susanna continued, "as you know. I am sure you all hear the fighting down here. Jack finds windowsills to read from in the many forgotten corners of this house. And Adam," she emphasised, "has been with Papa in his study for weeks. Papa has decided it is time for him to learn the trade, I suppose."

"You are not going to clean the silverware by tickling it," Grace interjected, changing the subject. Grace showed her the pressure she would need to apply to make the silver shine properly.

Even though Grace never liked to bring up the subjects that she didn't want to talk about, being Susanna's friend meant that she ought to inquire about what Susanna wanted or needed to say.

Grace looked to her left and placed a comforting hand on Susanna's forearm. "Susanna," she said softly, calling her friend by her first name after weeks of insistence, "you need not ever feel lonely. I have never abandoned anyone that I care about, so I hope you know that you may always find comfort with me."

Grace saw several looks, several emotions cross Susanna's face briefly, but never sticking. It was hard to pinpoint exactly what she was thinking. "I believe you, Grace," she said finally, her voice barely above a whisper. "I do," she said again, nodding her head. "Which is why I cannot understand ..."

Susanna liked to tease some of her thoughts at times, trailing off instead of finishing her sentence. It was almost as though she was afraid to finish the thought, and Grace grew increasingly frustrated. "You don't understand what?" she pressed. "Have I done something to you?"

"No, not to me." Susanna clamped her lips shut, her brows furrowing over her blue eyes, as though she were holding in something terribly troubling.

Grace's posture straightened as it became her turn to frown. "I have done something to someone else," she surmised. "Pray, what sin have I supposedly committed?" she asked in confusion.

Susanna looked around, watching for eavesdroppers, but the only servants around were Mrs Reynolds and her kitchen maids. They were far too busy with the Beresfords' luncheon to be paying any attention to what Grace and Susanna were talking about at the table.

"Adam," whispered Susanna. "The letter." She chewed on her bottom lip anxiously as the words escaped her mouth, as though she were speaking blasphemy.

But Grace's eyes flared, and she sucked in a sharp breath. "He told you about the letter?" she all but hissed.

Susanna looked helpless. "Well, of course," she nodded. "I had to help him with it ... it was an awful time for him."

Grace could not believe what she was hearing. Susanna had gone to the effort of befriending her ... and had all but confessed to being an accomplice in the letter that had all but ruined her youth. "It was an awful time for him?" Grace exclaimed, careful to watch the volume of her voice. Her hands began to shake, which made the silverware rattle in her hands. She put them down on the table and moved her hands into her lap.

"It was your letter then," Susanna said, disheartened.

"Well, of course it was," snapped Grace. "You knew all about it."

Susanna stared at Grace. "Why are you angry with me?" she demanded to know.

Grace forced herself to take a deep breath, not wanting to lash out, or say something that she would regret in temper. "I really struggle to believe that your brother had such a hard time with the letter, milady," she said tensely. The idea that Adam was the one who deserved sympathy made her blood boil.

"Well, he did!" Susanna insisted forcefully. "He was heart-broken! For months! How could you not think he would feel that way after that letter?"

"Oh, well, I am sorry that your brother's cold, unfeeling, unfaithful heart was hurt by that letter," Grace seethed, see-ing red, before immediately regretting her words as Susanna recoiled in shock. What was she thinking? She needed to control herself.

Susanna breathed shakily. "Adam is not cold, unfeeling, or unfaithful," she insisted. "You seriously misjudge him, Grace."

Grace looked back down at the silverware and clenched her teeth. "I need to get back to work, milady. I think that this conversation needs to end. We clearly share differing opinions on this subject, and any further discussion will only result in regrets. I suggest you go back upstairs."

"Do you not want to be my friend anymore, Grace?" Susanna asked quietly.

Grace forced herself to take another deep breath. Susanna would have still been very young when that letter was sent. Even if she had known about it, she would not have been in a position to do anything about it. Of course, Susanna would admire her older brother. Grace could not condemn her for that.

"I told you that I would never abandon anyone that I care about," Grace repeated her earlier words. "If you like, I may see you tomorrow."

Grace had been permitted a half day that Friday to attend to her mother, who was being visited by the doctor. As it was now the end of October, and two months since her fall, Doctor Carlton had returned to check on her.

Both Grace and Claire sat either side of their mother as the doctor looked over her leg. Mrs Denham was praying that she be allowed out of bed, as she was going absolutely mad in her confinement.

"I am satisfied that this leg has healed quite nicely, Mrs Denham," Doctor Carlton observed, feeling about her leg. "That does not mean you will be skipping and dancing any-time soon, but light exercise and some fresh air should assist in your healing. Short distances only as you build up your strength again."

"Oh, thank the Lord," declared Mrs Denham. "What a long recovery this has been. Might I attend the ball tomorrow evening, do you think, Doctor?" she asked. "It is the last public assembly before the winter, and I would so like a little entertainment."

Doctor Carlton smiled. "A carriage ride over, and you are to be seated," he insisted. "But I do not see why not." Doctor Carlton returned his instruments to his leather bag and clipped it shut. "I must bid you adieu, ladies."

"Thank you!" all three Denham women exclaimed at once as Claire volunteered to show the doctor out.

"I am so pleased for you, Mama," Grace said excitedly, squeezing her mother's hand.

"As I am, my dear," replied Mrs Denham. "As soon as I am able, I will return to Mrs Slickson's house. I am certain she would have you back in a heartbeat, and you would no longer have to work in that house. I do not care what you say, I can see it in your eyes, Grace. It grieves you to be there."

Grace couldn't stop her tears from falling from her eyes as soon as her mother had pointed them out. She fell into her mother's arms and felt immediately comforted as Mrs Denham began to stroke her hair.

"I am just being silly," Grace wept. "I found out yesterday that Susanna knew about the letter. She tried to tell me how hurt he was about it, but I don't understand how that is supposed to make me feel. Should I be happy that he has a conscience? Because all I want to do is slap him across the face whenever I see him."

Which, granted, was not very often at all. Grace believed that he actively avoided her.

"You will have to beat me to it, dear one," Mrs Denham assured her. "I imagine he will be in attendance tomorrow night, and I can tell you right now that your brothers and Mr Ellis will need to hold me back from him for causing you such grief."

Mrs Denham cupped Grace's face and brought her eyes up. With her thumbs, Mrs Denham brushed away Grace's tears.

"I am not so foolish to believe that the promise of a boy would stand the test of time," she whispered, "but he treated me so cruelly then, and he continues it now. Perhaps I could forgive him if he at least apologised to me. But whenever he does see me, he looks upon me as though I have just set him on fire.

"What makes it even worse is that his fiancée is coming to stay sometime in early November. He is engaged, Mama. How wicked of me to be thinking of another woman's fiancé with anything but indifference."

Mrs Denham frowned. "It is never wicked to feel, my Grace," she insisted. "Until he is man enough to own what he did, I fear there will never be peace in your heart."

Another set of arms wound themselves around Grace as Claire joined them. "Kate has left some of her old gowns for us," she said quietly. "Not old of course, but things she no longer wears as you know Mr Ellis likes to spoil her. I am sure there is something in our room that will make you feel beautiful tomorrow night. Adam Beresford will not be the only man in attendance."

Grace sniffed and smiled at her sister. "And neither will Arthur Slickson," she countered.

Claire blushed crimson at the mention of the gentleman that she desperately fancied. "Hush," she said bashfully.

"Dear me, Claire. What am I to do with you?" tsked Mrs Denham. "You are too sweet for Mr Slickson. You deserve someone with a heart as soft as yours."

"Mr Slickson is sweet," protested Claire.

Grace, for once, welcomed her sister's infatuation with Arthur Slickson as it took her mind away from her tears. She would be keeping an eye on Claire tomorrow, and that would hopefully keep her eyes away from someone else.

Chapter 11

G race fastened the very last pin in Claire's hair, satisfied that it was the prettiest that it had ever been, and her skills could not make it even more so. Claire was indeed terribly beautiful, and were it not for her lack of fortune, she would have been the object of affection for many a young man.

But, much like Grace, Claire's prospects were not grand, and she set her sights too high by fantasising about Arthur Slickson. Grace worried that Claire's naïveté would result in her falling prey to a young man with less than gentlemanly intentions. Claire would get her heart broken if she was not careful.

Claire's gown was a blush pink, the exact shade her cheeks seemed to always be in church. The contrast between her dress and her raven hair was lovely, and she looked every bit a princess.

Grace had selected a white gown that had belonged to Kate. It was simple, but elegant, with only a ribbon, cornflower blue in colour, around the waist as decoration. She had been drawn to the dress for exactly that reason, the cornflower description sticking in her mind unwillingly. Looking at herself in the mirror behind Claire, she could see that the ribbon did match her eye colour well.

"Claire," Grace said, shaking off any thought of him. "You must try to choose someone else to bestow upon your affection," she urged, frowning. "Mr Slickson is far too vain to appreciate someone as sweet and as lovely as you." She could think of other young men in town. More attainable men who would most certainly trail after Claire if she looked their way.

Claire blushed the colour of her dress and shook her head. "You are far too sceptical, Grace," she scolded. "There is much more to Arthur Slickson than his appearance."

Grace, having been the one to work within the Slickson household, was yet to see more to Mr Slickson then his own appreciation for himself. Could she be surprised by him? Grace doubted it. Either way, Arthur Slickson would never marry a girl as beneath him as Claire. Claire was simply too innocent to see this.

"Are you two presentable?"

Grace and Claire turned to their mother at the doorway. Mrs Denham was wearing her best Sunday gown and walking very tentatively, having only just regaining her ability to walk. When she saw her daughters by the dressing table, she clapped her hand over her mouth. "Oh, Claire!" she gushed. "When did you become a lady?"

At seventeen, Claire had not been permitted many opportunities to dress as she was. The previous summer had been the first time she had been allowed to attend public affairs. This would be her first winter ball.

She beamed at the praise and stood up from the chair. "Thank you, Mama," she said excitedly.

Mrs Denham's eyes then fell on Grace, and her expression softened to one of warm admiration. "And my good Grace," she said simply. "How beautiful you are." Holding her hands out to her daughters, she beckoned them. "Come. I am desperate for some conversation. Let us farewell your brothers and then depart."

"When you think of the society we had during the Season, Perry, I really have no idea why you would insist upon us attended a country dance," Cecily said distastefully as the Beresfords approached the assembly hall.

"Perhaps because it would vex you terribly, my dear wife," muttered Peregrine in reply.

Adam, who was walking behind his parents, Susanna on his arm, rolled his eyes. Pigs would fly before his mother found something that pleased her. Adam, on the other hand, was looking forward to the ball. He was looking forward to the music and the dancing, and the simple pleasures that a public assembly brought.

People from all over would be in attendance, including the servants in his own household. Including Grace.

Adam had been avoiding her, but it was not hard to when he had been cooped up in his father's study for days on end. Even then, he had not seen her since that brief moment weeks ago when it had been Mrs Hayes' birthday.

It was as though he had quickly become accustomed to her presence, addicted even, and his eyes longed to look upon her, at the extreme annoyance of his head.

The music behind the doors of the assembly hall was lively and jovial. The noise of conversation flowed, as did the laughter of old friends. How different the two sides of the door were, and Adam longed to be on the other, away from his quarrelling parents, and that much closer to seeing her for a brief moment.

"No, that will not be necessary," Cecily snapped, holding up her hand as an attendant went to give Susanna a dance card.

Susanna immediately pouted, her lower lip trembling as she frowned. "But Mother ..." she whimpered, "it's a ball."

"It's a country assembly, Susanna," Cecily said dismissively. "Were you to stand up with any man here, it would be an embarrassment. If you are to dance, it may only be with your brothers."

"Don't be ridiculous, Mother," said Adam, rolling his eyes. Knowing his mother cared so deeply about appearances, he continued, "Would it not be seen as charitable for Susanna to dance with whomever asks?"

Cecily glared at Adam over her shoulder. "No," she said curtly. "It will only cheapen her."

"What am I to say if someone asks me to dance?" Susanna protested. "Won't it be rude to refuse?"

"Susanna, you are the daughter of the Duke of Ashwood," huffed Cecily. "It will be rude of them to ask you." She turned her head back as the assembly room doors were opened for them.

Adam gave his sister a reassuring look. Once inside, he would ensure that she had a lovely time with the good people of Ashwood, the people that they had grown up with. They were the salt of the earth, and Adam, Jack and Susanna being associated with them could only be for the better.

The music, dancing, laughter, and conversation all stopped abruptly as all eyes turned to them. Adam disliked this greatly. He would have much preferred to slip into the assembly unnoticed, but his mother would never refuse an opportunity to appear superior.

"His Grace, the Duke of Ashwood, Her Grace, the Duchess of Ashwood, Lord Beresford, Lord Jack Beresford, and the Lady Susanna Beresford," called the attendant as the duke and duchess descended into the assembly.

Adam escorted Susanna, and Jack followed reluctantly behind them. Adam's eyes flicked around the room quickly, but they didn't find her.

The music quickly resumed, and the dancers returned to the middle of the floor, picking up where they had left off in the sequence. It was at the resumption of the dance that he spotted a raven-haired angel, for she could only be an angel, dressed in white and looking as ethereal as she was.

Her skin looked as smooth as porcelain, flushed from the exertion. Her pink lips were upturned in a bright smile as she enjoyed herself. But her eyes, her cornflower blue eyes, were as beautiful on her as the bloom on a Cornish hill.

How often he had thought about what her hair would look like out from underneath a maid's cap or the bonnet she wore in church. It shone like polished ebony, affixed in the softest feminine curls that framed her heart-shaped face.

In an instant his trance was shattered as she took the hand of a man, he did not recognise in the dancing sequence. The smile, the beautiful smile he had admired, was for him.

This sudden realisation came upon Adam like a punch to the gut, and it quickly brought him back to reality. He shook his head, refocussing his vision, just as his father's attention was claimed by the vicar.

Cecily made pleasantries before she quickly turned back to her children, focussing her eyes on Jack.

Jack had somehow already sourced a glass of champagne and was in the process of tipping it down his throat as Cecily demanded his attention.

"You are to be on your best behaviour tonight," she warned Jack in a low, hushed voice, glaring at him. "I do not want to see a drink in your hand after this one, and you are not to dance with any girl who does not have my approval."

Jack grinned wickedly. He had dressed well this evening, wearing a deep navy coloured coat, adorned with rich, brass buttons. His breeches and boots were dark, and he had bothered to comb his usually unruly dark hair.

He turned his head and tapped on the shoulder of the nearest woman to him. Cecily was powerless in her fury as the girl turned around. Adam recognised her instantly. Her similarities to her sister were uncanny.

She appeared shocked to have been approached by Jack Beresford, as though she had not realised how close she was standing to him.

"May I have the next dance, Miss?" Jack asked, as dashing as he could be, as he held his hand out to her.

She blushed, as only a girl of her age could, and looked quite flustered as her inexperience betrayed her. "We have not been introduced, sir," she replied softly.

Jack looked to Adam and Susanna for help, raising an eyebrow in hope that one of them knew who the girl was. Adam smirked at his mother's fury and stepped forward. "May I introduce Miss Claire Denham," Adam said politely. "Miss Claire, please allow me introduce my brother, Lord Jack Beresford."

"Denham?" hissed Cecily rudely, and Adam hoped that Claire's young ears missed it. "There's more of them?"

"There now," Jack said confidently. "We are introduced. May I have the next dance?" he asked again.

Claire looked over her shoulder very briefly, as though she was looking for someone, before her eyes returned to Jack. "I would be honoured, milord," she uttered nervously as she took his hand and curtseyed.

Jack could not leave them fast enough as he walked with Claire through the crowd of people to take their places as the next dance was to start.

"I should not have allowed him to come," Cecily said under her breath.

"He is twenty-three years old, Mother," muttered Adam in reply. "Jack will do as he pleases. What has he done but ask he sweet girl to dance?"

Cecily's attention was then claimed by the vicar as the music stopped. The dancers then applauded the musicians. Adam's eyes immediately found Grace again as she curtseyed to her partner. Something deep within him gave him the urge to follow Jack's lead, to walk right over to her and ask for the next dance.

But how could he? He could not be seduced into pain once more, no matter how beautiful she looked. As Grace walked away from her partner, Adam saw her notice Jack and Claire taking their place on the dancefloor. Her expression was neutral as she was claimed by her sister, Kate, before her eyes finally found him.

Adam saw vulnerability, hesitance, and hurt in her eyes they minute she looked upon him. He watched as her lips parted, as though she wanted to say something, but a room of people stood between them. Kate stole Grace's attention from Adam then.

"She was hurt by the letter, too," whispered Susanna, as though she was reading Adam's mind.

Adam, looking back instantly at Susanna, realised that his sister had clearly seen him staring at Grace.

"What are you talking about?" Adam uttered in confusion. How could Susanna possibly know such a thing. He saw guilt on his sister's face, and Adam's stomach immediately began to twist. "What have you been doing? Have you been speaking to her?" he demanded to know, his teeth clenching.

"Good God, Susanna, tell me you did not mention the letter," he hissed angrily.

Susanna squeezed his forearm. "Please," she begged. "Don't be angry with me. Grace is my friend."

Adam blinked several times as he comprehended that piece of information. "When did you and Grace have time to become friends?"

"That is irrelevant," Susanna dismissed. "I always wanted Grace to like me when I was younger. You know that as you spent so much time telling me to leave you alone so you could monopolise her time," Susanna reminded him. "But I like Grace. I do. She is kind, sweet tempered, generous, patient ... and I don't think she could ever do such a cruelty now. I asked her about the letter, and I hope you won't be angry at me for too long in finding this out, but when I did, she seemed to be deeply hurt by it."

Were they not in a room full of people, Adam would have exploded with anger at his sister. He felt such a humiliation at the thought of Susanna discussing his private feelings with her. "How dare you!" seethed Adam, glaring in a way that he had never done before. "How dare you share such private information with her."

Susanna frowned indignantly. "I was only trying to do you a kindness, Adam!" she protested quietly.

"No, you wanted Grace to like you," he retorted. "You told me so yourself," Adam reminded her.

"I defended you!" Susanna insisted. "Grace called you cold and unfeeling, unfaithful!" she persisted. "I assured her that you were not."

"Unfaithful?" Adam gasped, repeating the word as though it were a punch to the gut. Grace deemed him unfaithful? The sheer nerve, the sheer hypocrisy of that woman! "Do not ever discuss my private affairs with anyone again," Adam warned Susanna. "I don't care what your intentions are, Susanna, this is not something that I want repeated."

Susanna held onto Adam. "I won't!" she insisted. "But please, do not misunderstand what I say. I do believe that Grace was hurt deeply by the letter, too."

Adam wanted to laugh but feared such an act would draw too much attention. Grace hurt by her own letter? Preposterous. Unfaithful ... the word returned to his mind and it angered him to no end. He turned his head back to her, and she was still standing beside Kate, her fingers playing idly with the blue ribbon on her dress.

She would not apologise when they had met in the servants' quarters, and now she had spoken so brazenly to his own sister. Grace certainly had a lot to answer for, and Adam was no longer willing to put it out of his mind.

The moment he took a step away from Susanna, she whispered, "Where are you going?"

"To teach Grace the true meaning of faithfulness," replied Adam.

Chapter 12

The second dance had already begun, and Adam could hear the whispers about Jack and Claire immediately. It was news apparently, that the first lady Lord Jack Beresford stood up with was Claire Denham, a girl of no situation or consequence.

Adam wove around the crowd, managing to smile at people who curtseyed and bowed as he passed them. He barely had time to register the mothers who tried to put their daughters in his path. He noticed then that Grace and Kate were standing beside a seated Mrs Denham. There chairs all about the perimeter of the assembly hall, being occupied by those of a more delicate constitution.

Adam had always liked Mrs Denham. He had enjoyed her warmth as a boy, and how he had always felt welcomed and valued by her. He had admired how she mothered her children, and how she and her husband shared a loving union, one that he could have only dreamed of for his own parents.

He was momentarily saddened by the fact that she was now widowed, and how he would have paid his respects years ago had he known.

Mrs Denham was the first to notice his approach, and the first look she gave him after not having seen him in more than a decade was one of disgust, and it made Adam stop in his tracks. What had he done to deserve that?

Nevertheless, he persisted, and joined the party after inhaling a deep breath of courage. He cleared his throat and bowed his head respectfully to the ladies.

Kate raised her eyebrows in surprise, while Grace appeared very hesitant, nervous, and confused at his sudden coming.

"Mama, you remember Lord Beresford," she stammered. "Lord Beresford, my mother, Mrs Denham, and my sister, Mrs Ellis," she introduced, reacquainting them.

"Good evening, ladies," Adam said as calmly as he could manage, trying to keep himself from staring, and focussed on what he had meant to do. It did not help that being so near to her, he could truly appreciate the beauty the possessed out of that dreadful uniform. He averted his eyes from the curve of her throat and her smooth, elegant décolletage. "Mrs Denham, I hope you are feeling better and your injury is much improved," he said politely, offering her a smile.

Mrs Denham did not return the pleasantries, however, and merely scowled at him. This reception angered him, and the only explanation could be Grace had been telling tall tales. He had never done a thing to offend the Denhams. Why, as a boy, he had hoped on more than one occasion that they would allow him to live with them. He had always been on his best behaviour.

"Mama," hissed Grace, when she realised that Mrs Denham would not reply.

"Yes, much better," Mrs Denham replied reluctantly. "I thank you," she added, even more reluctantly, as though it pained her for the words to pass through her lips.

Adam needed to speak with Grace. There could no longer be any delay. But he knew he could not pull her aside and take her away for a private conversation. There were too many eyes, and there would be too many questions. Despite everything, Grace still had a reputation, and Adam was not so ungentlemanlike that he would tarnish that, no matter her past actions.

"May I have the next dance, Grace?" he asked, before correcting himself to, "Miss Denham." She was not in his employ at this moment.

Grace looked like a frightened rabbit, and both Mrs Denham and Kate were shocked at the invitation.

But Grace couldn't refuse unless she was otherwise promised, and Adam hoped that she was not. She stared up at him, her cornflower blue eyes wide with unease, but she nodded.

"I would be delighted," she replied, sounding anything but delighted.

The music for the second dance began to end, and Adam offered his arm to Grace. Her small hand shook as she extended it, placing it delicately on his forearm. The moment she was his, he led her away from her mother and sister.

"My sister tells me that you are now friends," Adam murmured under his breath, Grace's subsequent gasp letting him know that she had heard him.

"Is that why you have sought me out, milord?" Grace whispered. "Do you wish to put an end to that friendship?"

Ahead, Adam saw Jack extend his hand to Claire, asking her to dance the next with him. For a moment, Adam calmed, as he saw a genuine expression of happiness of his brother's usually sullen face. But this was quickly erased when another young man claimed Claire. Adam recalled his face from years ago, but he could not remember his name.

The look on Claire's face was evident that he was the man that she wanted to dance with, and she gave Jack her sincere apologies as Jack bowed to her and left, clearly disappointed.

Grace was watching the same exchange with disappointment. Perhaps she had wanted the connection between her sister and Adam's brother for reasons of benefit. Adam then admonished himself for the careless thought. Grace had never behaved in a way that was self-serving, and it was cruel to allow those thoughts now.

"No," said Adam, "so long as you do not fill Susanna's head with lies."

His words were cold, and perhaps her assessment of him had been correct as Grace looked up at him in shock. They took their place in the line of dances, Grace standing opposite to Adam, still reeling.

"I never lied," she mouthed emphatically.

Adam had to smirk. The musicians began to play, and he bowed to her, alongside the other men. The ladies in turn curtseyed to their partners, though Grace did not take her infuriated eyes off of him.

Adam took three steps in as part of the sequence, and uttered, "Unfaithful, you called me? Never!" he hissed, before taking three steps backward.

Grace followed suit, taking three steps in to meet him. "And you called me a liar?" she accused. "You are supposed to be a gentleman! That is why you went away. And you cannot even do the decent thing and apologise to me!" Grace spoke quickly, angrily, with the ire of weeks of pent up frustration, before she stepped back into line.

"Apologise?" snapped Adam, careful to keep his voice low as they met each other in the middle. Adam held his hands out for Grace's, and she took them, before they turned in a circle. "I owe you nothing. You, on the other hand, had the nerve to call me unfaithful after how callously and appallingly you behaved."

Adam and Grace came to stand next to each other as the couples moved in their lines. "I don't know how you could say such things to me now," Grace whispered shakily. "What you said to me is burned in my mind."

What was she talking about? Adam scowled down at her. "I have never said a cruel word to you," except for perhaps now, he silently admitted.

The line separated and they were once again standing opposite to one another. Grace's mouth was agape in shock as she comprehended his words, clearly not believing them.

"It is I who have never said a cruel word to you, milord," Grace retorted as they took hands once again to turn. "But you are not innocent. We cannot be friends, or anything else, as it is not proper," she said, as though she were reciting something.

Her eyes, her tone, everything made him feel as though this was supposed to mean something to him.

"You must understand that we are cut from two very different pieces of cloth," Grace continued shakily. "Do you think that I could ever forget such horrid words?" she asked him.

But at that moment, the music ended, and the dancers began to applaud the musicians. Both Grace and Adam participated in the courtesy, before Grace made the move to leave him.

His hand reached out to grab hers without him thinking of what he was doing. Adam was not letting her go until they finished this conversation, his previous reservations be damned.

Grace glared at him. "Let go of me!" she hissed. "Haven't you done enough?"

"No," snapped Adam as he glowered at her. "I haven't done anything." He pulled her hand onto his arm despite her protestations, so it at least looked as though he was to lead her back to her family, though he would take his own time in doing so.

"Stop making fun of me!" Grace demanded in a hushed voice. "How could you say those words to me and not apologise? I know a long time has passed, but it is the decent thing to do!"

Adam stopped, before looking down at her in utter confusion. Those words that she had recited were meant to be his? Where on earth had she got them from? "Grace, you are being ridiculous. I have no idea what you are talking about."

"Are you being deliberately coy?" Grace accused. "The letter!"

She could indignantly demand an apology from him but had the nerve to bring up her letter. Adam felt his fury bubbling in his chest.

"The letter," he repeated, shaking his head. "You are going to demand an apology from me, and then be the one to bring up the letter," he remarked in disbelief.

Grace stared at him. "Well, does not one deserve the other? Please, I am tired," she begged. "I have cried the last tears I ever want to over you. If you apologise for sending me that letter, then I promise to forgive you, and you can move on from me, which is exactly what you wanted."

Just as he was about to accuse her of being ridiculous again, he suddenly registered just what she had said. She was accusing him of sending her a cruel letter. Adam thought back to the countless letters that he had written her back then, the hours that he had spent planning, choosing just the right words, before pouring his childish heart onto the paper for her. Unfaithful, she called him, when he would have written her for years and years until the day they were reunited. In the dozens and dozens of letters that he had sent, never once had a sent her a word of cruelty.

He had been too busy thinking of synonyms for darling, dear, and my beloved.

"I really have no idea of what letter you are talking about," Adam said honestly, "but you cannot deny the words that you wrote me." He braced himself. "Do you think you are the only one with words burned into your mind? I don't want to write you anymore, you said. How silly I have been, you said. I am going to start my life without having an obligation to you, you said. You didn't want any part in my life anymore, and you told me that you wanted to move on from me." The words were truly etched in his brain, and it hurt something deep inside of him to repeat her words. "I don't know if I can ever forgive you for that, Grace, but an apology to me would be a start."

"Are you making fun of me?" Grace asked shakily, her eyes becoming glassy.

"No," snapped Adam.

"I never wrote anything of the sort," she protested, her voice barely above a fragile whisper. "I don't know what you are talking about. I only wrote you words of tenderness, faithfulness, and your last letter to me broke my heart."

Adam wanted to accuse her of lying again, anything to make sense of what had just been revealed, but he could see the sincerity in Grace's eyes. She was telling him the truth.

"But I received a letter from you," Adam reiterated, "telling me those horrible things, and you asked me to stop writing to you. Are you telling that you never wrote that letter?"

"No!" she cried, her voice raising slightly before she checked herself. "I never wrote you any such letter. You were the one to send me such a letter."

"I would never write to end our correspondence," Adam protested, "to end our friendship, our understanding, my promise to you." As soon as he uttered the words, he saw the recognition on Grace's face. She knew exactly what he was referring to. "Whatever letter you received was not from me."

"Well, whatever letter you received was not from me, either!"

They stared at each other in realisation, true comprehension of what had just been discovered between them. Neither one had severed their correspondence, but someone had.

To Adam, what was most important in this discovery was that Grace had never wanted to end their understanding. It had not been her choice, and every unforgiveable thought he had ever had about her filled him with immense remorse.

Grace. She was right here in front of him after so many years.

"Who could have done such a thing?" Grace asked softly.

Adam knew of only one person cruel and calculating enough to pull off such a ruse. And she had gotten away with it for twelve years. He immediately turned to where his mother was standing. She was still beside Peregrine, talking with the vicar's wife absently as she watched Adam with keen interest.

Cecily had an expression of disgust when her cold eyes flicked to Grace momentarily, before her attention returned to her conversation partner.

"I believe I know," muttered Adam tersely. Taking a breath, he tried to think of what to say next, what he could express to covey the magnitude of his regret. How could he even begin to make up for what his mother had done to her?

But before he could even begin to find the words, the music fell silent again, and the conversation in the hall stopped.

"Lady Ashley and Lady Sarah Ashley," announced the attendant, as two finely dressed women entered the assembly.

Chapter 13

Adam's eyes tore from Grace, whose mouth was still agape in shock, to the two ladies that had just been announced to the assembly. And there she was, standing at the entrance, her innocent eyes searching for him. Unbeknownst to Sarah, her fiancé had been about to realise a lifelong dream in the arms of another.

A thousand pounds of regret fell down upon Adam's head as he realised the magnitude of his actions. He had succumbed to his mother's pressure during the Season. He had finally engaged himself to someone she deemed worthy. When unbeknownst to him he would be reunited with Grace only a few months later. Only they were not reunited. He had beheld Grace for mere seconds, really, known her to have been honest and sincere in her affections for a brief moment before his obligations had caught up with him.

Upon returning his gaze to Grace, his beautiful, innocent Grace, he realised that she did not know the significance of the two ladies. She did not know the name of his fiancée. And he would have to break that to her and ruin this reunion in a mere flash.

But Grace was quicker than he had given her credit for, and upon seeing Lady Sarah and her mother being claimed by the duchess, the realisation was painted all over her face.

"Oh," she whispered, immediately putting distance between them, which Adam felt deep within his soul.

"You must promise that we will continue this discussion," Adam said under his breath, looking at Grace intently. "We must speak again."

Grace frowned helplessly. "What are you saying?" she asked, taking another step away from him. "She is who I think she is, is she not?"

Adam regretfully nodded. "Yes, but –"

"Then you must go to her," Grace instructed firmly, turning on her heel and darting away from him, back in the direction of her mother and sister.

Grace quickly disappeared into the crowd, and all Adam wanted was to go after her, but he knew he couldn't. He had meant what he said. They would speak again. He walked away as well, but in the direction of his own family, catching the eye of Lady Sarah almost immediately.

She smiled sweetly at him. It was the perfect adjective to describe her. Sarah was sweet. She reminded him of a mouse, with dainty, angular features. Her hair was a soft brown, and her eyes a dark green. She was average in height, standing at his shoulder, and her figure was draped in the latest high waisted fashions.

The daughter took after the mother almost exactly, though a few lines graced Lady Ashley's face to betray her age. She was a very elegant woman with excellent connections and had done everything in her power to put her sweet Sarah in the path of amiable gentlemen during the summer.

His own mother was beaming from ear to ear, heartily approving of their presence, which made him think that Cecily must have known they were coming. She had banknotes in her eyes now that they were come, and she could almost taste the twenty-five-thousand-pound dowry that was promised alongside Sarah.

As soon as Adam reached the party, Lady Ashley and Lady Sarah both curtseyed. He bowed his own head respectfully. "Lady Ashley, Lady Sarah, what a surprise. We had not expected you so soon," he murmured politely.

"The duchess wrote to hasten our arrival, milord," replied Lady Ashley. "She thought that Sarah would most enjoy the opportunity to stand up with you in front of your people."

"Was it a difficult journey, Lady Sarah?" Adam asked, turning his attention to Sarah.

"Oh no," replied Sarah, shaking her head. "I had not realised Hertfordshire was so near London in the grand scheme of things. You are quite fortunately situated. You must escape to town all the time."

Adam did not know if he would call thirty miles a quick journey, but he supposed it nearer than travelling to Newcastle. "Not as often as my mother would like," he replied with a small, dutiful smile.

Adam could sense her eyes, feeling her all the more powerfully now that they had realised his mother's probable cruelty. He longed to go back to her. Instead, he looked upon Cecily with hard, cold eyes, willing his mother to read his mind. He would be confronting her, make no mistake.

Cecily eyes narrowed at Adam's stare. "The music is not to my taste," she announced, "but the dancing has been quite animated. Adam, why don't you ask Lady Sarah to dance?" she urged.

Susanna was behind their mother, standing beside Peregrine. Her eyes were begging for news, having watched his display with Grace. He would not escape Susanna later.

At a loss, Adam lifted his arm. "Would you care to dance the next with me, Lady Sarah?" he asked.

Sarah gladly nodded, placing her gloved hand on his forearm. "I would be delighted," she agreed.

Adam hated the action immediately. He felt terribly guilty in an instant. Guilty for ever encouraging this union with Sarah, and guilty in knowing that he was hurting Grace again. Hurting her seemed like an unforgivable sin.

Hurting either of them was unforgivable, and Adam hated his mother in that moment.

"Are we a welcome surprise, milord?" Sarah asked tentatively, seeming to notice his cool mood.

Adam's head snapped down to hers, and he chastised himself, knowing that he had the heart of an innocent in his hands, and he needed to treat her with the kindness she deserved.

"I am glad to see you," he told her. Glad to be engaged, however, was another conversation to be had, and that time was not in the middle of an assembly hall.

When the music stopped, Adam noticed his brother out of the corner of his eye. Jack was standing away from the family party, so Adam excused himself to go and check on him.

Jack was not holding a drink but was merely standing on the edge of the hall, watching the scene before him.

"Are you well?" Adam asked him.

"I should ask you that, should I not?" he murmured. "I noticed your interlude with Grace. And that was before your fiancée waltzed into the assembly."

"Are you well, Jack?" Adam asked again, placing a hand on his brother's shoulder.

Jack scoffed. "Of course," he muttered. "I am only bored."

Adam followed Jack's line of sight quickly, noticing then that his gaze was focussed on Claire Denham, who was once again dancing with the gentleman that she had spurned Jack for.

"Do you know that man?" Adam asked him.

"His name is Arthur Slickson. Do not you remember him?" Jack answered all too quickly. "We were all in the school room together when we were little. Only he is not a boy anymore. She had danced with him three times."

The name he recognised, and he could not place it with the face he recalled.

"If you wish to, you could ask Miss Claire to dance again," Adam encouraged. "If it pleases you, Mother will hate it."

Jack chuckled at that. "No," he decided. "She didn't really want to dance with me anyway. The minute he asked for her hand, she leapt at the chance." He shook his head, before turning his attention to Adam. "What were you and Grace discussing so intensely?" he asked. "She looked quite distressed."

Before Adam could answer, he heard a yelp of pain from some twenty feet away. Mrs Denham had climbed to her feet and was suffering the pain of her leg injury. Grace and Kate were both trying to support her. The blacksmith, Mr Ellis, Kate's husband, had quickly come to his mother-in-law's aid and was helping her towards the door of the assembly hall. With her mother safely supported, an anxious Grace quickly went to fetch a devastated Claire away from Arthur Slickson. Mrs Denham struggled to walk, limping terribly, and the display, Adam could tell, was terribly embarrassing for her.

Much to his anger, he saw the sneer on his mother's face as she averted her eyes from Mrs Denham.

Adam's parents made it to midnight before they dutifully said their goodbyes to the few members of the parish whom they felt were high enough to speak to.

Cecily was a perfect hostess, riding in the carriage back to Ashwood House with Lady Ashley and Sarah, and personally showing them to their rooms when they arrived. Only after everyone had retired was Adam able to fish through his belongings for the very letter that he had so long believed Grace had sent him. He was certain that if he compared it to the others for long enough that he might be able to find slight differences in the handwriting.

Clutching the letter in his hand, Adam angrily made his way down the hall to his mother's bedroom. He knocked on the door twice, and he heard her beckon.

Cecily was sitting at her dressing table, pulling pins out of her hair. She frowned when she saw Adam. "Oh," she realised. "I thought you would be Naismith. But now that you are here, I really ought to tell you that you need to be more attentive to Sarah," she scolded. "You only danced with her once. Lady Ashley noticed that, I hope you realise."

Adam didn't hear a word she said as he slapped the letter down on her dressing table in front of her. Cecily jumped at the sound it made, before setting the last pin down on the table beside it.

"What's this?" she asked.

"You tell me, Mother," snapped Adam.

Cecily unfolded the letter and read it briefly, before discarding to the side. She then combed her fingers through her hair. "Why on earth would I want to read those silly love letters?" she muttered. Cecily had known of Adam's correspondence with Grace. He had received letters at his London home when he had been home on school holidays.

"That is not a love letter, Mother," said Adam icily. "That is the letter that Grace supposedly wrote me to end our understanding. Only Grace is not the one who wrote it."

Cecily said nothing as she leaned into her reflection, brushing something off of her face. "Really, Adam, I do not want to hear about that silly girl," she huffed. "It is highly inappropriate seeing as your fiancée is presently a guest at Ashwood."

"Did you write this letter?" Adam demanded to know.

"Stop it," snapped Cecily angrily. "It is late, and I am tired."

"Did you write this letter?" Adam pressed again. "You knew that no matter what happened, I would come back to Ashwood, and I would find her. You knew I loved her. You knew I would marry her one day. There was no changing my mind. So, you put a stop to it. You forged this letter. Tell me the truth!"

Cecily sucked in a sharp breath as she turned her torso and looked up at him. "Do you know, I have a good mind to sack her!" she exclaimed. "She is nothing but trouble. You can do so much better than her, Adam! Sarah is rich, she is titled, and she is a sweet girl! She will make you a wonderful wife! Why are you so blinded by an insignificant servant?"

Through clenched teeth, Adam said, "She is not, nor has she ever been, insignificant." His voice more of a growl now, he added, "I won't forgive you for this. You took her away from me, and I won't have you doing that again. Sarah is a sweet girl, but she isn't Grace. She is the only girl I will ever wed. That is a promise. That was my promise to her."

Cecily's eyes narrowed. "Do not threaten me, Adam. It will not end well. That is my promise."

Chapter 14

"Y**ou really need not fuss!**" cried Mrs Denham as Grace, Kate and Claire helped her into bed. "It is just a little ache!"

Grace could see the pain etched on her mother's face, and it was certainly not a little ache. She would need to dispatch a letter to the doctor in the morning. She was not ready to be out of bed, and it had been more than two months. Whenwould she be alright again? Would she ever be alright again?

"Claire, go and make Mama some tea," Kate instructed, sending their youngest sister down to the kitchen. "I will have Jim see you back to Ashwood House," she told Grace.

"No, I do not want Grace to go yet," insisted Mrs Denham. "Now that we are away from prying eyes," she shifted uncomfortably, "and more importantly, gossiping ears, will you tell me what was discussed between Adam Beresford and yourself?"

Grace could not even think of what had transpired, for all she could focus upon was the beautiful woman who had arrived late. The woman who had turned out to be Adam's fiancée.

Lady Sarah Ashley. Titled, wealthy, and impossibly lovely. What saddened Grace even more was the fact that she looked upon Adam with great affection. There was a connection between them, and Grace knew that it was entirely inappropriate to be speaking of it.

But her mother and sister were awaiting an answer. "You must not bring it up again in conversation," she said firmly. "I will tell you, and then it must be forgotten. Lord Beresford received a nearly identical letter to the one I was sent ending our understanding. Of course, it was not from me, just as the letter that I received was not from him. Someone intervened and ended our friendship, our ... someone put a stop to it. But it is entirely inconsequential now," Grace said quickly. "He is engaged. You all saw him dancing with her."

Kate smiled sympathetically at Grace, softly placing a hand on hers. "Dear Grace, we all saw him dancing with you," she uttered quietly.

"I don't know why I am so surprised," remarked Mrs Denham. "I honestly feel so foolish to have believed Adam capable of such a cruel act for so long. We need not think too long over just who the real culprit could be. I only know one so nasty."

"She never liked me," murmured Grace. "We all know this." Sighing, she stood up. "But what's done is done. I can forgive Adam now. I can put this behind me and get on with my role in his household." She would indeed be needing to maintain that employment for a long while, it seemed. Mrs Denham was in no shape to resume her employment. "I will return to the house now," she added for Kate.

Kate nodded. "I will tell Jim to escort you back." Sighing sadly, Kate pulled Grace into a tight embrace. "I love you so, Grace," she whispered in her ear. "You are the kindest, most selfless person I know. If I could but see you happy, I would be so fulfilled."

Ruby had not returned from the ball when Grace entered into their shared bedroom. It was a little after midnight, and the musicians would surely be playing for at least another hour or two. Balls were so few and far between, that Grace would understand if Ruby stayed until the very last song.

Grace changed out of Kate's dress, delicately folding it and laying it down on the end of her bed. She got into her nightgown before finding herself kneeling before her trunk of possessions. She unfolded several of the real letters that Adam had sent to her years ago.

Letters of hope with endless words of tenderness. She found her eyes brimming with tears as she read his dreams for them. Lord, she had not appreciated these words at the time. She had been too young to fully comprehend their meaning. But she could appreciate it now. Now that it was lost. Adam wrote so openly and honestly, with not a care for her station or situation. Nothing could have prevented him. Nothing could have prevented them.

Save for the letter that had been so maliciously concocted. Grace couldn't bear to read the words again, though she knew if she did, she would certainly find evidence of its falsehood now that she knew it was forged.

Tucking the letters safely away, Grace retrieved Adam's ring. She held the little, gold ring between her thumb and forefinger, admiring its shine still after so many years. Perhaps it was wrong, now, to still be in possession of it.

Her mind went to Lady Sarah, who was no doubt still dancing with Adam at the ball, or perhaps they had returned, and she would be sleeping on the floor below her. She was no fool. Sarah was the sort of girl that a man like Adam married.

Grace made the decision to return the ring. Adam had wanted to speak to her further, and they would, and it would be the last time that they talked.

There was a brief knock on Grace's bedroom door which made her jump. Whatever was Ruby knocking for? Grace quickly stashed the ring away and shut her trunk, before rushing over to the door.

"Ruby, why did you knock –" Grace began to ask as she opened the door, her words stopping when she saw the duchess standing in her doorway.

Cecily was dressed in her night things as well, though a duchess' nightwear was far more distinguished then Grace's oversized nightshirt. She was draped in flowing, white silk which looked as soft as a cloud.

"Your Grace!" exclaimed Grace. "Did you need something?"

Cecily didn't wait to be invited in, not that she needed to be in her own house. She walked into Grace's little bedroom, her nose upturning slightly as she took in the simple furnishings.

"I have a little opportunity for you, Grace," Cecily announced, turning around to face her, looking down on her with a calculating stare.

"An opportunity?" stammered Grace.

Cecily scoffed. "Don't repeat what I say, child. You are not a parrot," she scolded. She huffed, continuing. "But, as I said, I have an opportunity for you, which I believe you will find most ... helpful."

Grace remained silent.

"My son's fiancée has arrived to stay for the winter. Oh, I am so delighted," she exclaimed. "There is nothing lovelier than a society wedding. You will have to take my word on that, girl, as I am certain you have never attended such an occasion."

Grace prayed her face did not bear the expression of one that had just been verbally slapped over and over. "No, I haven't."

Cecily smiled, though it was more saccharine sweet than genuine. "I believe you to be a resourceful girl, Grace," she noted. "Clever, even. I suppose you would have to be in order to maintain your household after the sudden death of your father." Her tone became cool. "I do admire your commitment to caring for your family, Grace. It would only be too easy to marry a butcher and look after yourself, but you haven't."

"I have three younger siblings who would be without a home if I did such a thing, Your Grace," replied Grace as steadily as she could manage.

"Well, that brings me back to why I wanted to come and speak to you at such an hour," Cecily continued. "For the opportunity I have for you commences first thing tomorrow.

"I noticed your mother this evening, the pain she was in. It seems her injury is far from healed. She might not ever be properly healed. She may need to walk with a cane. All such things would render her useless as a housemaid. I certainly could never employ someone so ill-equipped to perform their duties. I am certain she will make up for that loss of income by doing laundry or mending or something to make a shilling or two for your family, but it will not keep you."

The same thoughts had been travelling through her own head regretfully. What if her mother was forced to use a cane? She would certainly be unable to work.

And if her leg was so poor, Grace wouldn't want her mother to exert herself like that! She would want her mother to rest at home. But that would mean never adding another income to their household.

"I am going to make you a lady's maid," Cecily announced, watching Grace carefully for her reaction.

"What?" gasped Grace. Of all the things Cecily could do, promoting her was certainly not what she had expected.

"I believe the words you are searching for are, "thank you for your great kindness, Your Grace"," Cecily said facetiously.

If Cecily had sent those letters, why on earth would she be giving Grace such an opportunity? This was indeed a kindness, so why would she bestow it upon Grace?

"Thank you!" exclaimed Grace. "I am most appreciative, Your Grace."

"I thought so," murmured Cecily. "With your mother in-capacitated, it will be down to you to ensure your family's survival, and what better way than through a wonderful household position. I am being most generous, I know. I could certainly find someone more qualified, but I thought to myself, who needs this most?" she asked rhetorically. "And then it occurred to me. Grace Denham."

Her tone returned to one of cunning, and a chill ran down Grace's spine. There was an ulterior motive. As much as it seemed this was a kindness, she certainly knew that Cecily was not a selfless person.

"You will receive an additional twelve shillings per week in wages. Does that sound fair?"

Grace gasped. An additional twelve shillings would make her income a little more than what she and her mother were both earning in the employ of Mrs Slickson. Oh, that would certainly help them greatly! "Yes," she said breathlessly. "Yes, Your Grace, that is certainly very fair."

"Good," said Cecily sharply. "I am glad we can agree on that fact." Her eyes then narrowed. "Now that I have bestowed upon you such a kindness, you need to ask me what you can do in return."

The ulterior motive, of course. Grace gulped. What on earth did the duchess want from her that she could not orchestrate herself?

"I have nothing I can give you, Your Grace," Grace mur-mured gesturing to her surroundings.

Cecily rolled her eyes. "I called you clever, child. Do not insult me by not assuming the same of me. My son is going to come to you," she said icily through gritted teeth. "As soon as he possibly can. I am certain you are already aware of this."

Grace said nothing, standing still as she stared at the duchess. She didn't know what to say. All she could assume was that Adam had already confronted his mother. Was this Cecily confirming her role in their separation?

"When he does, you are to send him away, once and for all," Cecily said firmly. "I have gifted you a blessing, child. You have a position among my senior household, and a generous income for someone of your age and station. I hope you understand, it would be far easier for me to have you sent away, but I will not." She muttered something under her breath that sounds like, knowing my son, he would only chase you.

Grace was frozen. What exactly did the duchess want her to tell him? To be cruel to him? To sever what kindness that had been restored to them?

"I cannot be cruel to him," she whispered.

Cecily merely smirked. "If you do not, I will have him disinherited," she threatened. "I will turn him out and he will have nothing. I have another son, you realise."

Grace gasped. What? Surely, she would not do such a thing to her own son. Surely disinheriting Adam was impossible!

"Why do you hate me so much that you would do such a thing to your own son?" Grace asked her, the words escaping her mouth before she could coherently understand what she was saying.

It was Cecily turn to freeze as she glared at Grace, for a split second, exposing a deeper level of emotion than her usual cool expression. There was more to the duchess than met the eye, and Grace couldn't understand why her disdain ran so deeply.

"My dear," she growled, "whether you understand or not, everything I do is to ensure my son's future. He in engaged to a woman equal to him in position and wealth. She is also young enough to believe herself in love." She exhaled sharply. "You are to attend Lady Sarah for the duration of her stay. You will attend to her every whim. Should you prove loyal and successful in this position, upon my son's marriage to Lady Sarah, your assistance will then go to Lady Susanna." Cecily sighed. "I don't care what you say to him, Grace," she said, continuing their previous line of conversation. "I trust that with your clever head, you will choose your family's survival over any chance of a future you might possibly believe you have with my son."

Grace swallowed loudly, finding her tongue. "I am my father's eldest child, Your Grace. I will always put my family first. It is my responsibility. I had already made the decision to put my past with Adam ... Lord Beresford ... behind me. You did not need to make any threats. You do not need to take anything away from him. I understand that he is engaged. I understand that Lady Sarah is far above me, and therefore far better than me in your eyes." Grace willed herself not to stutter. "Lord Beresford was my friend before any of this, and I do deeply care about his welfare. I respectfully ask you not to threaten him, or his birthright. I will not be responsible for that."

Cecily seemed to be surprised to hear such a speech from Grace. "I suppose you are cleverer than I thought," she noted. "If only my son could possess a little of your logic, Grace. Nevertheless, he will come to you. What will you say to him?"

Grace wasn't certain of what Adam would say to her when he did come. Cecily seemed to be acting pre-emptively. There was certainly not anything he could do anyway, was there? He was a man of honour, and he had asked Sarah to marry him. Grace would return his ring. That was all she could be certain of.

"I don't know," she replied honestly. "But I will not be cruel."

"Well," remarked Cecily. "This was certainly not the conversation I had expected from you. I had imagined a silly village girl filled with lust." She shook her head. "Regardless, I am a woman of my word. You will commence your new position tomorrow. Your income should certainly support your poor mother during her convalescence." She smiled briefly. "I am glad we had this chat, Grace. I believe we have a certain understanding."

Hope you enjoyed it! I wonder how this talk will indeed go! And I wonder what Cecily is hiding behind all of this ...

Oh wait, I don't have to wonder.

Lol, I just love that hehehe

Vote and comment!!

Chapter 15

Grace and Ruby were both awoken the next morning by the sounds of their bedroom door being opened. Grace had heard Ruby enter the room in the early hours of the morning, but she hadn't roused herself properly to tell her the news. Of course, her promotion to lady's maid would be the only piece of news she would be sharing.

She sat up in her bed suddenly, worrying if the duchess had returned to take back her offer, but instead Grace was faced with Mrs Hayes. She was carrying a black uniform, the same kind that she had seen Miss Naismith wearing.

"I am sorry to wake you both," apologised Mrs Hayes, "but I thought I would deliver your new livery, Grace. Or rather, Miss Denham," she corrected herself.

Grace's eyes widened. She supposed she would be called Miss Denham now as a lady's maid.

"New livery?" asked Ruby groggily. The poor girl was awakened with only three or four hours of sleep. "Whatever for?"

"The duchess has favoured Miss Denham," replied Mrs Hayes, a sense of caution in her voice. "You have best ready yourself now, Miss Denham. You will want to have enough breakfast in you for when the bell rings and you are forced to abandon your tea." Mrs Hayes laid the uniform down on the end of Grace's bed. While still bent over, she looked up into Grace's eyes. "You best be careful now, Grace," she warned in a whisper, only for her ears. "The duchess does not bestow gifts. There is always a price."

Grace nodded, even though she already knew the price. She knew exactly the price she would need to pay, and she was willing to pay it, not matter how it hurt her. She could withstand pain.

Mrs Hayes righted herself and went to the door. "I will see you both down at breakfast. Quickly now. This is our guests' first Sunday in church. I am sure there will be quite a spectacle about it." She then closed the door behind her.

"The duchess has favoured you how?" pressed Ruby, waking herself up further, sitting up in her bed.

"She asked me to attend Lady Sarah Ashley," replied Grace. "Just last night."

"Well," remarked Ruby, surprised, "that is lucky indeed. Are you trained as a lady's maid? Do you know how to fix hair? How to dress a lady?"

Grace pursed her lips awkwardly. "No," she confessed, "I am not trained, not in the way that I have travelled to France for courses. But I can fix some styles, and others I will learn. I can certainly dress someone."

Ruby didn't seem angry, but surprised, just as Grace had been momentarily before the duchess had revealed her ulterior motive. "Will you insist upon me calling you Miss Denham as we have to address Miss Naismith?"

Grace giggled before throwing her pillow across the room at her. "Don't be silly," she scolded playfully.

Ruby grinned, before tossing her red hair over her shoulders dramatically. "Please do feel obliged to practise fancy hairstyles on me of a night-time. Even in the morning, and I might tuck my hair under my cap. I would love to have something fine done to my hair."

"I might take you up on that offer," confessed Grace, before she climbed out of bed. She picked up her new livery and held it up against her person to measure the fit.

Mrs Hayes had been right. Grace had barely had a chance to sip her tea and take a bite of porridge before the bell in Lady Sarah's bedroom sounded.

She was now seated beside Miss Naismith at the breakfast table, much to her distaste. There were several curious expressions on the faces of the servants when she appeared dressed as she was, but a quick look from Mrs Hayes silenced the gossiping. Miss Hale was also at breakfast, sitting opposite Grace. She was the long serving maid to Lady Ashley.

Grace collected Lady Sarah's tea tray before making her way up the servant's staircase. As she ascended, she felt Adam's signet ring burning a hole in her pocket. She would inevitably see Adam today as it was Sunday, and he would walk by her in church. Would he make a scene? Surely not.

Though she and the duchess could agree on one thing. Adam would certainly seek her out. He was determined, and always had been. It was a trait that she had once admired. Now it made it her nervous.

Guests were housed on the same floor as the Beresfords, only in an opposite wing. Grace had never been in this part of the house before, not even when she had Adam used to run about the halls as children. She had to remember Mrs Hayes' instructions for finding Lady Sarah's bedroom.

When she reached the door, Grace felt her stomach seize. She didn't know what to make of this lady. She knew that she could trust herself to be perfectly attentive, but how would it feel later? This woman was to be Adam's wife. He had proposed marriage to her.

Resting the tray against her hip, she knocked on the door quickly. Grace heard a soft beckon from inside, so she opened the door and took back control of the tray.

The guest quarters of Ashwood House were expansive and luxurious, and Lady Sarah looked to be entirely enveloped by the sheer size of the bed she was sitting up in.

The young lady was smiling, albeit nervously, as Grace approached. As she came closer, Grace wondered at her age. She did look young, perhaps not yet twenty, and she had an endearing, youthful innocence about her. She was certainly very pretty, with bright, clear skin, lovely green eyes, and fair, brown hair. She understood Lady Sarah's appeal.

"Good morning, milady," greeted Grace politely as she set the tea tray down on the table beside the bed. "My name is Grace Denham, and I am to attend to you while you are staying at Ashwood."

"Good morning," replied Sarah. "I've never had a servant of my own before. Mama's maid, Hale, usually sees to me once she has been in with her."

Grace smiled as she poured the tea. "How do you take your tea, milady?"

"Oh, a little milk and sugar, I suppose," she replied.

Grace added a splash of milk and a sugar cube before she stirred it. Once she was satisfied, she carefully handed the teacup to Sarah.

She sipped the tea and smiled. "Thank you," she said gratefully. "I am frightfully tired after last night, but I thought it prudent that I look my best this morning. It will be my introduction into the parish, after all."

"Of course, milady," Grace murmured, taking a step back to assess the room, and to decide upon what she would need to do. They had arrived last night, so the trunk at the foot of the bed would be filled with Sarah's gowns. She wondered if anyone had thought to hang them. "Shall I unpack for you?" Grace motioned to the trunk.

"Oh, please," nodded Sarah as she took another sip.

Grace went to the trunk and knelt down, unfastening the two latches. Sure enough, there were at least a dozen gowns folded neatly that would indeed be creased. She was already planning on borrowing something from Susanna when she noticed a miniature portrait placed on top of a silver hairbrush on the other side of the trunk.

The artist had captured his hazel stare perfectly, alongside his very handsome features.

"Adam," breathed Grace.

"What?" asked Sarah.

"Oh, nothing, milady," said Grace quickly. "I only noticed the portrait you have packed." She quickly pulled out several of Sarah's gowns and hurried away with them to the wardrobe.

"Isn't it perfect?" sang Sarah blissfully. "It was a special request of mine the day after we became engaged. I asked my dear Lord Beresford to sit for an artist so that I might have a reminder of him during these months we were parted from one another."

Grace was so thankful that she was facing away from Sarah that she might not have seen the exact shade of green she was turning at hearing her refer to Adam as her dear Lord Beresford.

"How ... nice," Grace managed to say.

"He is terribly handsome, is he not?" Sarah gushed. "I thought he was certainly the most handsome of my suitors during my Season. I feel so fortunate that everything has worked out as it has."

"My warmest congratulations, milady." The words tasted awful on her tongue.

Grace finished hanging the gowns and focussed on controlling her face as she returned to Sarah.

"Shall we see to your hair, milady?" she suggested.

Sarah nodded, and put her teacup down on the tray. She climbed out of the bed and walked over to the dressing table and sat down. Grace fetched the brush from her trunk, careful not to stew on the miniature, before walking to stand behind Sarah.

Sarah removed the ribbon from her braid and allowed her hair to fall down her back.

"I hope we might be friends," Sarah said softly as Grace began to brush her hair. "I am away from home, and I don't know anyone here."

Grace met Sarah's eye in the mirror, and her face softened. "Of course, milady," she said, smiling as warmly as she could muster. Grace would be Sarah's friend, but she was sure the sentiment could not be returned. Could she bring herself to befriend the woman who was to be Adam's wife?

Was this part of Cecily's plan? Could she be so conniving? To force her to be in Sarah's presence every day to remind her of what she could not have. Of course, it was. Cecily was determined to remind Grace of her proper place. Brushing the hair of the future Duchess of Ashwood.

"Do you have any way in particular that you like your hair styled?" she asked Sarah, praying she would not say anything too complicated.

As Sarah told Grace how she wanted her plaits fixed, the door to the bedroom opened, and a fully dressed Lady Ashley entered the room. Sarah was very like her mother, though Lady Ashley possessed none of Sarah's innocence. She looked like any other mother that Grace had ever encountered in a ballroom or assembly hall. Determined.

"Good morning, Mama," greeted Sarah cheerfully.

"You are not dressed?" exclaimed Lady Ashley. "Quickly, child! You are missing a grand opportunity. Lord Beresford is downstairs in the dining room having breakfast."

Sarah frowned. "Why do I need to rush, Mama?" she asked. "I am telling Denham how I like my hair."

Lady Ashley did not even look at Grace, though Grace was not surprised. She had been a servant for a long time. They were supposed to be invisible. She raced over to the wardrobe and went through Sarah's gowns, gasping as she appraised each one. "But these are all creased!" she shouted. "Why did you not hang them up?" she accused Grace. "Lady Sarah cannot wear these. She would look like a pauper!"

"I beg your pardon, milady," apologised Grace, holding her tongue. "I only began attending Lady Sarah this morning. I hung them up almost immediately."

"She did, Mama," confirmed Sarah.

Lady Ashley huffed. "My darling, you must look your best. The duchess is very set on you and Lord Beresford spending lots of time together and I agree. Is that not what's best? He only danced with you once last night. You do not want him getting cold feet."

Sarah frowned. "Cold feet?" she repeated. "But we are engaged."

Lady Ashley selected a gown from the wardrobe and handed it Grace as she walked past her to Sarah. "That will need ironing," she murmured.

Grace laid out the gown on the bed before returning to start Sarah's hair.

"Sarah, nothing is final until you are standing before a clergyman," Lady Ashley said tiredly. "It has been some months since you last saw each other. You must still secure him. There are not many handsome young men in line to inherit such a rich dukedom. Believe me, I have searched."

Sarah looked quite dejected at her mother's words, and Grace checked her reflection in the mirror to make sure that her expression was neutral. She hated being privy to this conversation. She didn't like Adam being discussed as though he were a fish on a line.

"He loves me," Sarah told her mother.

The silver hairbrush slipped through Grace's fingers. "I am terribly sorry," she whispered, her eyes welling up as she knelt down to collect the brush. Adam loved Sarah. Had he told her that?

Lady Ashley seemed to read Grace's mind. "Has Lord Beresford told you that explicitly?" she asked.

"Well, no," confessed Sarah. "But I am certain he does. You do not need to worry, Mama. Everything will be alright. The next Duchess of Ashwood is in this very room."

Chapter 16

Grace managed to keep her composure as she fixed Sarah's hair as best she could. It turned out quite pretty in the end, and the collected the gown from the bed to take down to the laundry for ironing, promising to return as quickly as she could.

She made her way directly toward the passageway panel that would take her into the internal staircases, holding onto the gown tightly, as though she was channelling all of her nerves into it.

"Grace, I've been looking for you everywhere!"

Grace nearly jumped out of her skin when she heard her name being called, but she knew exactly who it was. She looked up to find Susanna running down the hallway towards her, still dressed in her nightgown, her blonde hair in rags.

"Good morning, Susanna," Grace uttered quietly, not wanting anyone, even if she couldn't see them, to hear her calling a lady by her Christian name.

Susanna looked at Grace's attire curiously as she slowed down to meet her. "Why are you wearing a lady's maid uniform?" she asked.

"Because I am a lady's maid," Grace said awkwardly. "Your mother gave me the position last night. I am attending Lady Sarah while she is here."

Susanna looked utterly dumbfounded, and Grace could appreciate her confusion. If one did not know of the duchess' ulterior motive, it would be hard to understand why she would offer such a position to a housemaid who had been in the household employ for only a few months.

"Mother spoke to you last night?" she checked once the initial shock had worn off.

Grace nodded. "Yes."

"My, she moves quickly," muttered Susanna under her breath before she shook off the thought. "I need two things from you Grace, or is it Denham now?"

"Please continue to call me Grace," she insisted. She didn't much like being barked at with her surname, even if it was a higher level of status among servants.

Susanna smiled. "Please tell me that you are not angry with me. You have had a few days to ... stop being angry with me, even if you said you weren't cross. You are still my friend, aren't you?" she asked hopefully.

Grace frowned. Susanna's initial line of questioning made all the more sense now. Susanna had been under the impression that Grace had treated her brother awfully. She was protecting Adam, just as Grace would protect any one of her siblings. "Of course, I am not angry with you," she promised. "and yes, I still want us to be friends."

Susanna breathed a sigh of relief. "Good," she said gratefully. "Now, tell me, your sister, Miss Claire, her hair last night was simply lovely. Did you do it?"

Grace smiled slightly. Perhaps she was not so terrible at hair as she thought she was. "Yes, I did," she confirmed. "I did think she looked really pretty last night."

Susanna lifted her hands to her hair and pulled at a couple of the rags. "Would you be so kind as to help me with my hair this morning?" she asked eagerly. "Mother's maid usually does my hair, but her styles are terribly boring. I would so like your taste."

"I would love to help you, Susanna, but I need to go down to the laundry," said Grace regretfully, holding up the gown in her hands. "Lady Sarah's church dress needs ironing."

Susanna pouted. "Oh, please?" she begged. "We will not be leaving for church for at least another two hours. That is plenty of time to fix my hair and to iron that dress, don't you think?" Susanna didn't give Grace much opportunity to rebut before she had seized her arm and was running with her back towards her bedroom.

Grace gulped as she ran with Susanna towards the bedroom where the duchess would still be abed, but luckily, she did not emerge. Susanna pushed open her door and motioned for Grace to go inside.

"I must go after you," Grace told her, frowning.

Susanna rolled her eyes and gave Grace a push, knocking her inside the bedroom. "Now, you aren't cross with me, remember?" she prompted, before she suddenly pulled her own door closed and shut Grace inside.

"Susanna, what are you doing?" Grace exclaimed as she tried to open the door again, but found it locked.

"I am afraid Susanna's little charade was intended to help me get you alone."

A chill, which was becoming all too familiar, ran down her spine. Grace turned around slowly to find Adam standing by the armchair that sat in front of Susanna's dormant fire. He was already dressed for the day, his coat the shade of green that reminded her of emeralds. But she could not dwell on his appearance for too long. Panic soon set in.

"Are you mad?" she hissed. "What will people say if they knew I was alone in a bedroom with you?" Her eyes flared as she cupped her hands over her mouth, dropping Sarah's gown on the floor in the process. "What will Mama say? Oh, she would be so ashamed of me! And Claire would never be able to get married, and she would hate me!"

Adam frowned. "Grace, do you ever believe I would allow your reputation to be tarnished?" he asked in disbelief. "No one is going to find you in here. Susanna is looking out for us. But even if they did, it would give me an excuse to marry you all the more quickly."

Grace took a step backward, knocking into Susanna's bedroom door as she stared at him. "You should not say such things!" she snapped.

Adam nodded, allowing that. "I understand things are a little complicated ..."

"Complicated?" repeated Grace, before she remembered the duchess' jab about her sounding like a parrot.

"I told you that we would finish our conversation," Adam reminded her. "Please, would you sit with me?" he asked earnestly.

Grace shook her head. "No, I think it is wise that we keep as much distance between us as possible. Lord, I might throttle Susanna."

Adam actually laughed lightly. "Do not blame her. It was I who sent her. I wanted to speak to you before my mother would have a chance to."

Grace realised that she'd already revealed that the duchess had spoken to her to Susanna without realising it. Adam would certainly find out. But Grace needed to think quickly. The duchess had demanded that she put an end to this once and for all.

Despite Cecily's wishes, Grace knew that she needed to end it for her own sake. She had only heard one too many stories over the years of powerful lords having their way with servants, all the while forging some of the most glamorous, wealthy connections through marriage. She knew how this would end, and it wasn't up to Adam no matter how much he might have wanted it to be. Lords did not wed servants.

They would both lose.

Grace felt inside her pocket and pulled out Adam's gold signet ring. She fiddled with it for a moment before she found the courage to cross the room to him. "I thought that you ought to have this back," she said softly.

Adam held out his hand curiously, before gasping quietly when she dropped the ring into his palm. "You kept it?" he realised, before he looked down at her and met her gaze. "Why would you return this? I gave this to you."

"You gave it to me when you believed you were free to do so," she murmured. "But you are not anymore, and it's not appropriate that I have it when your fiancée is here."

"Grace, you don't know what you're saying," Adam said hoarsely, his hand making a fist around the ring. "I didn't know the letter was a forgery then, and I allowed myself to pushed by my mother ..."

Grace took a step backward, the action appearing on Adam's face as though she had struck him. "I do know what I am saying. I am not a silly girl, Adam. I do have a head on my shoulders, and I do know how this world works. It does not work in favour of dreamers. At the end of the day, when everything is said and done, rent must be paid, food must be purchased, family must be taken care of." Grace hated that her eyes began to well up. "My mother might not be able to work again," she said fearfully, "but should she have to? She has raised five children and nursed her husband, and she deserves rest."

"I know you are not a silly girl, Grace," Adam said firmly. "You were never silly. I know you are clever, and kind, and generous, and I honestly wish I was as good an elder sibling as you are. I have much to learn from you.

"But being the elder sibling does not mean carrying around the weight of the world on your shoulders without allowing anyone to help you. You are not weak if you allow someone to take care of you."

Grace's eyes narrowed. "Weak?" she snapped. "Do you honestly think me so fragile that I would be afraid of weakness?" she asked in disbelief. "I am afraid ..." she took a breath, "... of a lot of things. Things that I cannot control. Things that are out of my control."

Adam sighed exasperatedly. "And I am afraid that I am going to say something stupid to upset you, to make you so angry at me that I cannot finish what I wanted to say to you. You know that about me, Grace. You know I am determined."

Grace forced herself to take another breath. She was at risk of saying something hurtful as well, and she had promised herself that she would not be cruel.

"I made you a promise that one day I would return to Ashwood and I would marry you," Adam said slowly, carefully, "and I want to keep that promise. I was hurt, and angry, and cold when I first saw you upon my return, and I am furious at my mother for separating us and costing us such precious time. But I want to put that behind us. I promise you that I will sort everything. Sarah is a sweet girl, but she isn't you."

Grace could see the hope in Adam's eyes. It was the same hope that he had written her about so many times. He was untouched by the cruelties of the real world. He knew not the reality of selling virtually everything of value so that there might be a roof over his head and bread on the table.

Adam didn't know that he couldn't promise her these things. He didn't have the blessing of his parents. He certainly would never get it. And though she was uncertain if

Cecily's threat to disinherit him was true, what sort of person would she be to risk that? Where would they be if Adam was disinherited? He would have nothing.

Her head knew the right choice. She had a wonderful opportunity as a lady's maid. And if she worked hard enough, she might be able to find a position somewhere else, with another lady who paid just as well. With a little economy, her mother wouldn't have to overexert herself. If they economised a little further, Claire might have a small purse on her marriage.

Her head knew this.

But her heart? Her heart ached to look into his hopeful eyes. It was though he was dangling a perfect future in front of her, as though it was attainable. As though there were not a dozen obstacles preventing it. If she leapt into his arms, Grace knew that Adam would hold her, that he might kiss her if she asked him to.

"But we were children then," Grace said softly. "We don't know each other anymore, not really. We have grown up, and so much time has passed. We are different people."

"I long to know you now if you will let me," Adam declared. "I am not asking to settle everything right now. I know that would be very overwhelming. I only want to know my friend again, and when you are ready, we can have another ... conversation."

Grace shook her head frustratedly. "No, you are not listening to me. It is not as simple as that."

"How am I not listening?" Adam asked, furrowing his eyebrows. "What don't I understand?"

"Everything," Grace said breathlessly. "And that is not your fault."

The door suddenly opened, and Grace gasped so hard that she about lost all the air in her lungs. But it was Susanna. The shock alone made her want to run.

"I'm not eavesdropping," she assured them, "but you should know that Mother went to her last night," she told Adam. "She got to her already, so please fix that, will you?" Susanna then shut the door again, quite obviously listening.

"My mother spoke to you already?" growled Adam, shaking her head furiously. He pinched the bridge of his nose with his thumb and forefinger. "What did she say?"

Adam clearly hadn't noticed that she was wearing a different uniform, but Grace wondered if gentlemen ever noticed such things. "She didn't say anything I didn't already know," murmured Grace. "But she made me Lady Sarah's lady's maid."

It was then that Adam looked upon her dress with an expression of realisation. "Why on earth would she do that?" he asked himself under his breath. "What sort of game is she playing?"

"With this income, I might be able to keep my mother from further hurting herself. I have a family to feed, to house," she explained quietly. "Your mother's condition if she gave me this position was that I send you away once and for all."

Adam practically glowered at her. He looked as though he was trying very hard to control his temper. Grace was unsure if it was she that he was angry at now. "You don't think that I would feed your family?" he asked rhetorically. "I would have them live here if that was what you wanted."

But did he not see how impossible that was? "Your money is not your own," Grace retorted shakily. "Your money belongs to your parents, and ... and ..." Tears fell from Grace's eyes, and Adam caught them before they could reach her cheek. She unwittingly leaned into his touch, closing her eyes for a moment. Her senses quickly returned, and she looked back up at Adam. "Please," she begged. "I was ready to forgive everything, to move on. Won't you let me?"

Could he not see that she was trying to protect him, too?

Chapter 17

Adam heard Grace's words, her pleas. But he couldn't let her go. Not when they had only just found each other again.

He knew his mother would do whatever she could to keep them apart, only he hadn't imagined that she would have worked so quickly. At what hour must she have called upon Grace last night to give her this position?

Not for a second did Adam believe that Cecily had acted out of generosity. Grace had but confirmed it herself when she had revealed his mother's condition. He did not blame Grace for accepting, either.

Grace would have been eighteen years old when her father died. To learn to cope with grief at such an age, as well as having to find a way to provide for her family, was simply unimaginable. Lord, it made him angry that he had not been with her to help her.

She would not make a selfish decision. She would not choose him if it meant her family might suffer. As much as he wanted to take her by the hand and pull her towards what he wanted, Adam understood her hesitation.

Adam's heart ached as he looked upon her beautiful, tear stained face. Her brows knitting together as she vulnerably frowned, her pink lower lip trembling, her narrow shoulders shuddering as she tried to control what would be sobs.

Adam had loved Grace long before he had known what love was. Everyone knew, he was certain of it. He followed her around helplessly, potentially annoying her into being his friend. But once she had, there was no separating them. Not until the day he had left for school.

After all the years, even though he had been heartbroken, Adam had never forgotten Grace. As much as he might have wished otherwise, she was never far from his thoughts, and he wondered about her often. Having her back in his life the way there were now wasn't good enough. He needed more.

She was right when she said that they didn't really know each other as adults. Adam simply wanted the chance to get to know the lady she had grown up to be. The destination he was confident in. Somehow, sometime, she would be walking into church as his bride. But he looked forward to the journey there in the meantime.

"I am so sorry, Grace," Adam said sincerely. He took a chance and grabbed hold of one of her hands. She was shaking and he calmly opened her palm, slowly tracing the lines there. Her shaking slowed, and then stopped, as she watched his index finger intently.

"You haven't done anything wrong," whispered Grace. "You don't need to apologise. I feel like I am the one spoiling everything."

"You are not spoiling anything," he promised. His mother was the one to blame for that. "No, I am apologising for engaging myself to another." He watched as Grace bit down on her bottom lip. She did not look up at him but continued to watch her hand. "If only I had delayed ... just another summer," he uttered regretfully. "We would have come home, and I would have seen you, and there would not be such an added complication. I will end it, I promise you."

Grace gasped and snatched her hand away, her cornflower blue eyes returning to his, this time flared with panic. "No!" she cried. "Adam, your engagement is not what is stopping everything ..." she trailed off, and he could read on her face that she was having a bitter thought about it despite her words. Grace took a deep, calming breath. "Your mother told me that if I did not send you away when we spoke, that she would disinherit you," she revealed fearfully.

Adam felt like something burst inside his brain at the sheer lunacy of her statement. His mother had threatened to disinherit him. The only way he would not be the next Duke of Ashwood would be if he were to spontaneously die. He knew Cecily Beresford was cold, but cold enough to plan a murder? He did not think so.

But Grace did not know that, and Cecily had put that pressure, that onus, on her. It was yet another injustice that infuriated him.

"How could I live with myself if such a cruel threat came to pass?" Grace continued, sounding so fragile. "You would have nothing, and forgive me, but I do not think you would do well if you had nothing. You are very accustomed to a certain way of living."

Adam found himself chuckling. "You do not think I would find employment in a mine or somewhere, come home with a face blackened by soot?"

Grace laughed tearfully, and it pleased him greatly to hear that sound. "No!" she exclaimed.

Adam stepped forward and Grace froze, wary of what he was about to do. He leaned closer and watched her anxious eyes. Not yet. Not while he was still engaged to another. He pressed his lips to her forehead, lingering a little, before he pulled away.

"My mother cannot disinherit me," he told her quietly. "She was trying to frighten you, and she succeeded. I am going to speak to my father. He has more sense than my mother. Please, will you be patient? I promise it will all be alright."

Grace nodded, though she did look a little uncertain. Adam supposed he felt the same way. The immediate future was a little uncertain. But he knew what the end looked like, and he was willing to do whatever necessary to get there.

"I need to go down to the laundry," Grace murmured. "Lady Sarah's gown needs ironing ... Susanna wanted me to fix her hair, as well, but I suppose that must have been a ruse."

"Ignore Susanna. I do." Adam grinned.

There was a sudden bang on the door and Adam laughed. He knew Susanna would be eagerly listening to any bit of news on this front.

Grace blushed and hurried back to where she had dropped Sarah's dress. After picking it up, she rushed over to the door and rapt on it lightly. "Susanna, let me out," she instructed. The door opened and Grace looked back at him, and for the first time, Adam saw a glimmer of hope in her eyes.

Adam had not been able to do anything before church that morning, and it had not helped that his mother used their guests as a shield to prevent any confrontation and positioned Sarah so that she could walk into the service on Adam's arm.

Grace was sitting with her family, but she didn't look his way for long. Adam found it hard to concentrate on what the poor vicar was saying as Sarah kept leaning over to whisper, "What page is he reading from?" every three minutes. Every time she did, he noticed someone within the church whispering as they stared. Was this something that she had been told to do? Had his mother encouraged this behaviour?

When they returned to the house, Cecily had planned a grand Sunday luncheon. The first to welcome Lady and Sarah Ashley to Ashwood.

"Father," Adam said quietly as they walked into the drawing room to wait while the servants prepared the dining room. "Might I have a private word?"

Peregrine frowned. "Can it wait?" he asked. "Luncheon is about to be served."

"No," replied Adam, shaking his head. "I am afraid this is an important matter, and I would rather discuss it with you now, seeing as Mother is occupied." He nodded towards Cecily, who was standing in front of one of the family portraits, no doubt exaggerating their importance.

Peregrine then nodded and started towards the drawing room door and Adam moved to follow.

"Where do you two think you are going?" Cecily called, her voice a cheerful charade.

"None of your business," Peregrine snapped under his breath.

"Away, Mother," replied Adam tersely. "We shall return shortly for luncheon. Not to worry."

Cecily's eyes flared as she looked between her husband and son. "No," she said pointedly. "What a thing to do, to abandon your guests," she scolded, before putting on a laugh. "I will not hear of it. Adam, you are to escort Lady Sarah into the dining room."

"Why, will she get lost?" Peregrine again muttered, only for Adam to hear.

As much as his parents' disdain for each other had angered and frustrated Adam over the years, he had never been more grateful to have his father so disagree with his mother. Surely, Peregrine would see his side. Together, they would go against Cecily and end her reign of terror.

"As I said, Mother, we will return shortly," Adam said again, before motioning for his father to go.

Peregrine stopped at the stairs and thought for a moment, before deciding against them, as though climbing them was too big of an effort. Instead, he made his way into the library, shutting the door behind Adam, and taking a seat in one of the large, wingback armchairs.

"What did you want to speak to me about?" Peregrine asked calmly.

Adam was not about to dance around the subject. He decided to get straight to the point. "Grace."

"Ah," realised Peregrine, leaning back into his chair.

"Did you know that Mother separated us? She forged two letters, sending one to each of us, to end our understanding?"

Peregrine shook his head. "No, I do not much concern myself with what your mother does with her time," he murmured. "I do know that you were very fond of little Grace when you were a boy."

"I'm not just fond of her, Father. I love her. We have only just discovered Mother's deception and I want your blessing to pursue her."

Peregrine leaned an elbow on the arm of the chair and pursed his lips. "What about Lady Sarah?"

"You know how Mother urged me into that engagement," Adam retorted. "Sarah is a sweet girl, and she will no doubt find another suitor, but I can't marry her. I won't be happy with her, and I am certain she wouldn't be happy with me. How could she be when I am in love with another?"

Peregrine actually smiled. "Happiness," he chuckled. "What has happiness to do with marriage?"

Adam sat up straighter, suddenly concerned at his father's odd opinion. "Everything," Adam said slowly. "I know you don't love your wife. Would not you have led a happier life if you had married a woman that you loved?"

"You may be a man, Adam, but you are very naïve." Peregrine shook his head. "Have I not spent these last weeks teaching you all there is to know about the running of this estate? Money makes the world go around. Without money, our titles mean nothing. Of course, I didn't love Cecily. I barely knew her when we were engaged to one another. And now that I do know her, I can't stand her. Would that have changed my decision? No. My father used her dowry to clear several debts against the estate and we have been able to prosper for many years."

Adam stared at his father in disbelief. He could not believe that after nearly three decades of marriage to Cecily that he would not be screaming at Adam to choose happiness over a marriage of convenience.

Peregrine sighed. "Adam, I am not heartless. Of course, I wanted happiness. That is what we seek elsewhere once there are children to secure your line. Why not set Grace up with apartments in London?" he suggested. "You could visit her whenever you like."

Bile rose in Adam's throat as the idea left his father's lips. He launched out of his chair and was halfway across the room when he managed to exclaim, "You want Grace to be my mistress?"

"What is so shocking?" barked Peregrine. "If you want her so badly, then surely that is an acceptable solution."

Adam about threw his head into a wall. "That is not acceptable. I cannot even fathom the thought; it is too insulting.

I would never degrade Grace in such a way," he seethed. He thought back to Grace's fears that her reputation would have been compromised had they been caught together in Susanna's bedroom. He would never again be able to look her in the eye if she ever heard such an idea.

"Adam, sit down," Peregrine instructed, firmly enough that Adam obeyed.

He reluctantly returned to his chair, sitting down before he glowered at his father.

"Grace Denham is a very pretty young girl," he allowed, though his tone unforgiving. "I understand why she has caught your eye. But she is a servant. The scandal alone of marrying a servant would be great. But to weather such a scandal as a new duke is simply unthinkable."

As Adam was about to refute his father's claims, he suddenly comprehended a certain detail. "New duke?" he repeated, looking up at his father and frowning. "What do you mean?"

Peregrine pressed his lips together firmly. "You mother was relentless in securing you a match this last summer for a reason. She wanted a strong match for you, one with a large dowry to secure any destabilisation following what was inevitable."

"Father, you're speaking Greek," stammered Adam. "Please, explain to me what you are saying."

Peregrine laid a hand on his stomach. "When you and Jack were away at university, and Susanna was away being finished, my physician discovered a mass on my liver. I was operated upon by one of the best surgeons in London, and the tumour was removed. In July, my physician found that the mass had returned, only this time there were more." Peregrine touched his neck, as though there was a mass there as well.

Adam was frozen still, his brain not quite wanting to think the horrible truth.

"I had not wanted to tell you or your brother or sister yet," continued Peregrine quietly. "I don't know what I was waiting for, but here we are. I am going to die, Adam. I don't know when, but I feel dreadful some days. You are going to inherit sooner than you thought. You are not going to bring about a scandal of that magnitude as this house enters into mourning," Peregrine said coolly. "You are not going to bring about a scandal of that magnitude ever. We are not common, Adam. We are not a family for the papers. We are a family who can trace their lineage back to the Norman conquest. You, my son, will not ruin us. You will make a respectable marriage and you will pass the title on to your own son."

His father was dying. Adam felt his heart crack, as though it were made of fragile glass. One sudden movement and it would shatter into a thousand pieces.

Peregrine stood up and kissed the top of Adam's head, placing his hands there afterward. "Perhaps you will not love your wife. Perhaps you will grow to love her. But I can guarantee you one certainty. You will love your children, and you will do anything to prevent them from choices that will make their lives even harder, especially when they must face the cruelty of death."

Chapter 18

Grace never heard what Adam's father had to say. Adam never told her. Though the fact that he was still engaged to be married answered her own question.

Adam did not seek Grace out for a conversation, a clandestine meeting or anything for weeks. On that Sunday after the ball he had promised her that he would speak to his father and then nothing.

Adam wasn't being cold. He wasn't being cruel. If he were so, Grace could be angry, frustrated ... resigned to the fact that nothing was to come about. Something was wrong with him. Something was wrong, and Adam was carrying that weight around on his shoulders.

The only time that she saw him now was every other Sunday in church. There was something missing from his eyes. He didn't smile. There was anxious tension in his brow.

She supposed she was frustrated as nobody seemed to notice anything was wrong except for her. Grace was not in a position to ask questions. She could not go and knock on his door and check to see if he was alright.

Her one inquiry had been to Susanna, who had told her that Adam had said that everything was fine. That had been four weeks ago.

Susanna was her only ally. She could not ask anyone else for fear that they would make dangerous connections. Grace desperately wanted to go to Mrs Hayes. Adam had always looked up to her like a mother, but not even she seemed worried. Of course, that could have been because Adam kept to his father's study.

Listening in on the conversations of valets told Grace that the duke and Lord Beresford were spending quite a bit of time together. Grace didn't know if this was particularly odd as Adam had been spending that time with his father before she had noticed that something was wrong.

Grace felt helpless as she tried to listen for any scrap of news, and she wished that she could go and find him. She wished that he would come and find her, to confide in her, as he always had done as a boy.

Perhaps the most frustrating part of her day was her time spent with Lady Sarah Ashley. Personally, Grace thought Sarah was a lovely young lady. She was everything a high-born girl ought to be. She was well-mannered and spoken, well-read and walked with a regal sense of balance. She was proficient in her needlework and could delight company with her ability to speak both perfect French and Italian.

Of course, the latter virtues Grace only knew by the praises of her mother.

What was frustrating about their time together was Lady Sarah's ignorance. She claimed to love Adam. She thought he was perfect. She could not find fault with him, and often confided in Grace about her feelings.

Her ignorance, and innocence, was evident, Grace felt, in her inability to read just how uncomfortable her confessions made her lady's maid.

Lady Sarah thought everything was perfect, and she did not seem to mind that her fiancé spent nothing more than a few moments a day with her. Grace thought it absurd. If it were her, she would want to marry someone she could not wait to spend her time with.

Sarah was occupied with planning her wedding, an occasion of which the duchess could spare no expense.

It infuriated Grace, really, that this girl claimed to love Adam and yet could not see that there was something terribly wrong. Were she a little more observant, Sarah was in a position to solicit an audience with Adam. But she never thought to.

Grace put the finishing touched on Sarah's intricate hairstyle. She had definitely improved, and she had taken up Ruby's offer to practise on her. Ruby often had a very fine style tucked up under her cap.

Sarah admired herself in the mirror and smiled with satisfaction. "Lovely," she complimented. "You have such a delicate touch, Denham."

Grace smiled. "Thank you, milady," she said quietly.

"Do you think that you would continue to be my maid after I am married?" Sarah asked. "I don't know where Lord

Beresford and I are to live yet, but as a married woman, I will need a maid. I would so like for her to be you."

Grace's eyes widened and she did her very best to compose herself quickly. She could not imagine anything more painful than serving Adam's wife. It was challenging enough serving Adam's fiancée. "I am terribly sorry, milady, but the duchess had bid me to Lady Susanna when you leave."

Sarah pouted, but nodded with acceptance. "Well, I have enjoyed having you as my maid, Denham, and I shall enjoy our time until I am wed."

Grace picked up the hairbrush and comb that she had been using to fix Sarah's hair and popped them in the dressing table drawer. "Are you nervous about marrying Lord Beresford?" she asked.

Sarah hesitated before shaking her head. "I suppose I am not," she decided. "I always knew that I would be engaged by the end of the past summer. I will be one and twenty next year." Sarah tsked at the age.

Grace would be four and twenty the following year.

"He is everything I desire in a husband. Handsome, sensible, gentlemanly, titled ..." she trailed off.

Grace thought about the four adjectives that Sarah had used to describe Adam, and how two of them referenced his appearance and his rank. It annoyed her.

Grace knew that if she thought about it for much longer, her feelings would start to show on her face. She changed the subject. "Shall we dress, milady?"

That afternoon, Grace carried a parcel of material up the servants' staircase. It had been ordered by Lady Ashley for

Sarah to view, so that she may pick the fabric for her wedding gown. To be carrying such fabric twisted her stomach, but Grace moved as swiftly as she possibly could.

As she came out into the hallway, she heard a thud and a shout from behind her, back towards the main staircase. She certainly could not ignore it. Grace turned around and made her way towards the noise.

When she came to the main staircase, she was shocked to see the duke on his knees, three steps from the landing. He was leaning on one hand, the other dripping the banister, as he made the effort to regain his feet.

"Your Grace!" she cried. "Please, let me help you! Or let me fetch someone to help!"

"No, no," snapped the duke. He looked up to see who was standing at the top of the stairs, and his eyes widened a little in surprise as he recognised her. "Grace Denham," he murmured. "Just give me a moment." Peregrine pulled on the banister, trying to right himself, but he appeared weak, as though he did not have the strength.

He looked thinner in the face, Grace noted, his skin looking paler, though the growing December gloominess was contributing to all of their complexions. Peregrine looked as though he needed something hearty to eat. In truth, he reminded her of –

"Oh, it's no use," huffed Peregrine suddenly. "Help me," he demanded, motioning for Grace to come to him. "You will tell no one," he ordered.

"Of course, Your Grace," she promised, setting down the parcel and rushing to the duke's side. Grace did not know how much help she could be. Thinning as he was, the duke was still much larger than her.

Grace went to his right side, with Peregrine immediately wrapping his arm around her. Grace felt his weight completely, and her legs nearly gave way. But she was determined not to fall. She lifted with all her might and helped to get Peregrine to his feet.

"I need to rest. Help me to my bedroom," Peregrine grunted lethargically, not thinking of the position he was putting Grace in with such a request.

Grace knew the sensible thing to do would be to ring the bell for his valet, but she could not very well refuse a duke's instruction. Grace left the parcel of fabric behind and allowed Peregrine to continue to lean on her as they made their way in the opposite direction to where she had been going. The duke's bedroom was the very last room at the end of the long hallway, something that Peregrine felt it necessary to complain about.

When she opened the door, Grace was astonished at the sheer size and grandeur of the room. It was positively enormous, and had furniture positioned about to simulate six different rooms. The bed was the largest, finest feature, and boasted a spectacular golden canopy that hung from the ceiling. The luxurious drapes surrounded the bed. Grace released Peregrine momentarily to pull them back so that the duke could lie down.

Peregrine exhaled, as though he was in pain, as he laid down on his bed, stiffly stretching his limbs, grimacing.

"Your Grace, shall I send for the doctor?" Grace asked quietly. "I will ring the bell for Mrs Hayes and Mr Cole. Surely they will know what to do."

"No," uttered the duke. "No, I have no need for a doctor, or for anyone else. I very much know what is wrong with me."

Grace gasped as the words left his lips. He knew something was wrong?

"Tell me, Grace. How long did your father live after the doctor diagnosed him with an incurable mass?"

Grace immediately paled, her blood running cold in her veins as she thought back to her own father's dying days. Mr Denham had been suffering with a terrible cough for a while, to the point where he would bring up blood. The doctor had initially thought it was consumption, but upon further examination, a mass had been discovered on his stomach, and the doctor believed the two were connected. Her poor, dear father had suffered so, and he had not lived long once he had begun to cough blood.

She looked over Peregrine Beresford with the deepest sympathy when she understood that the same thing must have been happening to him.

"Your Grace ..." she whispered.

"No, no, I won't hear that tone," he scolded, shaking his head from the pillow.

Grace's heart then broke terribly for Adam when she realised just what he had been burdened with. She knew his pain exactly, and she so wanted to take him into her arms, to take that pain from him.

But his father was going to die, and there was nothing she could do to erase that pain.

"Do you know how to read, Grace?" Peregrine then asked.

"Y ... yes, of course," she stammered.

"Good." Peregrine motioned to the book that was on his bedside table. "Read to me, please. The page is marked."

Grace picked up the thick book and read the title.

Dante's Divine Comedy.

She had not heard of this book before, though she supposed she was not as well-read as many other women.

"Do you know it?" Peregrine asked.

"No, Your Grace."

"Dante writes to illustrate a soul's journey to God through hell, purgatory, and finally to heaven. I have read Inferno and Purgatorio, and I have finally made it to Paradiso. But it tires my eyes." Peregrine sighed. "Beatrice, Dante's beloved muse, is to lead him through the nine spheres of heaven. Please, read to me," he urged.

Grace nervously eyes the door, which she had purposefully left open. But she could not deny the duke his wish. She took a seat in a chair near his bed and opened the book to the marked page.

"As to the King," Grace read, "who makes his will our will. And his will is our peace; this is the sea to which is moving onward whatsoever, it doth create, and all that nature makes. Then it was clear to me how everywhere in heaven is Paradise."

"Ah," sighed Peregrine contently as he listened.

Grace read until she had finished the Canto, realising exactly why a man might read such a text at this point in his life.

Grace returned the book to Peregrine's bedside table gently when she thought that he had fallen asleep.

His tired eyes were closed. But he had not drifted yet, and uttered, "You will come back to read some more tomorrow. I must finish."

"Of course, Your Grace," Grace whispered softly as she walked quietly from his bedroom. The moment she was out into the hallway, she closed the door behind her, and looked for any onlookers. Thankfully, she saw none.

As she was alone, she clapped her hand over her mouth and stifled a violent sob. It was as though a wave of suppressed grief had suddenly overcome her as she knew what was to be.

Chapter 19

Grace's heart bled for Adam. And for Jack and Susanna. What a secret to be hiding, what a burden for Adam to carry all the while knowing that his father was to die an imminent and painful death.

To know he was in pain, and to know his exact pain, about killed Grace. It killed her that he had been suffering and she had not known until now how to help him. Even then, she did not know how to help. There was nothing she could do to prevent his pain. She could only understand it. And she wanted to let him know that she understood his pain, and that she would support and be there for him as he grieved.

Grace needed to speak to Adam alone. Never had she ever sought out to speak to a man alone before, but she needed to find a way now. If the duke was in bed, then he was not in his study. Adam had been spending every day shut away in there with his father, so she hoped that meant he was by himself.

Grace hurried back to the stairs and collected the material that she had left there, before walking swiftly back towards Lady Sarah's bedroom. What excuse could she make, she wondered?

Grace knocked on the door twice and heard Sarah call out for her to enter. Sarah was sitting at the writing desk, an unfinished letter before her, as she stowed the quill away.

"The material your mother ordered has arrived, milady," Grace reported, gesturing to the parcel in her hands.

"Oh, wonderful!" cheered Sarah, abandoning the desk as she came to receive the parcel. Grace placed it in her hands and Sarah brought it over to the bed to unwrap. She immediately made a sound of satisfaction as she lifted the first sample. It was a pale blue silk that looked as though it would be as soft as a lamb. "Beautiful!" she exclaimed. "What do you think, Denham?" she asked, holding the rectangle against her neck. "Does it suit me?"

Does the fabric that could be made into a gown to be worn by Adam's wife look nice? Grace had to swallow her first, second, and third thoughts before she managed to say, "Lovely, milady!" with a smile.

Sarah seemed satisfied with that answer as she picked up a satin that was a darker blue, cornflower blue. Grace's eyes narrowed. What had made Sarah make that choice?

"What do you think of this one?" she posed, holding it up against the lighter silk. "Cornflower blue is Lord Beresford's favourite colour, did you know? He told me so at a ball in London. He was being terribly coy as I asked if he appreciated the colour of my gown, and he said that he never appreciated any colour as much as he did cornflower blue. Other colours seemed dull in comparison. It is his favourite, and always would be."

Grace almost felt like shielding her eyes. She knew that if Sarah held such a fabric up to her own complexion, that she would see the connection. But then, it was such an odd connection for anyone to make except for Grace. Adam had been the one to describe her eyes as the colour of cornflowers, and it warmed her terribly to know that even when they were estranged, he still cherished that connection.

She then realised that she had not responded to Sarah's story. "Oh, what an odd colour to enjoy," she stammered, before adding, "I prefer the paler silk. I don't think that is your colour, milady, if I may be honest."

Sarah pursed her lips, before nodding in agreement. "Yes, I think you are right, Denham," she replied. "I don't see the appeal. Perhaps I could send for some cornflowers to add to my bouquet?" she thought. "I wonder if they will be in season."

Grace could feel her calm temperament threatening to explode as she worried about Adam. Now that she knew the truth, worrying about flowers and dress colours seemed ludicrous. Sarah really knew nothing about Adam save for his favourite colour, and even then, such information had been shared after she had tried to seek a vain compliment from him.

She would scold herself for thinking ill of Lady Sarah later.

"Will there be anything else, milady?" Grace asked, praying to be dismissed until it was time to change for dinner.

Sarah looked up from her samples and smiled. "No, Denham. You may go," she allowed.

Grace curtseyed thankfully and begun to plan how she might sneak into the duke's study without being seen. Though at least she would not be missed as Sarah would not be ringing her bell again.

Just as she reached the door, Sarah called out, "Oh, wait!"

Grace gritted her teeth and took a deep breath before turning around. "Yes, milady?"

Sarah laughed as she shook her head. "I just remembered that I lost a button on my lavender spencer coat ... the one I wore out yesterday. Would you mind taking it downstairs to mend?"

Yes, I do mind, Grace thought bitterly, as I need to go and comfort the man you are supposed to be in love with.

But she nodded, and smiled, as though she was grateful for the busywork, and fetched the aforementioned spencer coat from the wardrobe, before curtseying once more, and leaving the bedroom.

Grace slipped back inside the servants' staircase and made her way as quickly as possible down to the kitchen, thinking of a plan as she went. She needed to find Ruby. The kitchen was a madhouse as Mrs Reynolds and the kitchen maids prepared their nightly feast of delights for the Ashleys. Footmen carried silverware and serving trays, and to move about was to weave in and out of people's ways.

But luck was on her side for once when she was Ruby absently staring a cup of tea at the dining table as she flipped through that morning's paper. Grace surprised her by sitting down on the bench seat next to her, placing the spencer coat down on the table.

Ruby jumped. "My God, Grace," she gasped. "Where did you come from?" She shook her head and turned her torso a little.

"I need a favour, and you cannot ask me any questions. Please, will you help me?" Grace begged quietly, taking hold of Ruby's hand and squeezing desperately.

Ruby frowned. "Well, of course," she agreed suspiciously. "And by questions, you mean not any questions now, but you will explain to me later in our room?" she clarified.

Could she tell Ruby about her connection with Adam? Grace trusted her to be discreet … but with a secret of this nature? If word got out, Grace would lose her position, and that was something she could not afford, something her family could not afford.

"I can't tell you now," said Grace apologetically. "But I promise that I will tell you when I am able to."

Ruby appeared disappointed, but she reluctantly accepted. "I suppose so. What do you need?"

Grace placed her right hand on the spencer coat. "I need you to mend Lady Sarah's coat. It's missing a button. When you are finished, leave it in the laundry and I will come and collect it."

Ruby's jaw dropped open. "Mend a button?" she repeated, before frowning. "Well, how terribly dull, Grace," she complained, before her expression turned. "But then, this is what you are supposed to be doing now. What are you up to? Please tell me!"

"No questions, remember?" Grace reminded her. "Mend it and leave it in the laundry for me. Thank you!" She then got up from the bench seat and walked back towards the stairs.

The duke's study was on the same floor as the bedrooms, but in another wing entirely. Adam had once told Grace that the original study had been in a room adjoining the duke's bedroom, which in turn connected to the duchess' bedroom. Apparently, Peregrine had not liked being so accessible to his wife, and so he had the study moved down about a mile of hallway.

Grace navigated her way through the interior walls, trying to remember where each door came out. She passed several servants, though as Grace was now a lady's maid, and of a higher rank, they didn't question her.

When she came to the panel that she wanted, she pushed it open, and poked her head out in the corridor. It was vacant, but it was the corridor she had wanted. What she hated about the hallways at Ashwood House was how wide and tall they were. Every sound was magnified. She had often felt this as a child when she was somewhere, she was not meant to be.

Grace walked with purpose, coming up with a believable lie should anyone stop her.

I was tasked with asking Lord Beresford's colour preferences for Lady Sarah's wedding gown.

Was it ridiculous? Yes. Was it plausible? Also yes.

But thankfully, Grace did not happen upon anyone as she reached the study door. She knocked on it quickly.

"I am not seeing anyone!" shouted Adam from inside. "I require nothing."

If he was not seeing anyone, then he was alone. Grace ignored his demand and opened the door, quickly slipping inside and shutting it behind her.

Adam was sitting behind an enormous desk. Grace had thought Adam a very tall gentleman, but he was completely engulfed by the large, mahogany behemoth that had the nerve to call itself a desk. His head was focussed down on the book that he was writing in. In fact, he had stacks of books around him, which contributed to his small appearance.

The room itself was long and rectangular, with book-shelves wrapped around three walls. The fourth featured two large west-facing windows which were opened to the afternoon sun.

"For God's sake, go away," Adam snapped, not looking up from his work. "You have no right to be in here. I did not ring the bell."

"I know," said Grace breathlessly, not realising that she had been holding her breath for quite some time as she had hurried up the hallway.

At the sound of her voice, Adam's head snapped up. Grace had not been this near to him in weeks, and she could see the signs of struggle and pain so much more plainly. There were dark shadows underneath his hazel eyes, and permanent lines of concern and anguish in between his brows. His cheek and jawbones looked a little more prominent, as though he had lost weight.

"Grace," he breathed. "What are you doing in here?"

"I know about your father," she replied, not knowing any other way to put it.

Adam did not ask her how. He didn't question her at all. He merely stared at her, his frown increasing, his eyes becoming glassy, his lower lip trembling, as he fought to control what he was feeling.

But he needn't. Not with her.

Grace was already breaking all the rules, so she didn't worry a wit as she ran to him, around the desk, before sitting herself on Adam's lap and wrapping her arms around him tightly as the first of his violent sobs escaped his chest. He abandoned his work and wrapped his arms around her as well, holding onto her as though he was clinging to dear life.

Grace would not cry. She would not. She cuddled his face to her chest and stroked his head comfortingly, willing him to be alright. "I'm sorry," she whispered. "I'm so sorry." She kissed his forehead before increasing the tightness in which she held him.

Adam sobbed, so violently that he shook Grace with him. She could feel that the front of her dress was now wet with his tears, but she didn't mind. He had been hiding this for a month, and he needed to feel.

Grace wasn't sure for how long she sat on Adam, or for how long that he cried, but his hold on her never eased, and he wouldn't let her go. In that moment, she had nowhere else on earth that she would have rather been.

"I know your pain," she uttered softly as his sobs eased. "It might seem impossible, that no one could know what it is like, but I do."

She knotted the fingers of her right hand in his hair and held her hand like that on the side of his head. Adam leaned into her touch.

"Even though you are grown up, though you feel grown up, you have always felt the security of having your parents in your safe place. You are out in the world, exploring for yourself, but when you need it, when you need them, need him, he is ready to take you back in and show you the way," Grace whispered. "Safety and security are not something that we realise is essential to us until it is threatened.

"Because you realise you will be alone. And you might have thought that you knew what it was to be alone because you have been out in the world. But now that your safe place, your security is changing, is disappearing," is dying, "you are now realising that you don't know what it is to be alone. He is not just going away. You won't see him, you won't hear his voice, you cannot go to him when you face a problem that requires his advice, and that is the most frightening thing in the world, to know that experience is coming.

"And it is not selfish to feel these things. It is not selfish to think of ourselves when we are faced with the prospect, the reality, that we are going to lose someone we love dearly. For we are the ones who have to live without them. We are the ones who need to find a way to survive. We are the ones who need to find a new way to feel safe in a world that is changing."

Adam was quiet, though he still had a vice grip around Grace's waist. He was listening. Grace could feel the warmth of Adam's breath on her neck, knowing that he was calming down.

"It will hurt," she continued, her voice unwillingly breaking. "It will hurt in places that you did not know you could feel pain. And it will continue to hurt you. You will feel as though you are in a treacherous sea, out of your depth as the grief hits you like waves, over and over. You will cry more tears than you ever thought yourself capable of crying. You will punish yourself for every cruel word, every smart remark, and every time you ever had an unkind thought. You will hate yourself for choosing others over him. Choosing to spend time with your friends rather than having a conversation with him. And when you have finished punishing yourself, you will miss him with every part of your soul.

"And then one day, as you will think of him every day, you will remember something, and it will make you smile. And another day you will laugh. Until a time comes when thinking of him does not bring you immeasurable pain, but great pride in knowing that you loved him, and he loved you. Grief is not something you will move on from or forget. It is something you learn to live with. And it is the hardest lesson ever learned. But you will learn it, and you will survive, because you are not alone. Not ever."

Grace exhaled a shaky breath as memories of her own father filled her mind. She could still see him taking his dying breaths as she, her mother, and her four siblings crowded around his bed. But the memory changed.

"Papa," Grace whispered nervously to her father as she watched the couples take their places for the first dance at the annual winter assembly. "Why has nobody asked me?"

Mr Denham smiled wickedly. "What young man could ever compete with a father for the affection of his daughter?" he quipped as he extended his hand, with Mrs Denham slapping him playfully as he did so. "May I have the first dance, Miss Denham?"

Grace beamed up at her father, looking into his kind, blue eyes. Townsfolk had always complimented Mrs Denham at passing on her looks to her three daughters, but Grace knew that she had inherited the violet tone in her eyes from her father.

"Yes!" she said excitedly, placing her hand in Mr Denham's as he led her out onto the dancefloor.

A tear rolled down Grace's cheek as she thought back to the first and only winter ball that she had attended with her father. She had been seventeen then, and he was gone by the time the assembly had been held the following year. She wasn't sad to think about it now. She remembered the pure joy she had felt, the pride she had felt, at dancing with her father.

"Look at me," murmured Adam as he shifted his head off of Grace's chest.

Grace turned her chin down and looked upon Adam. His eyes were red, but the lines between his brows were gone.

"If I learned anything by growing up in Ashwood, imposing on your family, it was that your father adored you," he uttered simply, his voice hoarse. "If I have learned anything since coming back to Ashwood, it's that I cannot survive without you. The world might be on fire, but when I look at you, I know there's hope for me."

Chapter 20

Grace laid a hand delicately on Adam's cheek, feeling the prickle of his jaw against her skin. "I am sorry I did not come to you earlier," she said softly. "I knew something was wrong."

Adam smiled, albeit sadly. Lord, his smile was quite possibly her favourite of Adam's features, and she wondered when she would see it again. How long had it been in her own bereavement before she had been able to laugh properly again?

"How could you have known?" he said simply. "In fact, how do you know?" he realised, asking curiously.

"I came upon your father in on the stairs whilst on an errand for Lady Sarah. He was struggling, and so I helped him to his bedroom," explained Grace. Adam grew rigid, as though he wanted to go to his father. "He's alright," Grace assured him. "I helped him into bed, and then he asked me to stay and read to him awhile. That is when he told me. Or rather, he asked me how long it had taken my own father to die of the sickness." Grace was not sure of how Peregrine had known the cause of her father's death, but then the doctor who was treating him might well have been the one to treat her father. Perhaps he had shared his knowledge of similar patients with the duke.

"Ah," said Adam, in a tone barely above a whisper. "He hasn't told anyone aside from me, and Mother, of course," Adam revealed. "In learning of my father's condition, Mother set about marrying me off. I now know why she was so persistent during the Season," he uttered distastefully. "And Father revealed his condition to me when I went to speak to him about you."

Grace figured as much. Adam's behaviour had changed about then, and she never did learn of the outcome of that conversation, even though the results were glaringly obvious. Otherwise she would not have just spent time picking out wedding clothes for another.

"I won't insult you with the solution that he offered me," Adam muttered angrily. "I would not want your ears to ever hear such filth."

Grace recoiled slightly and her eyes widened. Adam reacted to her movement, pulling her back close to him.

"Don't ever pull away from me, please," he begged quietly.

Grace nodded, knowing that there was not much that Adam could do that would turn her away from him.

"My father bade me marry her," Adam said sadly. "He doesn't see marriage as I do, and it honestly bewilders me considering the match he had. He told me the scandal it would bring to wed a servant would be too much as I inherited and took my place in the House of Lords." He gestured to the books and papers before him. "My father has practically spent our entire time back at Ashwood teaching me how to run this estate. The short version of the story is that it requires a lot of money, and much of ours is tied up in investments, land, dwellings, Susanna's dowry, my mother's dowry and our trusts upon her death ... my father called Sarah's dowry liquid cash."

Adam shut his eyes for a moment and took a breath.

"And I hate him. I hear this, and I hate him. And then I hate myself for having such wicked thoughts knowing that he is dying. And it hits me over and over again that he is dying, every day, the knowledge kills me. Despite everything, our disagreements, my father is dying, and I don't know what to do. I can't help him. I can't do anything." Adam's voice was on the verge of cracking, and so he stopped, trying to control his emotions.

Grace understood Adam's anger, and his subsequent guilt.

"I love him," Adam continued after a quiet moment. "He is my father and I love him. I know he only wants what is best for me, for what he is to leave behind. And he's ... dying ... and it's going to kill me, Grace." Adam let out a frustrated cry of pain as he held her tight, resting his forehead against her collarbone.

"It's not going to kill you," she promised as she held him. "I know it feels as though it will, but you will survive this. And I will be here to support you, I promise. I won't leave you." That thought about killed her.

Grace had been listening to his every word, and she knew exactly what Peregrine was meaning. It had been what Grace had thought all along. Dukes did not marry their servants for many reasons, but mainly because money meant everything. Without it, these grand old estates would cease to exist. It took wealthy brides, like Sarah, to marry into these families and bring with them extraordinary lump sums of cash. Grace had no idea of Sarah's dowry, but she imagined it to be a very large amount.

Furthermore, unsuitable marriages brought about scandal. It was such a word filled with vitriol, Grace thought. Scandal meant a loss of connections. Connections were what brought about these sensational matches. Were Grace to be elevated, she would never be received. It was not something that she at all minded, but the follow-on affects would be great indeed.

Jack and Susanna would be the immediate victims.

And lastly, with a villainess such as Cecily out to thwart her, Grace knew that she would have no hope at all.

All she could do was remain as Adam's friend. She had always been his friend, and a friend in this time was the most important thing. Watching him marry ... well, she hoped that pain would one day ease as all pain did.

"I will always be your friend," Grace promised. "I mean it. You will not face this alone."

Adam let out a breathy chuckle. "My friend?" He shook his head. "How is this choice not my own?" he asked rhetorically. "As a child, it seemed like the simplest thing in the world. You were the best thing in my world. The absolute best part of my day, every day. It made simple sense to me that when we were grown up, I would marry you. You don't know this, but I kept a roll of parchment in my bedroom. I started it when I was eleven or so. Counting down the days until your sixteenth birthday. It was the day I was going to propose to you."

Grace's eyes widened as her cheeks flushed. She certainly hadn't known that. Lord, what if he had asked her to marry him then? They would have been married for seven years by now. Would they have had a family?

"But I suppose we all have to grow up, don't we?" she uttered softly. "The real world is not as fanciful as we imagine it to be when we are children."

"No, it certainly isn't," Adam agreed. "I meant what I said, Grace. I cannot do without you, I cannot do this without you, and that is the most selfish request I could ever make of you." He looked into her eyes deeply, as though he was committing the way she looked into memory. "By God, I adore that colour a little more every time I see it," he murmured. "You say I will survive, but I know I won't if I do not have you by my side."

"And I told you I would be," repeated Grace tenderly, "as your friend." As the realisation settled within her, she knew that their current embrace was not exactly indicative of friendship, and yet Grace had no desire to leave him. However, her head prevailed. "I should go," she whispered.

Both of their heads suddenly turned when they heard the sounds of heels walking down the long corridor. Only one person could walk with such pride and purpose. Grace gasped, the blood running from her face entirely.

"She cannot find me in here!" Grace panicked. "I will be sacked!"

Adam thought quickly and pushed Grace down. "Under the desk," he instructed. "Quickly, and don't make a sound!"

Grace scrambled to get onto the floor before crawling into the small space reserved for the duke's legs. She heard Adam fumbling with something on the desk, no doubt trying to create the appearance that he had been working.

Cecily didn't knock, instead opening the door to the study and marching inside.

"Mother, this is a private room," Adam snapped disinterestedly.

"You are not the duke yet," retorted Cecily.

Grace had to stifle a gasp, before Adam slammed his foot on the ground and stood up, unknowingly treading down hard on her hand. Once again, Grace concealed a cry of pain

"Must you be so callous?" exclaimed Adam. "Your husband is dying. Please do not speak of such things without finding a little tact first."

Cecily huffed. "It is your dear father who brings me here. A … servant … discovered him on the stairs. Word will no doubt fly about the house now."

"You ought to have a little more faith in the servants," replied Adam.

"Regardless," said Cecily, "it is time. He is looking dreadful, and I doubt he will be up and about very much anymore. Questions are sure to be asked, and I think that you ought to tell your brother and sister now."

Adam sat back down in his chair, but Grace didn't hear him respond. He may have nodded.

"You get a handle on Jack; do you understand me?" Cecily warned. "I won't have him making a scene or running off to London to make a mockery of this family while his father dies." She tsked. "I will inform Lady Ashley and Lady Sarah. The nuptials, I believe, will need to be brought forward. We cannot have a wedding in full mourning. Otherwise, it will not be an occasion to write about."

"Mother, tell me something," Adam interjected, disregarding her previous statement.

"What?"

"Did you ever love Father? Even if for a brief moment at the beginning."

"No," Cecily answered immediately, not needing a second to think about the question.

Grace winced but placed her hand on Adam's knee in comfort. He subtly pulled his own hand underneath the desk and placed it atop hers, rubbing his thumb over the back of her hand in a curled pattern.

"Did you ever love anyone?" Adam wondered in disbelief.

Cecily took a few steps towards him, to the point where Grace could see the shadows of her feet under the small gap between the desk and the floor. "Did you think you were the first person to ever give up someone for the future of your family?" she posed curiously.

Adam said nothing, and Grace believed he was just as surprised as she was. Cecily had given someone up. She had loved someone. Perhaps what was even more shocking was that someone may have loved her.

"Ensure that Jack knows how to behave," Cecily ordered. "I will go and speak to your fiancée." Cecily turned around and left the study, closing the door behind her.

Adam shoved his chair back and pulled Grace up to her feet before him. "I am so sorry. Was that your hand I trod on?"

"It's alright."

Adam lifted the hand of hers that still had a red boot mark and he placed a soft kiss there. As she was standing, he looked up into her eyes, memorising Grace as he had before, as though he was preparing to lose her.

Chapter 21

Word spread throughout the house quickly. So much so that by the time the bell rang for Grace to assist Lady Sarah with dressing, all the servants were aware of the duke's illness and the fact that he was to now keep to his room.

Gossip was rampant. Mr Cole and Mrs Hayes could not do a thing to stop it. The death of a duke and the inheritance of his son was always a time of great change, and people hated change. Ashwood House had not known any change in twelve years. Grace wished that she could assure them all that they would be safe with Adam.

Adam would always do the right thing, even at the expense of his own happiness.

Ruby had mended Sarah's spencer coat and had left it perfectly folded in the laundry as Grace had asked her to. Grace collected it and took it back up the stairs to Sarah's bedroom.

When she knocked on the door and entered the bedroom, she found Sarah sitting at her dressing table with Lady Ashley standing at the wardrobe, pulling gowns with a frustrated expression on her face.

Grace quietly placed the coat on Sarah's bed and went to her at the dressing table, pulling the pins from the style that she had fixed that morning. Sarah smiled at Grace in the mirror.

"Do whatever, Denham," she murmured, before turning to her mother. "What's the matter, Mama?"

"None of these gowns now seem fit for a duchess," Lady Ashley complained. "Far too plain, too simple," she added distastefully.

"They are all new this year," Sarah reminded her. "You made Papa spend a fortune."

Lady Ashley scoffed. "On the wardrobe of a bride, not a duchess. My dear girl, this is such wonderful news! You need to be seen this minute as a matriarch, not a girl."

Grace's hands froze over Sarah's head as she heard the words leave Lady Ashley's mouth. She certainly could not mean that the duke's imminent death was wonderful news, could she? Surely her ears were hearing things.

"Mama, please," muttered Sarah, embarrassed as she watched Grace cautiously.

Grace made an effort to control her face knowing that Sarah was aware of her.

"I cannot help that I am excited!" Lady Ashley protested as she finally settled on a gown. She carried it over to the bed and laid it down beside the coat. "It is not every day that one's daughter becomes a duchess. Obviously as you were marrying the heir, I knew it would happen someday. But to have it happen so soon? Oh, Sarah dear, it is all I ever wanted for you! You will be a young, beautiful duchess! Every door in England will be open to you!"

Grace now knew that her ears had not been deceiving her. Lady Ashely was glad about the duke dying. She then wondered if such a feeling was a mortal sin and God would strike her down dead because of it.

Sarah's cheeks were flushed. "Mama!" she exclaimed. "Go and dress! Denham can ensure everything is ready for me in here. I will be fine. Go!" she insisted.

Lady Ashley eventually nodded, coming over to kiss her daughter on the cheek. "Oh, I am so proud of you," she said quietly with a smile, before leaving the bedroom, closing the door behind her.

"I am terribly sorry," Sarah said bashfully. "What an awful thing for her to say."

"You needn't apologise to me, milady," Grace said politely. Really, a lady never needed to apologise to a servant, so she did appreciate it coming from Sarah.

Sarah turned her body in her chair, taking her head away from Grace's hands so that she could look at her properly. "No, really," she insisted. "The duke is your master and it was entirely wrong of her to be saying such things. Are you alright?"

Grace's eyes widened in genuine surprise. Was she alright? Of course not. Would she confess such a thing to Sarah?

Certainly not. "Yes, milady," she said calmly. "We are all dreadfully sorry to learn of the poor duke's condition."

The words felt meaningless, even if they were genuine. Grace wanted to help Adam, and she would do so by being there for him, but she could also help him in another way. Whether she liked it or not, Sarah was going to be his wife. Perhaps she would regret doing this later, but she needed to try. Grace knelt beside Sarah's chair.

Sarah looked a little taken aback but moved a little closer to listen, furrowing her eyebrows.

"Five years ago, I lost my own father to the same illness," she revealed quietly, in perhaps the sincerest tone she had ever used when speaking to Lady Sarah Ashley. "It is a dreadful death, and I would not wish it on my worst enemy."

"Oh, dear Denham, I am so sorry to hear that," she said sympathetically.

"Thank you, milady. I don't know when the duke will die, but I fear he is not long for this world. His death will hurt this household immensely."

Sarah nodded slowly; her expression serious.

Grace took a deep breath. "You must be ... sensitive ... with Lord Beresford. He will need time, and he will need understanding ... and he will be hurting in so many different ways. But he loves his father, no matter their differences, and this loss will change him." Grace's breaths were so shaky and nervous that she was afraid she would not get her words out, but she had said them, and the prayed that Sarah took heed of them.

Sarah inhaled a deep breath as she sat back in her chair. She thought for a long moment before she spoke. "Do you speak from experience, or do you know Lord Beresford well?"

Grace stood up and smoothed out the skirt of her dress as her fingers knitted together in front of her. "Experience, milady," she said truthfully. It certainly was not a lie, even if the other part of her statement was true as well.

Sarah nodded calmly as she turned her attention back towards her reflection. "Do you know, Denham, I never noticed the colour of your eyes before now," she murmured quietly. "What an unusual blue."

Grace's eyes dropped as she concentrated on Sarah's hair. "Thank you, milady," she replied softly.

Dinner had been quite the disaster. Susanna could not stop weeping. Jack was nowhere to be seen. Adam looked as cheerful as a gravestone. And poor Lady and Sarah Ashley had a front row view to the spectacle.

Cecily Beresford had noticed a change in Sarah since she had spoken to them that afternoon and informed them of the duke's failing health. She was quieter at dinner, more observant, though there was much to see.

Lady Ashley had been trying to discuss appropriate wedding plans seeing as they now needed to move up the date, but Adam had been absolutely disinterested in the conversation and could only tend to his sniffling sister, and even Lady Sarah did not feel the need to contribute.

Cecily had ended the night with a thumping headache and an overwhelming desire for a sherry.

Why? Why did this all need to be so difficult? People died all the time. It was tragic, she was well aware. Death was indeed something to mourn over. But weddings, matches like Adam and Sarah, were society dreams. Such an agreeable match was to be revered. It did not matter that they were not in love. Nobody in their circle was in love when they married. But did it mean that the weddings were droll affairs? Absolutely not.

Her son infuriated her. There were a dozen other girls that Cecily could have matched Adam with, but she had selected wisely. Sarah was rich and lovely. There were plenty of rich trolls on the lookout for husbands as well, so she had done her son a service.

Cecily was the last to go upstairs but stopped herself nearly halfway up when she saw Adam leaning against the banister, looking down the hallway towards Sarah's bedroom. Could it be? Could he be interested in his fiancée? What a change! Cecily crept up the remaining stairs so that she could peek down the hallway, but her face fell when she realised who he was really watching.

Grace Denham had let herself out of the servants' passageway and was walking down the hallway towards her lady's bedroom. She had not seen Adam and did not know that she was being lusted after.

The minute she was inside Sarah's bedroom, Adam bounced off of the banister and went to walk in the direction of his own room. But that was when he spotted his mother watching.

Cecily could see the remnants of a longing smile on his face, though it quickly disappeared as he looked down at her.

"I didn't see you there, Mother," Adam murmured.

"No," replied Cecily as she made her way up the rest of the stairs to the landing. Cecily looked up at her son's face, and she did feel a keen sense of sadness. Adam did look dreadful. He was very tired, owing to Peregrine's senseless concealment of his illness, as he had been sleeping poorly. He definitely looked a little thinner, and his once cheerful eyes were very empty. "Do I need to move her on?"

Adam's eyes narrowed and his jaw clenched. "What?" he snapped.

Cecily almost winced at the sudden harshness of Adam's tone. Adam rarely used a civil tone when they spoke, but whenever his precious Grace was mentioned, he became a Neanderthal. "Will she be a distraction?" Cecily repeated calmly. "Do I need to find her a position elsewhere?"

"A distraction?" Adam scoffed, pinching the bridge of his nose with his thumb and index finger. "Mother, every mo-ment of my life when I consider myself to have been truly happy, Grace was the cause. You took her away from me once. You do it again and I will follow her, this estate, my inheritance, be damned."

Cecily wanted to accuse her son of being dramatic, but she knew that he was telling the truth. Every memory that she had of Adam laughing and smiling as a boy was because he was running about with Grace Denham. She would not deny that the girl had made him happy.

"Would you do it over again if you had the choice?" Adam suddenly asked her.

Cecily frowned. "What?"

"You told me earlier that I was not the only one who had to give up someone that they loved for the future of their family. You loved someone, Mother," Adam reminded her. "If you could make your choice again, would you choose Father, or him?" he posed.

Cecily had not intended to reveal that to Adam. She had said it in temper, in frustration, and she had hoped that it had gone in one ear and out the other as so many things that she said seemed to when it concerned her children.

But his question shocked her, affecting her immediately as memories that she had once long locked away bubbled to the surface.

"What a senseless question," Cecily stammered. "One cannot go back, so there is no point in discussing such matters."

Adam's hard eyes softened as he exhaled. "Mother, I would be the last person to judge you if you said you would make another choice. In fact, if you said as much, I don't think that I would be able to explain the respect I would have for you."

Cecily's heart hammered in her chest as her mouth parted without words. But she could not say what he wanted her to say. "Goodnight, Adam. I hope you will behave more courteously and willingly tomorrow as we discuss wedding plans." With that, she walked swiftly past her son and marched down the hall towards her own bedroom.

Tears. She had tears falling down her cheeks. She had not cried in years ... in fact, she had not cried since ...

Cecily practically slammed her bedroom door shut behind her and eyed her bedside table immediately. She rushed over to it and pulled open the second drawer, throwing the clean, folded handkerchiefs over her shoulders as she searched for it. Then, at last, her hands felt something hard.

She had carried this with her, kept it by her bed, for nearly thirty years ... ever since she had painted it. Once upon a time, one of Cecily's many accomplishments as a young debutante was her painting skills. As a young lady, she had often occupied her time by painting pictures of her sisters playing out in the garden.

Cecily had grown up with four sisters, she the eldest of them all. Her father was a merchant, of common stock, and had deep ambitions of continuing to raise himself up in the world. Her mother was a lady and had brought great disgrace on her family when she had lowered herself to marrying a man such as her father.

For love. Love faded, as she saw with her parents, and her mother grew to resent her father for his business gambles that often left them skint.

Her maternal grandmother, Lady Susan Kentworth, had taken pity on her eldest granddaughter, Cecily Simpson. She had seen great potential in Cecily, and so had funded her excellent education. Cecily had attended the best boarding schools, and finally, the finest finishing school in the country, to ensure that she could be presented into society properly as a granddaughter of the Kentworths, and not a daughter of a failed merchant.

About the time that she had come out at age sixteen, her mother reconciled with her own mother, and they set about together in making the finest match they could for Cecily. For whatever match Cecily could achieve, her four sisters were bound to benefit. Without Cecily's fine marriage, they would be left to marry tailors or bakers. Her father certainly could not afford a decent dowry.

Lady Susan had entrusted a thirty-thousand-pound inheritance to Cecily, a sum so grand that her mother had about fainted when she had heard it. Such was the faith that her grandmother had had in her. Of the thirty, ten thousand was to be put in trust for her children upon her death.

Well, with such a temptation of thirty thousand pounds, Cecily was the object of every gentleman's affection. Cecily was young, beautiful, and had very old, strong connections through her mother's family.

But the prize of the Season was Peregrine Beresford, the recently inherited Duke of Ashwood. He was ten years her senior, quite handsome, and Cecily had thought herself in love with him. Or, what she imagined was love. Her mother and grandmother were experts in this game, and they orchestrated every single move that she made during that summer Season.

Cecily, so swept up in the balls, the gowns, the jewellery, and the idea of a title, that she hardly knew herself when she accepted Peregrine's proposal come summer's end.

And that was that. She had done her job, served her purpose at sixteen-years-old. She was to be married. She was to be a wife, to produce the duke's heirs. She was happy, or at least that was what her grandmother had told her to feel.

The engagement was announced, and it was only a short while before her mother had helped her to pack her possessions before they travelled to Hertfordshire for the wedding.

Considering it was only thirty miles from London, Ashwood was a very small village, and it seemed hard to believe that such a great estate could be positioned here. But great it was, and Cecily had been astounded at the sheer size of it all.

"And you, dear Cecily, will be her mistress," her mother had told her excitedly.

They had been received by Peregrine and his own mother, the soon to be Dowager, and Cecily had worried that her intended did not look very pleased to see her. Her mother, and shortly after her grandmother, had assured her that all gentlemen appeared disinterested before a wedding.

Cecily's own nerves had definitely gotten the best of her. She had lost three inches from her waistline and all of her gowns were swimming on her, especially her wedding gown. There was no dressmaker in the village, and Cecily couldn't send all of her things to London. So, she had made a special trip to the tailor.

She had thought that a tailor ought to be able to help a little. She had not realised just how much that tailor would change her life. She had walked into his shop and had stopped dead in her tracks. Never had she stared so openly at a man before, but never had she seen a man as handsome as he.

He was young, still with youthful with his teenage years, though he was dressed as a young man in a smart suit. His hair was dark, and neatly combed, his smile kind and inviting. But his eyes, oh, his eyes. The looked like the sea off of Dover at sunrise. Never had she seen such gorgeous eyes before.

And she was not the only one who stared. He stared openly at her as well, in a way that no man would have ever dared before. He nearly tripped over his own feet as he rushed around his counter to reach her, bowing awkwardly.

Cecily had blushed as red as a rose and stammered over her own words as well. She had never spoken to a man like him before, especially unchaperoned as she was.

But that had been it. It was love at first sight, and whatever affection she had convinced herself into feeling for Peregrine she knew wasn't real.

His name was Edward. He had insisted that she call him Edward, just as she had insisted that she be called Cecily. Such an intimacy felt right. Whatever was between them felt right.

Cecily used the excuse of her needing her garments altered and fixed to leave the house whenever she could. And when that didn't work, she simply said that she was going for a walk for some exercise. She used any excuse to meet with Edward, and she fell deeply, passionately in love with him. Edward was clever. Far too clever for his trade, but such was his lot in life. He was charming and witty and considerate. He listened to her, inquired about her, and was actually interested in what she had to say. Cecily realised during this time that she had never felt important before.

She had thought that she was important to her family, but she realised that it was her marriage that made her valuable, and not her as a person.

Edward made her feel as though she was worthy of true affection and care. And it wasn't long before they were making plans. They would elope, and Cecily would take her inheritance from her grandmother to find them a house and help Edward to start a business somewhere else.

It was in the woods behind Ashwood that Edward had kissed her for the first time, and he had told her that he was in love with her.

Four days before her wedding to Peregrine, Cecily had made the fatal mistake of confiding in her mother. She had told her mother everything, believing that she would understand. She, too, had ignored her mother's wishes and had married for love.

Her mother had been understanding, reasonable, and had promised her daughter that everything would be alright. She would sort it out. And Cecily had believed her. So much so that she had packed her things ready to run with Edward after church that Sunday.

Cecily could still vividly remember the odd look on Edward's face during that last church service. He wouldn't meet her eye and Cecily began to worry that something was dreadfully wrong.

She did not have to wait long to find out what it was as the marriage banns were read out by the vicar. Edward's name was announced, and for the briefest of moments Cecily thought that her mother had arranged for her name to be called alongside his.

But it wasn't her name. It was another's. He was engaged to another.

Cecily's heart split open in her chest and she bled out in that church. She had never experienced such heartbreak before, and her mother told her that Edward was reasoned with. She and Edward were cut from two very different pieces of cloth. He could never have made her happy. Cecily was born to be a duchess, not a tailor's wife.

Cecily had hardened herself on that day, and she had gone through with her own wedding to Peregrine, discovering only weeks later that he kept apartments for two favourites in London and would spend a month at a time visiting them. As much as it should have, it did not hurt her. Nothing Peregrine could do would hurt her.

She bore his children, and after the third, she put a stop to his visits, having no desire to spend any time with him. Peregrine, too, reciprocated, and preferred the company of his women in London.

And while he was in London, Cecily was forced to watch. For thirteen years, she watched as Edward fell out of love with her, and in love with his own wife. She watched as he became a loving father five times over.

To Catherine, Claire, Peter, Jeremy ... and Grace, his eldest and his favourite.

She watched as her own son was welcomed into their home, time and again. She watched as Edward would play with Adam, as he would laugh with him, before sending him home so happily that it would force Cecily to snap.

Adam would shout at her. He would wish that she was as kind as Mrs Denham. He would wish that his parents could be like Mr and Mrs Denham. At least they loved each other. Adam never knew that every time he spoke such things, he chipped a piece of her away.

Cecily watched as her own son began to walk in his mother's footsteps. How like Cecily Adam was, and he never even knew it. He had such a large, open heart, ready to love whomever he pleased. And his choice was quickly made.

Cecily was resentful of Grace Denham before she had even known the girl. She was the daughter of the woman who had the life that Cecily had desired for herself. But she had the eyes of the man she loved beyond reason. Cecily had once heard Adam describing the colour as that of cornflowers, and she recalled her own description of the colour years earlier.

Cecily had needed to separate them. Any further and Adam was going to be as hard as she was. Adam couldn't marry Grace, the same as Cecily couldn't marry Edward.

Finally, after thirteen years of watching, suffering, Cecily had convinced Peregrine to take them away to London. She had given a few valid reasons, of course, but to be away from Edward and his family was what her heart needed. And she truly hoped that the separation would help Adam to forget about his attachment to Grace Denham so that he could one day make a suitable match that would make him happy.

But her son was a constant young man, and a faithful one at that. With the help of one of his school masters, she had intercepted an outgoing letter of his, and an incoming letter of Grace's.

Both were filled with childish, romantic notions of their impossible future. Cecily had sincerely thought that she was doing both of them a service when she had severed their communication.

They would certainly forget about each other. They wouldn't get to the maturity that she had been at when she had fallen properly in love. Adam wouldn't feel the pain that she had felt, and Grace would long be forgotten to him.

Estates, dynasties, were born, made and maintained by smart matches worth a lot of money. Cecily knew that. Her own money had fed the Ashwood estate greatly. But there was such emptiness in it.

The only thing worse than heartbreak over a beloved lost to another, was the loss of that beloved altogether. Cecily had read Edward's death announcement in the newspaper, the newspaper, of all places. She could still vividly remember herself crawling into a ball and crying such tears that she might have drowned herself. Every part of her felt broken, even after all these years.

DENHAM, Edward. P. May 23rd aged 41. of Ashwood, HERTFORDSHIRE. husband of Mrs Ellen Denham. father of Grace, 18, Catherine, 16, Claire, 12, Peter, 10, and Jeremy, 7.

Cecily had attended Edward's funeral incognito, sitting at the back of the church underneath a black veil. She had been distraught, her grief made only worse by the fact that she had never truly had him. She watched his wife grieve him at the front, supported by her five children, who grieved terribly also.

Cecily unfolded the death notice, which she had kept since that day five years ago wrapped around the miniature of Edward that she had painted. It was so like him, except for his eyes. She had not been able to mix the colour quite exactly. But she could see his face clearly in that painting, and it grieved her to this day.

Adam had asked her a question. If she could, would she go back and make another choice?

Her original plan had been to prevent Adam from such pain, but whatever connection she had thought severed was clearly not. Cecily could not be certain of Grace's attachment, but her son's was as clear as day. Cecily knew that she could force him. She knew that Peregrine would force him. Peregrine had spent his life thinking about money and being as a man and seeking carnal pleasure elsewhere, such things as love in marriage were inconsequential to him.

Cecily's lower lip trembled as she thought about Adam in pain. She knew that she did not show it well, that she was a hard woman, hardened by choices that were made for her, but she did love him. She realised now that she was taking the same path as her mother once had.

Adam had confided in her, just as Cecily had confided in her own mother. Of course, Adam was not as innocent as Cecily had been, but the intention was the same.

If she could go back, would Cecily have made another choice?

Cecily looked down at Edward's face and felt her eyes fill with tears.

Yes.

Chapter 22

The next morning, Cecily did not ring her bell for Naismith as she usually did. Instead, she put on her robe and went through what had once been the duke's study and entered into Peregrine's bedroom.

It was a passageway that had been used for two centuries by the dukes and duchesses of Ashwood, and yet Cecily believed that this was quite possibly the first time that she had used it. She certainly had never taken it upon herself to visit her husband. Not once.

It made her laugh, really, to remember that Peregrine had arranged for his study to be moved some years ago as though Cecily would have a desire to disturb him.

Peregrine was still in bed, and it shocked her a little for a moment before she saw the soft rises and falls of his chest as he breathed. He did look awful. His skin was pale, and as thin as paper. She could see every vein underneath it. The sickness was eating away at him and he had lost a considerable amount of weight in the last month or so.

It astonished her that neither Jack nor Susanna had realised their father was ill. Susanna, perhaps, was too much of an optimist to think the worst. Jack was often far too busy with his nose buried in a book as he flouted responsibility to notice anyone else.

As Cecily took a seat in the chair near Peregrine's bed, Cecily wondered if she would have been able to ever love her husband had she not met with Edward Denham. Perhaps she might have. Perhaps if she had been more loving, Peregrine would not have had to seek comfort elsewhere.

She did not at all blame Peregrine for his choices. Once she had lost her heart to Edward, she could never open it again for him, especially not so soon after having it broken. She never gave Peregrine a chance. She had hardened herself, becoming an entirely unpleasant person to live with, to protect herself from being hurt in such a way again.

Peregrine had developed a dislike for her that could only be in response to her behaviour towards him. Though he had never been cruel to her. Their marriage had been doomed from the moment they stood at the altar.

Really, from the moment that Cecily had confided in her mother. Peregrine might have been like Sarah in the beginning. He could have been kind and sweet to her if she'd taken the opportunity to notice. But Cecily had changed him. Just as Adam would change Sarah.

Selfishly though, Cecily did not really care about Sarah Ashley's feelings at the moment in time. Adam was walking along a precipice and he needed help. He needed someone to say that happiness was important, that love was important. Her son deserved the life that Cecily had so wanted for herself.

And perhaps God was giving her an odd sort of second chance in being able to pave the way for her son and Edward's daughter.

The idea made the hair on the back of her neck stand up, it shocked her so. Never in her wildest dreams could she have believed that she would ever even consider allowing such a match. She had spent so much of Adam's life preventing such a union.

Her reasons for preventing the match still stood. Grace was nobody. She was poor. She was low born. She was a servant in their own household.

Though Edward was a tradesman, he shared the same characteristics with his daughter. And yet it hadn't mattered to Cecily. At sixteen, she was prepared to bake their own bread and sweep their own floors.

Just as Edward wasn't nobody to Cecily, Grace was not nobody to Adam. And God forbid, if she prevented their marriage, and the poor girl died ... she never wanted any of her children to feel as she had five years ago.

"Perry," Cecily uttered, stirring her husband from his slumber.

Peregrine's eyes fluttered open lethargically and he turned his head towards the sound of his name. He looked upon Cecily indifferently, and then with a confused expression. He, too, was aware that Cecily had never visited him in his bedroom before.

"What are you doing in here?" he asked drowsily. He tried to sit up a little, but he lacked the core strength.

Cecily immediately stood up and went to him, leaning over him to fetch the pillow from the other side of the bed to help prop him up. "I need to talk to you about Adam," she said quietly. She took a seat on the edge of the bed beside him.

"What about Adam?" Peregrine inquired.

"He's miserable," Cecily stated simply.

Peregrine sucked in a shallow breath as he nodded his head once. "He's tired," he replied. "I know he is. I have been working him hard to prepare him."

"He's not just tired, Perry," Cecily reasoned, frowning sadly. "He is being marched rapidly towards a wife he doesn't love by both of us."

Peregrine stared at her, a true look of shock upon his face. "Well," he said in amazement, "and pigs might fly."

Cecily tsked as she rolled her eyes. "I know that I am not the right person to be discussing felicity in marriage ..."

"No," Peregrine agreed, interrupting her.

Cecily took a breath. "I am sorry, Perry," she said sincerely. "I am truly sorry for how I have behaved towards you in all our years together."

Peregrine looked as though he might have remarked about the pigs again. He had certainly not been expecting an apology from Cecily, nor had she ever believed she would offer one. But he didn't make fun of her. Instead, he uttered, "That is very big of you, Cecily."

"Our son has forced me to reflect upon my life a great deal," Cecily continued. "To think about what it might have been like had I been able to choose."

"Choose someone else, you mean," Peregrine surmised calmly.

Cecily wasn't going to lie. She nodded. "Yes. What might my life have been like had I not been forced into a marriage by my family?" she posed. "What might your life have been like had you had a wife who could love you as you deserve."

Peregrine shook his head. "I do not have any regrets in my life," he informed her. "And like you, I have spent a lot of my time these last months reflecting. While we may not have been a love match, Cecily, I have three children whom I love, and our marriage ensures that I leave them a healthy and strong estate, a legacy for them to be proud of."

"I do not regret our children," Cecily agreed, "even though Jack vexes me more than he pleases me," she added. "I am glad that I became a mother. But I do have regrets, Perry," she said sadly. "I wonder what my life might have been like had I married for love. I know I would not be the hard, cold woman I have become. I know because of how I behaved, you have spent much of our marriage hating me ... and that only made me resent you."

Peregrine pursed his lips and thought for a moment. "I never hated you," he countered, "I never particularly liked you, but I never hated you."

Cecily huffed, for some reason his wording making her smile. "I never made you happy. I could never have made you happy, Perry. I honestly do not know if I could ever make anyone happy again. And I worry for Adam because he is so like me." She watched as Peregrine's eyebrows rose. "That surprises you, doesn't it?" she guessed. "You probably think that Adam is nothing like me. Adam is warm, he is loving, he is caring, he is dedicated and passionate and headstrong. He would go to the ends of the earth for those he loves, and he is exactly like I was when I was a young girl. He does not realise how like his mother he is."

"You are worried Adam will become as you are now," concluded Peregrine.

"I am not worried," replied Cecily. "I know he will become like me. In a year, in five years ... in time I won't recognise him. Adam will do as you ask, Perry," Cecily said softly. "If you tell him to marry Sarah, he will. But do not we, as his parents, have a responsibility to encourage him to be happy? My parents never did, and I am certain yours did not, either. Must we repeat their mistakes?"

Peregrine thought for a long while, leaning back against his pillows and staring up at the canopy above him. "It is the responsibility of the eldest Beresford son to ensure that the estate is maintained through a wealthy marriage," he stated simply.

Cecily's heart sank as she heard Peregrine's decision. It did not surprise her, really. It was the way of things and did not she know the way.

"So, let us hope that Adam's eldest son falls hopelessly in love with an heiress, shall we?" Peregrine continued, chuckling quietly to himself.

Cecily nearly choked on her own tongue a she gasped.

Peregrine found her expression all the more amusing. "The estate is in good condition," he said simply. "Susanna is taken care of, your pension and trust are ensured, and Ashwood's investments ensure a wealthy income. Perhaps some of the plans that I had for Sarah's dowry will not come to fruition, but, as I said, our future grandson may yet marry rich." He laughed again to himself. "Oh, the scandal." He smirked and shook his head. "The scandal will be great indeed."

If there was one thing that Cecily had learned in all her years as once of the highest peers in England, it was how to handle a scandal, and how not to handle a scandal.

"You leave society to me," Cecily murmured.

Peregrine took a deep breath, or at least as deep a breath that he could manage. "I am glad to have seen this side to you, Cecily," he noted. "Compassion was not a trait I thought you possessed, and I am glad to be wrong." He smiled, his weary face now struggling. "So, I must ask you also extend that compassion to our middle child."

Cecily's posture straightened. "Jack will have my compassion when his immediate reaction to something not turning out his way is not getting drunk and destroying something," she said distastefully.

Peregrine nodded, reluctantly agreeing with her. "Jack has a lot to learn," he allowed. "He needs to find his purpose. It wasn't the clergy, and he is surely not disciplined enough for the army. If you can mend fences with Adam, then you can find an olive branch for Jack, as well."

Cecily knew that Peregrine was right. Once Adam had hopefully ended his years of hating her, she would need to turn her attention to Jack. What career could he make out of a penchant for whiskey and books, she wondered?

"I still know your mind, Cecily, even if we have not seen eye to eye on many things," Peregrine muttered. "Compassion," he emphasised. "You know how not to handle Jack. Learn from that." He was quiet for a minute before he said, "She is a good girl, Grace Denham."

Cecily silently agreed. No matter how she had tried to dislike her, Grace Denham had certainly taken everything in stride. She had to admit ... she had not known many daughters in her lifetime who would support her family as she was. She was a responsible girl ... a responsible young woman.

Peregrine did not notice the tear that fell down Cecily cheek as she thought of Edward in that moment. Silently, she promised him that would treat his beloved daughter right.

"Go and fetch our son, will you?"

Adam did not think he had ever seen both of his parents in his father's bedroom before now. It was a little unsettling, and that was on top of the twisted nerves he was feeling at being summoned at such an hour. His first thought had been, terrifyingly, this his father was taking his last breaths.

He had quickly pulled on breeches under his night shirt as he had followed his mother into Peregrine's bedroom. His father looked paler this morning, and Adam's breath caught in his throat as he wished him a good morning.

Cecily looked as demure and as calm as Adam had ever seen her, especially in the presence of his father. He could quite possibly count on one hand the number of civil conversations that he had witnessed between his mother and father.

"Sit down, Adam," Cecily gestured to the chair by the bed as she sat down on the edge of the mattress.

Adam did so suspiciously.

"Your father and I have been discussing your marriage this morning," Cecily informed him.

Adam resisted the urge to blaspheme. After everything, his mother had run to his dying father to get him to insist on the marriage to Sarah. Lord, he could curse that selfish woman.

"You needn't have bothered," Adam snapped quietly. "I know your wishes."

"Listen to your mother, Adam," Peregrine demanded.

That was definitely the first time that he had heard those words from his father. He straightened his posture as he looked at his mother curiously.

Cecily folded her hands in her lap, as though she was mulling over what exactly to say to him, and Adam could not help but be pessimistic. Surely not ...

"Believe it or not, Adam, but you are very like me," Cecily revealed to him. "When I was younger, before I got married. It startles me sometimes how much of myself I see in you." Cecily's eyes narrowed upon Adam's expression. "And that might sound ludicrous, and you might not want to hear that you are like your horrid mama, but you are. And I worry that you will grow bitter and cold as the years go on, as I did in a marriage that was not of my choosing."

Adam sat frozen.

"No need for drawn out details, Cecily. Tell the boy the news he wants to hear," Peregrine hurried, "or I might die while waiting for you to get to the point."

As Adam and Cecily stared at Peregrine, he laughed at his own wicked joke.

Cecily huffed, before returning her attention to Adam. "We want you to be happy," she said simply. "Your father and I have agreed not to repeat the choices of our parents. In saying that, we are giving you the choice."

Adam blinked several times, hard, making certain that he was awake and not dreaming. He had to be hallucinating. There was no way that these two people, who looked like his parents, could be them. "I think I'm having a stroke," Adam spluttered. "What are you saying?"

Cecily looked to Peregrine, who said, "We are saying that if you like, you may choose your bride," he said simply. "I still firmly believe that a match with money is a smart match, but your mother has been quite your champion. I want to leave you knowing you are happy, Adam."

"Mother ...?" Adam stared at Cecily, who offered him a slight, kind smile.

"Will Grace make you happy?" Cecily asked Adam simply.

A wave of elation erupted throughout Adam's chest as he burst out of the chair and got to his feet. Would Grace make him happy? Yes, he was certain of it. Adam wanted nothing more than the time to court her properly, so that they could know each other as adults before he proposed to her, which he would inevitably do. God, he wanted nothing more than to run upstairs and bang her door down to tell her the news, to beg her to let him court her.

"Yes!" exclaimed Adam. "Yes, she will. I ... I cannot believe this!" Adam raced over to his mother and kissed her hard on the cheek, causing Cecily to gasp and steady herself. "Thank you, Mother, sincerely!" Had she listened to him? Had she thought over what he had said to her on the stairs the evening before? She had to have done. He then bent down and kissed his father on top of his head. "Thank you, Father."

"This is your mother's idea," Peregrine replied, "so you mind her," he instructed, "and respect her. I expect it."

Adam looked back at Cecily, who did indeed appear very bashful at the unusual praise of her husband. "I will," he promised her, promised them both.

"You must not race off to Grace," Cecily interjected. "Things must be done properly. You must see to Sarah first."

Chapter 23

Adam faced Sarah on the twin settees positioned by the fireplace in her bedroom. She sat beside her mother as chaperone. Sarah appeared very nervous, and not at all put together as she usually was. He had surprised her, as it was still very early.

Really, he should have waited, but when was an appropriate time to break an engagement? The sooner they both understood their futures, the better. He could not let Sarah think there was a future between them for a moment longer.

"Lady Sarah, I am terribly sorry to hurt you," Adam said sincerely, his voice low. "But I cannot go through with this marriage. It will not work between us."

Sarah allowed her lip to tremble for a moment before she concealed her face with her handkerchief as she buried her face into it. Lady Ashley, however, did not conceal her feelings. Her eyes flared in a moment of pure rage.

"What is the meaning of this?" she hissed furiously, putting a protective arm around her daughter. "How dare you!"

Adam did not know what to say to make anything better. He knew nothing he could say would make it better. They both had a right to be angry. But he honestly could not feel guilty for feeling deliriously happy in that moment. He had spent the last month in utter misery, and he knew there were incredibly dark days ahead. For this brief moment, he wanted to be happy.

"I am sorry," Adam repeated. "I am so sorry," he added, looking upon the quietly weeping Sarah. He did feel very awful for hurting Sarah, as she didn't deserve it. She was young and beautiful, and she believed herself in love. Adam hoped that when she really fell in love, she would know that she had not lost anything to Adam.

"We had an agreement," seethed Lady Ashley. "Your mother and I had arranged everything! My husband is arranging my daughter's dowry as we speak! The engagement was announced!"

"And I beg you to please blame me," Adam offered. "I will wear whatever repercussions there are."

"Who else would I blame?" spat Lady Ashley.

"Is it her?"

Both Adam and Lady Ashley looked at Sarah, who had pulled her handkerchief away from her face to look upon Adam. Her eyes and nose had quickly become red.

"Who, darling?" pressed Lady Ashley.

But Sarah didn't answer her mother. She simply looked upon Adam with sad, quizzical eyes. "Is it?" she asked again. "I ... I hadn't suspected until ... it all made sense ... you even called me Grace once at a ball in London ..."

Adam nearly choked on his own tongue. Had he? Sarah certainly hadn't said anything, and he certainly didn't remember doing that. But it simply displayed how deep Grace was in his veins. Even when they were estranged, she was never far from his thoughts.

"And when she spoke of you yesterday," Sarah continued, her voice a little stronger now, "and I saw her eyes ... it wasn't only the colour that clicked, but the care she had when she ... she wanted me to protect you ..."

"Darling, who are you talking about?" Lady Ashley demanded to know.

"Denham, Mama," Sarah cried. "He's in love with her! And she's in love with him!"

Lady Ashley gasped in shock as her angry glare returned to Adam. "Oh, good Lord!" she spat. "A servant! What a vile little vixen!"

"That's quite enough," Adam said firmly. "I won't stand for any member of my household being the recipient of slander. It is not warranted." If she continued to label Grace foul names, he would certainly lose his temper. "Sarah," he said again, "I am sorry. I am so sorry for the pain I have caused you. If you would like to speak again a little later when you have had a chance to think, I understand. But if you would never like to see me again, I understand that, too. Lady Ashley, if you would like to have a discussion with my mother, I trust her to help you understand." Adam never thought he would use his mother and trust in the same sentence, and yet he had. He stood up and bowed his head, though it felt quite silly. "I will leave you ladies. Good morning."

Adam shut the door to Sarah's room and immediately started back towards the family's hallway, and the concealed panel he knew was there that would lead down to the kitchen. He knew there was a panel along this hallway, but he wasn't entirely sure which one it was, and he did not want to waste vital time pushing on walls when he wanted to get down to Grace.

Grace ate her breakfast quickly, becoming accustomed to needing to consume her food in a timely manner for when Sarah's bell rang. The general demeanour of the servants at breakfast that morning was quiet. They had all gotten over the initial shock of the duke's diagnosis, and were all internally preparing for when the house would move into full mourning. Grace had no idea what that would look like, but she did not spend much of her energy thinking about it.

Her thoughts never strayed far from Adam, as well as Jack and Susanna. If she could, she wanted to help all three of them. She had overheard Mrs Hayes fretting to Mrs Reynolds about Susanna's weeping, which had been passed on to her from the footmen at dinner the evening before. Grace wondered when she would get the opportunity to comfort her friend, to offer her the same comfort that she had given to Adam yesterday.

She quickly scraped the last remnants of the porridge out of her bowl and took the last sip of tea as the bell rang. Sarah seemed to always be the first awake, and so Grace was the first to leave the table.

Mrs Reynolds motioned to the tea tray that had been left on the benchtop for her as usual, and Grace smiled in thanks as she took it and went towards the stairs. As she diverted towards the back of the house where Sarah's bedroom was, she heard the faint sound of quick footsteps on the stairs. Someone was in a hurry, she mused. Grace balanced the tray against her hip as she pushed her way out into the hallway and closed the panel door behind her.

Grace walked up the hallway towards Sarah's room, balanced the tray once more and knocked twice, before letting herself into the bedroom. Sarah was not in bed, nor was she at her dressing table. Grace frowned as she quickly looked around the room before finding Sarah sitting by the fire with her mother. Sarah was in tears.

Grace abandoned the tea tray on Sarah's dressing table and raced over to Sarah, kneeling down before her. "Milady, are you ill? What's wrong? Would you like me to send for the doctor?"

"How dare you," growled Lady Ashley, in a tone that Grace had never been on the receiving end of before.

She stumbled backward in shock, falling on her rear before the fireplace. "I beg your pardon?" she gasped.

"My pardon is denied," snapped Lady Ashley as she protectively rubbed her daughter's back. "How dare you," she repeated. "Don't you know your place?"

"Milady, I am not at all certain of what you are accusing," Grace stammered. "What have I done?" Grace immediately tried to retrace her steps between when she had last served Sarah to now, and she could not think of any way in which she had behaved inappropriately. Yes, she had offered Sarah advice, but that had been meant with genuine kindness.

She had certainly held her tongue when Lady Ashley had celebrated the duke's illness the day before. But Sarah had apologisedon her mother's behalf. Surely that was not what was making Sarah upset.

Lady Ashley laughed mockingly. "What have you done?" she repeated with a sneer. "You have bewitched the future Duke of Ashwood!" she cried. "That is what you have done! You are a whore and I will ensure that every door in London is closed to you. Mark my words! He will not get away with this!"

Grace recoiled from such an assault of words, an expression of pure horror on her face.

"Mama!" wept Sarah, but her mother ignored her.

"You will leave this house!" ordered Lady Ashley, pointing to the door. "The duchess will not allow you within twenty miles of this estate when I am finished with what I have to say! Get out, you filthy girl!" she screamed.

Grace could barely concentrate on anything as a terrified panic set into her very bones. She scrambled to her feet and rushed to the door, not understanding at all what has just happened! She hadn't done anything! She didn't know what they were talking about. She was Adam's friend. She had promised to be his friend! They both knew he would marry Sarah! Tears streamed down Grace's face as she realised that the duchess would absolutely abide by Lady Ashley's wishes. Cecily did not need an excuse to dismiss Grace, and with no position, her family would be turned out of their house.

Adam was thoroughly out of breath when he reached the kitchen, but he discovered that the servants were all seated down at breakfast, with the exception of Mrs Reynolds and the kitchen maids, who were busily preparing the family's breakfast.

They all turned to look at him with amazement, as a half-dressed Lord Beresford was not a usual occurrence in the morning. His eyes hurriedly looked over all the faces, searching for Grace's, but he did not see her.

"Forgive me," he puffed. "Good morning, everyone."

He received a startled greeting from the servants who looked to be trying to all get to their feet at once to bow and curtsey.

"No, please," he begged, holding up his hand. "Mrs Hayes," he called out, and his childhood nanny left her seat to meet him at the staircase.

"What is it, dear boy?" she uttered quietly. "You look quite ... excited."

Rather odd, he knew. "Please, where is Grace?" he asked her. "I need to speak with her this minute."

Mrs Hayes had a suspiciously look about her as she replied, "She has gone up to Lady Sarah, of course. The bell rang."

Adam paled. That was not good. Grace was certainly walking into hellfire this minute, and he could not go in there after her. It would be too insulting on poor Sarah. "I need to borrow a housemaid," he uttered. "I need someone to meet me upstairs."

"I will send Ruby in a few minutes," replied Mrs Hayes. "She is nearly finished her meal and I wouldn't disturb her as that would not be fair."

Adam nodded. "Alright, thank you, Mrs Hayes."

"Is everything alright?" Mrs Hayes inquired.

"Just send Ruby, as quick as you can," begged Adam, before he raced back up the stairs as quickly as his legs could carry him. Lord, he would need to practise this if it were to become a regular occurrence. How did the servants do it all the time? As he made his way to the panel he knew of, he suddenly wished he had waited for Ruby, as she would have been able to show him the way.

Grace nearly fell down the stairs, she was so distraught, barely able to put one foot in front of the other. She had been so good. She had taken everything that the duchess had thrown her way. She had kept her mouth shut and she had worked hard for months!

What was she going to say to her mother? How ever could she look her in the eye again?

She bumped into Ruby on the stairs, who promptly fretted over her with great concern.

"Grace, what's wrong?" she cried.

"I can't ..." she sobbed. "I need ... Mrs Hayes."

Ruby chewed on her bottom lip as she frowned, before her eyes flicked upstairs. "Yes, yes, go and see Mrs Hayes. Oh, I would come with you, but Mrs Hayes said I was needed upstairs." Ruby hugged Grace tightly, before they separated.

She was certain that the other servants heard her coming, though Grace could not control her sobs as she stumbled into the kitchen. She was certain that she looked ridiculous, but she needed Mrs Hayes' help.

The kind housekeeper was quickly on hand, pulling Grace away from prying eyes, and into her sitting room.

"What's happened? Did he find you?" pressed Mrs Hayes.

Grace hysterically shook her head, having no idea what Mrs Hayes was talking about. "Please, Mrs Hayes," she whimpered. "Please, you have to help me! I promise, I never did anything wrong! I never did anything inappropriate, but Lady Ashley called me such vile things, and it isn't true, any of it! Please, you must speak to Her Grace. I beg you, please! If I do not have my position here, my family will be out on the street!"

Grace could barely breath as she began to hyperventilate, and Mrs Hayes was hushing her as calmly as she could, drying her eyes with her handkerchief. "Just breathe, in and out," she instructed calmly.

Grace sucked in as many breaths as she possibly could, feeling as though she was not getting enough air. But she concentrated, trying her best to calm herself, to take controlled breaths. "Lady Ashley sacked me!" she finally confessed. "Please, Mrs Hayes. She said she would go to the duchess, but I never did anything wrong."

Mrs Hayes looked very unimpressed as she pursed her lips. "Dear Grace, Lady Ashely does not have any power to sack my maids," she assured her. "I will make your case to the duchess, do not fret. If she will not have you as a lady's maid, then I will take you back on as a housemaid. You needn't worry. Now, you have had quite the morning. You are in not state to work today. I want you to go home to your mother for the rest of the day. Come back for dinner, and I will have everything settled, I promise you." She cupped Grace's cheeks affectionately and brushed her tears away with her thumbs. "Go home," she urged.

Grace felt like bursting into a new wave of tears as every possible emotion flowed through her body. "Oh, God bless you, Mrs Hayes!" wept Grace.

Mrs Hayes smiled kindly, before she released Grace from her sitting room.

Adam waited in the hallway, growing more and more annoyed every second Ruby did not appear. While he waited, he kept watch over Sarah's bedroom door, willing Grace to appear so that he would not need Ruby's assistance.

He couldn't hear anything, but that was not necessarily a good sign. Lady Ashley could be stabbing Grace with a letter knife and he wouldn't know it. The thought shocked him, and he was about prepared to burst into the bedroom when a panel in the wall suddenly opened. For future reference, he immediately committed its location to memory.

The red headed housemaid who had helped them when Jack had made a mess in the library appeared and was quite startled by Adam immediately starting towards her.

"Good morning, milord," she greeted, curtseying nervously.

Adam could not have cared any less for formalities at that very moment. "I need you to go into Lady Sarah's bedroom and make up an excuse for Grace to come out. Tell her you need help with a task," he instructed firmly. "Please," he added.

Ruby frowned, and Adam was not sure how she had misunderstood his request.

"But Grace isn't in Lady Sarah's bedroom," she replied.

"What?" he snapped. "Where is she?"

"Well, I saw her on the stairs as I came up here," stated Ruby. "She was awfully upset about something. She wanted to speak to Mrs Hayes. In fact, I was going to check on her after I had seen to whatever needed my attention here."

Adam was about to bang his head against the wall. In fact, he did, and he immediately regretted it. And then he registered what Ruby had said about Grace being upset. Lady Ashley had been cruel, and he was not at all surprised. Sarah could stay until she wished to leave, but if that woman had said something unforgivable to Grace then he would personally pack her things. Or light them on fire.

Grace was innocent in this.

"I need to see her. You are dismissed, Ruby. I am sorry for wasting your time," Adam said frustratedly as he raced to the panel that Ruby had just come from. Ruby was close behind him. Adam had never run up and down so many steps in his life, and once again he startled the servants as they were finishing their breakfast.

Grace was not at the table, and Mrs Hayes was just taking her seat again. Before she could properly sit down, she saw him, and straightened her posture.

She hurried back over to him with an understanding look on her face. "She was in quite a state," Mrs Hayes reported.

"Where is she?" Adam demanded to know, not at all caring if the other servants heard him.

"Lady Ashley dismissed her," replied Mrs Hayes. "I am not certain of the circumstances, but Grace was adamant that there was no wrongdoing on her part, and I believe her. I will be speaking to the duchess a little later, but I sent Grace home for the day as she was in no condition to work, the poor girl. I told her not to worry as I fully intend to bring her back as a housemaid."

Adam hissed. No wonder she was so upset. He knew exactly how much Grace's income meant to her family. "How long ago?" Adam pressed. "How long ago did she leave?"

"Not five minutes ago," said Mrs Hayes quietly.

"I will bring her back, Mrs Hayes," Adam said determinedly. "Not as a housemaid, but as a future duchess." He left Mrs Hayes with a wide, gaping smile, and stormed across the kitchen, past the table full of servants with similar expressions of absolute astonishment. Adam pushed the kitchen door out of his way and took off at a run.

Chapter 24

Adam felt as though his lungs might turn inside out as he pushed himself to sprint off in the direction of the village. Grace would have left through the side entrance and all the way around the Ashwood estate to the road. He prayed that as she was walking with much shorter legs, he would catch her quickly before he collapsed from exhaustion.

He kept his eyes ahead, searching through the dense trees as he ran, checking to see if Grace had taken a wooded path, but he hoped she was too sensible to walk alone through there.

Adam was grateful that the air was wintery, and he was not running in high summer, but as he puffed, it felt as though he were inhaling a dagger over and over.

But then he finally spotted her. Grace was walking along the edge of the main road back into the village, a few miles from her home. She had not even stopped to collect a coat or anything from her bedroom and was simply wearing her lady's maid uniform. Adam then realised that he was only wearing a thin shirt and breeches, and had nothing to offer her for warmth, as not even he had thought to collect a coat before running about the house like a madman.

"Grace!" he shouted. "Grace, stop!"

Grace jumped and spun around, looking for where her name had come from. When she saw Adam running towards her, Grace's jaw dropped open in shock.

"Adam?" she called, though the distance between them made her voice faint.

Adam finally reached her a minute later, his legs like lead beneath him as they buckled. He all but fell into the ditch between the road and the wood as he sucked in raspy breaths. "You ... have ... no ... idea ... what ... a ... wild ... goose ... chase ... I ... have ... been ... on," he puffed.

Grace fell to her knees beside him, kneeling her black skirt into the dusty road as she put a hand on his shoulder. As he looked into her eyes, he could see how upset she was. Her lashes were slick with tears, and her eyelids were red and swollen, as was her nose. Her cheeks were tear stained and flushed. She was absolutely devastated to have been dismissed, and the sooner Adam could stop himself from dying on the side of the road, he wanted to end her pain, just as she had tried to help his.

"You shouldn't be out here," Grace warned in a fragile, shaky voice. "I don't know how ..." She bit on her lip nervously. "Well, perhaps I do, I might've given her an inkling ... but Lady Sarah thinks that there have been inappropriate relations between us." She hiccoughed. "Her mother called me ... a ..." but Grace could not bring herself to say the word.

She covered her mouth with her hand as she tried to stifle a sob. "You need to go back there and fix it!" she urged. "Lady Sarah was so upset ..."

"Sarah was upset because I ended our understanding this morning," Adam explained, his voice sounding a sight more human. He righted his posture a little and shuffled closer to Grace, his movement kicking up a little dust from the road.

Grace's eyes flared as all manner of shock crossed her face. "You did what?" she gasped. She could not have separated herself from him quickly enough as she practically flew to the other side of the road, her skirt covered in grey gravel dust. "Adam!" she exclaimed. "What on earth were you thinking?" she accused. "I know you said your mother couldn't disown you, but I certainly think she will try now!"

Adam could not help but smile as he watched Grace panic. He had not been amused in a long while, and he knew it would be brief. But he wanted to enjoy this moment. He would remember this. "I don't think she will," he murmured.

Grace stared at him, her eyes the size of saucers, looking as though she were watching him grow a second head. "We are discussing your mother, am I correct?" Before her expression changed to that of anxiety. "Oh, please say you are not doing this for me," she begged. "I told you I would never leave you," she promised, clapping her hands together. "I told you I would always be your friend."

Grace suddenly paused when she saw Adam's expression, and a wave of confusion crossed her face. She frowned.

"Why do I feel as though you are teasing me?" she asked tentatively. "This is not the moment to tease me. I have had a dreadful morning and I have to go and tell my mother that if Mrs Hayes cannot convince the duchess to take me back as a housemaid, that we will have no money for food, let alone the rent!"

Grace placed her hands on her hips and stared at him, arching one of her eyebrows as she waited for his response.

Alright, he allowed. Perhaps this was not the moment to enjoy her squirming. They would have years. "Grace, my parents gave me their blessing," he said simply, and he waited for the message to sink in.

"Their ... blessing?" repeated Grace, her voice soft and delicate. "My goodness, Adam. Do not be coy!" she demanded. "Blessing for what? You are allowed to take up cross stitch?" she huffed facetiously.

Adam chuckled. "No, my dear Grace." He shook his head. "They gave me their blessing to end my engagement, as they now understand and accept that there will only be one person who could ever make me happy." He was still shocked himself, so he did not blame Grace at all for looking as though she would need it said again.

Her brows furrowed vulnerably as her eyes watered, and she turned away from him to shield her face. No. Adam launched towards her, taking her hand away from her mouth and using the other to turn her chin back towards him. "Please, don't hide from me," he said softly.

"I don't understand!" she whimpered. "Just yesterday you told me that your father bade you marry her!"

There was certainly a lot that Adam did not know, a conversation that had taken place between his parents that he was not privy to ... and certainly his mother had had some sort of epiphany. But he would not question it. His prayers had been answered. In a period that would bring him, them all, great sorrow and woe, he would be grateful for the joys.

"I don't know everything," replied Adam honestly. "But I will not look a gift horse in the mouth. My parents spoke this morning, that I know, in what will perhaps be the most civil interaction I have ever witnessed between them. They told me that they did not wish to repeat the mistakes of their own parents."

"They want you to be happy?" Grace breathed, her voice breaking on the last word.

Adam nodded, a broad grin spreading across his face as he looked down at her. "My mother was quite our champion, I am told. She asked me if you, Grace, would make me happy. And you know the answer to that." His thumb brushed over her cheekbone, wiping away a falling tear, an action which brought a smile to her lips. How beautiful she was when she cried happy tears. "I know you will always be my friend, Grace, and I firmly believe that in a blissful partnership, friendship is an important foundation. But I could never be content with just your friendship, with you being so close to me, and yet so far."

Grace let out a sob, though it was combined with a joyful laugh. Her smile was growing by the second as she looked up at him. "I don't believe this," she whispered. "They would let you choose? They would let you choose me?"

"My choice has always been you," he promised. "Even when we were apart, no one could compare. We were fated to find each other again, Grace. They understand now. My parents, they understand. My mother, my father, they're on our side now."

"Your mother still terrifies me," Grace whispered, a raspy giggle escaping her chest.

Adam chuckled. "Well, now she will terrify anyone who has something to say against us," he said with conviction, not entirely believing that he could be saying these words. Out of curiosity, the curiosity that he had had since first seeing her again in the upstairs hallway, Adam reached behind Grace's head and removed the white cap that she wore over her hair. He found the large hairpin underneath her bun and pulled it out, letting her long, dark hair tumble down to her waist. "Beautiful," he murmured in admiration.

Grace's already flushed cheeks reddened further as she combed through her ends with her fingers.

"I love you, Grace," he uttered.

Never had he seen such an expression of elation on her face before now. Grace's gorgeous eyes sung with happiness as she beamed up at him, her smile melting away any hint of nervousness that she had been holding within.

"I want to remember this exact moment," he said softly. "You looking as you do right now, knowing that I love you." Lord, he hoped he would never forget her face as she heard those words for the first time. "Because ..." Adam paused, feeling as though his words were struggling to free themselves, "... it will be a long time before I will be able to make you smile again."

Grace knew exactly what he meant, and she immediately wrapped her arms around his waist, laying her head against his erratically beating heart. She fit just perfectly as he rested his chin on top of her head.

"I will take care of you," she promised quietly.

Adam smiled as he closed his eyes. "We will take care of each other," he corrected, "even though I know ..." he stammered, "... I will be quite hopeless soon." He pulled away slightly only so that he could look down into her eyes once more. "Until I can fulfil my promise, may I court you, Grace?"

"Court?" repeated Grace with a burgeoning grin. "Do you mean to take me on chaperoned picnics, walks through the village with my sister five steps behind us, tea with my mama ..."

"Yes!" cried Adam. "Yes to all! Every bit of it, every proper outing there can be, just as soon as I can, as I am able." Adam closed the distance between them and pressed a soft, chaste kiss to her lips, enough to surprise Grace, and for her cheeks to flush once more. "Might we walk together to your mother's?" he suggested. "When she saw me at the assembly, she looked as though she wanted to behead me, so I sincerely hope that now at least I might be welcomed inside."

Grace giggled. "She was under the impression that you so cruelly broke my heart. But yes." She nodded. "Might we tell her?"

Adam allowed Grace's small hand to slip inside his as they began to walk in the direction of the village. "Let's."

Once Cecily had been dressed and was now properly presentable, she made her way towards the guest quarters to pay her apologies to Lady and Sarah Ashley. Naismith, who had been downstairs at breakfast, had reported the goings on of the morning to her.

She was not at all surprised that Adam had run about the house like a headless chicken with how excited he had been. She was also not surprised to hear of Lady Ashley's anger, though she was unsure of what it had been directed towards Grace Denham. Despite everything that Cecily had done previously to ... break her ... she had risen to every occasion. From all reports, Grace had been an exemplary lady's maid.

Oh, Cecily knew she would have her work cut out for her in time as she needed to prepare that girl for the cruel world that was the aristocracy.

Cecily knocked twice on Sarah's bedroom door out of courtesy, before she heard movement on the other side. The door was opened by Lady Ashley, who wore a hard expression on her face as she looked momentarily reprieved to see her. "Oh, Your Grace," she greeted. "I feared it might have been that horrid maid returned to beg our forgiveness. Please tell me you have come to report that your son has seen sense!"

Lady Ashley opened the door properly and allowed Cecily to enter the bedroom.

She noticed immediately that Sarah was abed, weeping softly into her handkerchiefs. Cecily immediately realised in that moment that Sarah was far too young to be wed. She was certainly not mature enough, and she certainly couldn't love Adam, not really. Adam had barely given the girl any attention. If this was how she clung onto a potential match, she had much growing up to do.

"No, I am afraid I am not here with news of Lord Beresford," replied Cecily. She imagined Adam was in the middle of his engagement at that moment, or something along those lines, and she would have news later. "I merely came to inquire after Lady Sarah, and to ensure that we may part as friends," she added politely.

Lady Ashley frowned in shock. "What?" she gasped. "You mean to tell me that you approve of this nonsense? Your son passing over my daughter for a ... whore who lifts her skirts for anyone!" she hissed.

Cecily pursed her lips with displeasure. While she may have had her own fair share of dishonourable thoughts about Grace Denham, she was not of the mind that she would tarnish a young girl's reputation out of spite. Particularly not Edward Denham's favourite daughter. "My dear lady, my son was pressured into this arrangement by my husband and me. We have since agreed that Lord Beresford ought to choose his own match. My son has never behaved in-appropriately with anyone," no matter where his thoughts may have been, she knew Adam would behave respectfully, "and I can say the same for every one of my household staff. Especially Grace Denham."

"I cannot believe this!" exclaimed Lady Ashley. "I cannot believe this. We have been corresponding for months, you and I!" she cried. "This was a match that would have been exceptional for both of our families. We were in agreement that this was what was best!"

Cecily nodded. "Yes, I know. But I have since come to understand that it is not my place to decide what is best for my son. He is five and twenty ... and do you know what?" Cecily sighed. "He has known what was best for him since he was all of seven years old.

"My husband and I are terribly apologetic for the pain that has been inflicted. I am certain Sarah will recover in due course." Cecily was definitely certain of that.

"You approve then?" remarked Lady Ashley. "You approve of your son, the future Duke of Ashwood, and a serving girl? A nobody ... a poor, insignificant nobody about to assume your position." She scoffed.

Cecily would not deny that the idea would take some getting used to. She had not necessarily thought of anyone assuming her position, but then, she had been prepared for Sarah to be the duchess. She could prepare for the eventual reality.

"My son will love, honour, and respect his wife, and that is what I approve of," Cecily said plainly. She would approve of the rest later, once she had a chance to offer some education.

"She will never be seen," Lady Ashley declared. "She will be a laughingstock! She will drag your good name down to the gutter with her!"

Cecily's patience was wearing thin, and she had had about enough of Lady Ashley's ridiculous insults. She walked past her and went over to Sarah's bed, looking upon the girl with pity. "Oh, cheer up, young lady," she urged. "I promise, your heart is not broken."

Sarah's lower lip trembled. "It is," she insisted. "I never realised their connection before yesterday, and I feel a fool! Lord Beresford even called me Grace once!"

Cecily rolled her eyes. Dear Lord. "Yes, well it seems my son can be a little ... focussed on one thing in particular." She would have throttled Peregrine had he ever called her by the name of one of his women. "Trust me, dear, you will soon be quite mended from this experience. I hope, in fact, it helps you to choose someone you might actually be happy with."

Cecily realised then that she knew someone who could do with a little growing up. Perhaps, together, they would make a fine pair after a long engagement.

"You know, my younger son, Lord Jack, is quite unattached." Lady Sarah would certainly be an excellent match financially for Jack. His future income was dependent on his marriage.

"A second son?" exclaimed Lady Ashley in disgust. "A second son for my daughter?"

"Mama!" cried Sarah, before she looked over at Cecily apologetically through her sad eyes.

Cecily knew that she would probably have the same reaction were Susanna to be attached to a second son, though she hoped she would approach the situation with a little more tact. She was reminded of Peregrine's urging that she be compassionate towards Jack. He couldn't live up to Cecily's expectations if she had none. "My son has great potential," Cecily told Lady Ashley. "He is Cambridge educated, and

the second son of a duke. He is a fine match for any lady."
Well, he could be, at least.

"No titles, no inheritance, no land," hissed Lady Ashley.
"Not fine enough for Sarah!"

"Well," Cecily remarked, clapping her hands together. "I
fear I am out of children, then. Good day, ladies."

Chapter 25

Perhaps it was not still as early as Adam had thought, as the village was very much awake by the time Adam and Grace walked through it. Grace was now holding Adam's arm, a more appropriate display of courtship, and it was very much noticed by everyone who walked by them.

Adam was happy for the rumours to spread. They would certainly be true. They were courting. They would be engaged in time, and then they would be married. The thought alone still completely struck Adam as incredible. Lord, he would need to find a way to thank his mother. Yet another thought that was truly baffling.

Grace wore the most blissful smile upon her face as she knocked on her mother's door, before letting herself into the house. "Mama!" she called. "It is me!"

The scent of baking immediately filled Adam's nose as they went into the kitchen. He had not been in this house since he was a boy, and yet he seemed to remember the way. When once it had been Mrs Denham who was always a fixture in the kitchen, this morning it was Claire.

Claire wore a plain grey dress with the sleeves rolled to her elbows, and an apron protecting her clothes from the flour. She stood before the bench, kneading dough, with a fresh loaf having just been pulled from the oven.

The moment Claire saw Grace, she paused, smiling, but her expression immediately changed when she saw Grace's companion. Her mouth dropped open, and Adam mused that the sisters looked remarkably similar when they were surprised.

She quickly wiped her hands on her apron before pulling it off and laying it down on the bench. "Good morning ... milord," she greeted quizzically as she hurried around the bench to curtsey before Adam. "Grace?" Claire's eyes flared at her sister, as though she were communicating by thought.

Grace laughed, as though she understood, and Adam realised they perhaps they could communicate by thought.

"Miss Claire, please do not feel the need to curtsey," he assured her. "I am the one imposing on you this morning."

Claire smiled nervously, before seizing Grace's hand and pulling her towards the stairs, and quickly out of Adam's sight. "You look awful and yet you are smiling!" he heard Claire hiss. "Why were you crying if he is with you?"

But Adam could not hear Grace's reply as their voices were quickly muffled as they reached the upper floor. And Adam was left on his own in the kitchen. He would have put water on for tea ... yet he had no idea how to do that. He had a

Cambridge education, and yet he would not know where to begin when it came to boiling water on a stove.

Adam was not alone for long, however, as the quick footsteps of a couple descending the stairs sounded, though they were much too rambunctious to be the steps of young ladies.

And he was correct as two young men joined him in the kitchen. The older of the two looked to be no more than fifteen or sixteen years old. He was growing, and would be tall, and looked to be quite strong, as though he laboured regularly. His hair was dark, the same shade as his sisters, and he wore it down to his chin, where it curled slightly at the ends. He had to have been Peter Denham, whom Adam had not seen since he was all of three.

The younger of the two was still very much a boy. He was untidy in grass stained breeches and a shirt that had had one too many holes mended. His dark hair was scruffy and unkempt and had most certainly not seen a comb in many moons. Jeremy Denham had been a baby when Adam had left for school. It was hard to believe that he was now this old.

"Good morning," greeted Adam. "My name is Adam Beres—"

"We know who you are," interrupted Peter. "I'm Peter and he's Jem." Peter nodded to his younger brother. "It's my job as the man of the house to make sure that men aren't sniffing around the skirts of my sisters, you know." He folded his arms across his chest and looked upon Adam sternly.

Adam greatly admired his gumption. He knew that were it a suitor Susanna's that had come to call, he would be doing exactly the same thing. "And rightly so," he agreed.

"Are you going to treat Grace with respect?" Peter demanded to know.

"Mama spent an awful long time saying that you were a piece of work, you know," Jem added.

Adam, of course, had his own mother to thank for the many years of incorrect appraisal that he had received within the Denham house. "I will always treat your sister respectfully," he promised. "She deserves nothing less."

Slower steps now sounded on the stairs, and the three men were shortly thereafter joined by Grace, Claire, and Mrs Denham, the latter of whom was using a cane to support herself with. Both Grace and Claire hovered over their mother and helped her to sit down at the small dining table. Adam had noticed over the last month that Mrs Denham's condition was taking much longer to improve, and the cane had been a new addition in the colder weather.

The last time that they had spoken at the ball, Mrs Denham had held a very poor opinion of Adam. Now, the kind woman was smiling at him. Adam had always greatly admired Mrs Denham and had often looked to her and his nanny for maternal affection when his own mother was distant or standoffish. Mrs Denham had always welcomed Adam into her home with love and warmth.

"Good morning, Mrs Denham," Adam greeted courteously, bowing his head to her.

"Good morning, Lord Beresford. I would curtsey, but I am sure you understand," she said apologetically.

"As I said to Miss Claire, there is no need," he assured her. "Are you well?" he inquired, though knowing the answer already.

Mrs Denham pursed her lips. "The chill in the air is giving me some bother this morning," she replied. "But I have been making myself useful with some mending and altering tasks for neighbours."

"Well, I certainly hope you will call on me if there is ever a need," he urged.

Adam realised that he would soon be Mrs Denham's landlord. The Ashwood estate owned many of the buildings in the village, and the Denham's house was one of them.

Adam's eyes flicked to Grace. She was watching him with a coy, though happy, smile on her face. "I trust Grace has told you as to why I am here this morning."

"Oh, no," lied Mrs Denham. "Please, enlighten me."

Adam smiled. "Obviously, there has been many years of misunderstanding between us, but I am so grateful that Grace has come back into my life, and that we have been able to find our way back to each other. This morning, I asked Grace if I could court her, and she has accepted."

Claire was positively gleeful, and there was a very cheerful smile on Mrs Denham's face. Even Peter and Jem appeared pleased.

"I know Grace will not have disclosed this detail out of courtesy for my family, but I will tell you anyway, because word will get out soon. This will not be a short and a cheerful journey," he warned, doing his best to mask his emotion as it quickly began to overwhelm him. Grace seemed to read this immediately and she came to his side, placing a hand on his arm. "My father is very ill," he disclosed. "He suffers from a mass, a disease which will take his life. I am not certain when, only that it will happen. And when it does ..." Adam stopped himself, one word from his voice cracking. He inhaled a deep breath.

"Dear Adam," uttered Mrs Denham in a devastated voice. "Oh, my dear boy, don't we know your pain."

Adam could not help but grimace as he nodded.

"Claire, dear, put the tea on this minute," instructed Mrs Denham, and Claire left her side for the kitchen. "We shall sit down to breakfast."

As Peter and Jem were sent for dishes and cutlery, Adam could not help but overhear a private comment meant for Grace.

"You cannot live in that house, work in that house, if you are courting, Grace," Mrs Denham warned her daughter quietly. "It is not appropriate. And I hate that I have to ask you this, as I am the mother, but what shall we do? I cannot go back to Mrs Slickson yet."

Adam had not even thought of the propriety of he and Grace living under the same roof, and he supposed that Mrs Denham was right. Grace would have to cease her employment at Ashwood House. Which then begged the question of income.

"We'll manage, Mama," Grace promised her, kissing her mother on the cheek. "We always do. I will sort everything."

Adam could see on Grace's face that she had not realised that either and that she was beginning to stress, as the onus of this household was on her shoulders.

This was a burden that Adam would take away and ensure that she never had to worry about again.

After breakfast, Adam and Grace thanked Mrs Denham for her hospitality, and Claire was instructed to chaperone them both down to the forge so that they could tell Kate and Jim Ellis.

Kate had been just as excited for Grace as Claire had been, and Adam enjoyed seeing Grace joyful with her sisters, while he enjoyed conversing with the blacksmith, Jim Ellis, who was perhaps the tallest man that Adam had ever encountered.

When Peter arrived a little while after to work in the forge, Jim hooked up a horse and cart for Kate to drive both Adam and Grace back to Ashwood House.

They arrived back at Ashwood House in the midmorning. Considering it had only been a few hours since he had left the house, and with everything that had already happened on that day, Adam could hardly believe it was not even noon.

As they walked around the estate to the servant's entrance, Grace murmured, "Do you think it alright that I am returned to quickly? Despite everything, Lady Ashley still dismissed me. Mrs Hayes said she would speak to your mother, but she might not have had a chance yet. Even then ... I don't know if I will be able to return to work here ..."

"Grace, I do not want you to worry about your position, your income, anything," he insisted. "I told you once that I would never neglect your family, and I know what your income means for them. No guest can dismiss you from my house. While the details are still being organised, I know of at least one young lady who could do with your company."

Grace immediately nodded her head, smiling sympathetically. "I do want to look in on Susanna," she agreed.

When they entered the kitchen, the breakfast dishes had been cleared, and the servants had all dispersed to go about their daily duties. Those who were about the kitchen all immediately stared at Grace and Adam, looking between them with expressions of shock, interest, intrigue and excitement.

But none were as happy as Mrs Hayes as she materialised before them with a look of pure elation. "Oh!" she cried, putting a hand on both Adam and Grace's cheeks. "I always knew you both were lost to each other, ever since you were little ones, I knew!" she gushed. "But I am glad you are returned quickly, Grace," she added. "The duke has requested you go up and read to him again just as soon as you returned."

Adam wondered if his father really wanted a reader, or if he wanted to speak with Grace alone. He trusted that neither one of his parents had changed their minds. Even if they had, he had monumentally destroyed his engagement anyway. He would remain optimistic.

"Oh, of course." Grace nodded. "I will go directly." Just as soon as Grace started towards the stairs, Ruby appeared from the laundry and spotted them both.

"Grace!" she shouted excitedly across the kitchen, her decorum disappearing.

"Ruby!" scolded Mrs Hayes. "I never want to hear such shouting again! You are in the presence of Lord Beresford. Do not forgot your manners."

Ruby hurriedly curtseyed and apologised before she raced over to Grace and seized her arm as they made their way upstairs together.

Mrs Hayes shook her head. "Are you engaged?" she asked quietly. "If, as your once devoted nanny, I may ask."

Adam smiled. "My once devoted nanny may have anything," he promised. "No, but we are courting." Adam greatly wanted to traditionally court. As a boy, he had imagined returning to Ashwood and doing just that. He had no idea now how courting would be, but they would find a way.

"I am glad to hear that all the same," replied Mrs Hayes. "After so long, you finally have your Grace."

Adam smiled contently.

Adam could hear Grace's voice through his father's bedroom door as she read him Dante. Perhaps he really did want a reader. The door was ajar, and Adam left them, choosing to then knock on his mother's bedroom door. When no one answered, Adam checked to see that Cecily was not inside.

He checked in the ladies parlour, the library, the dining and drawing rooms, before giving up on locating his mother at that moment. When he decided to turn to his work for the day, he found Cecily sitting at his father's desk in the study.

"Mother?"

Cecily was concentrating as she sifted through paperwork, clearly trying to locate something. The pessimist in Adam thought it could potentially be his father's will that she was searching for, though she would have no luck in finding it. Peregrine's will was safely in London with his solicitor.

"What are you doing?"

"Aha!" cried Cecily as she secured whatever document she had been looking for. She then looked up at Adam. "You are back a lot sooner than I had thought you would be. Did you speak with Grace?"

"Yes," confirmed Adam.

"And?" she pressed.

Adam owed his mother a great debt, he knew, and so he needed to show her gratitude. "And we are courting," he replied, coming towards the desk and sitting down in the chair before it.

Cecily smiled. "So, why do you look as though I have smacked you across the bottom?"

Adam shook his head. "Forgive me," he said. "I am very happy, very grateful to you and Father."

"Well, I am glad, if you can believe it. I am," said Cecily as she organised the papers on the desk that she did not need. "To answer your first question, I was looking for a document to help me solve a problem ... mend a fence, if you will. It is a private matter, and I will not be telling you anything further."

Mend a fence? Adam never thought Cecily would be the type to make amends, but he would certainly not get in her way.

Cecily stood up from the desk and walked around it. Adam rose as well. When she came before him, Adam hugged her, for quite possibly the first time in his life. Cecily was quite rigid at first, though she quickly softened and returned the gesture, holding onto Adam tightly.

"I won't forget this, your kindness, Mother," he promised. "But I do need to talk to you about something."

They parted, and Cecily frowned. "What is it?"

"Lady Ashley dismissed Grace –"

"I heard," interrupted Cecily, tsking. "She and Sarah are departing tomorrow morning. I would give them both a wide berth."

Adam certainly would. "My issue is, now that I am courting Grace, it is no longer appropriate for her to live here, let alone work here. Her family solely depend on Grace's income, and without it they will be in grave trouble. I want to find a way to pay Mrs Denham a pension without her thinking of it as charity. Her husband died before his sons were old enough to take over his trade –"

"Yes, I know," Cecily interrupted again quickly. "Do not fret, Adam. This is something that I have been thinking about this morning, and I do think I have a solution. Will you leave it to me?"

Adam was making a habit out of trusting his mother. He nodded.

Chapter 26

Cecily had never made a habit of travelling into the Ashwood village. When she had been a young bride, the experience had simply been too painful. She often blamed her disinterest in the village on it being too simple, the society being too demeaning ... anything to avoid seeing Edward and his growing brood.

The ball some weeks back had been her first foray into the local society with the exception of church in over a decade.

Cecily had never visited the Denham home before. It was a tired looking building, with missing shingles, faded shutters, and in desperate need of repair. She had never known anything less than a fine home from the time that her grandmother had stepped in to ensure her future.

There was a fluttering in her stomach as she looked out of the carriage window. What would Edward have said could he have known she was about to call upon his widow. Cecily had never spoken a word to Mrs Ellen Denham. Not one word.

Adam had spent much of his childhood visiting in this house and she, herself, had never stepped foot on this street.

Cecily's way of life, way of thinking, had been ingrained into her. She had been brought up to believe that someone of her status ought to live a certain way, ought to marry a certain man, ought to socialise with certain people. And when her heart had been so broken for daring to step out of such a life, she had retreated back, and immersed herself back into what she thought was the right way of being.

Cecily had brought up her children to expect the same, to live the same way. Though how she had monumentally failed.

Adam was always going to return to Ashwood. He loved it here, and he would always love Grace. As Cecily had now allowed herself to feel what she had felt in her youth, she knew it wasn't falling in love, choosing who to love, that was the enemy. It was the expectations of society, and the limits it placed on people who possessed a certain rank. She could not do to Adam what her own mother had done to her.

Cecily could not allow Adam to become like her.

It was her job, her responsibility, as Adam's mother to help him. Cecily knew that she hadn't been an exemplary mother for much of her children's lives. But she would be better.

Grace worked hard. Cecily knew this. Cecily's maid watched Grace constantly and had reported every little titbit of news back. But all Cecily learned was that Grace was a diligent worker. Whatever Cecily had done to dampen her, to push her, to get rid of her regrettably, Grace had risen to the occasion. And it was for this very reason. For the very people who lived inside this house.

When Edward had died, his eldest son, Peter, had been only ten years old. He wasn't old enough to have learned his father's trade, to take over his business and to support the family. No, Grace was left to support her family. A young girl of eighteen, forced to abandon any ambitions for herself.

Grace's actions had allowed her next sister in age, Catherine, to marry. Cecily had seen her with her husband in church. The younger girl, Claire, was a very pretty prospect for some village boy as well. She would be able to marry as her elder sister provided for the home.

Selflessness was not a quality one often found in debutantes. But it was a character virtue that Cecily had grown to admire, even if she was at first reluctant. Grace would need Cecily, and perhaps she did not realise it yet, but in accepting Adam today, she was effectively feeding herself to the wolves. Cecily would help her in a way that her own mother should have helped her as a young girl.

And she would begin by calling on her mother.

Cecily's door was opened by the driver, and the step was let down. The moment Cecily was out of the carriage, the front door of the Denham home was opened, and the youngest daughter, Claire, stood in the doorway, mouth agape as she wiped her hands on her apron.

She was an attractive girl, and she could understand why Jack had been quite taken with her at the ball for all of ten minutes, though Cecily did believe Jack had been more interested in vexing his mother then tempting his dance partner.

Claire's large, blue eyes were wide, and she wore her dark hair down, with a few pins holding the front tendrils away from her face. She had flour in his hair, which turned the dark, charcoal colour a bright white.

"Close your mouth, dear. You will catch a fly," murmured Cecily, to which Claire abruptly closed her mouth.

Claire seemed to recover some composure, and she stumbled into a curtsey as Cecily approached. "Y – Your Grace!" she exclaimed. "This is a surprise." Her expression suddenly changed to one of worry. "Oh, dear, are you here for Grace? Or for Adam? I mean, Lord Beresford!" she stammered. "You mustn't be angry at Grace!" Claire insisted. "She had done everything she was told, and she works so hard –"

Cecily held up her hand. "Calm yourself," she instructed coolly. "My son and your sister are both at Ashwood House at this moment. I am her to call upon your mother." Cecily did not ask. She did not want to be refused, even if there was only a miniscule chance this young girl would refuse a duchess.

Mrs Denham suddenly appeared beside her young daughter, supporting herself with a cane. She had once been a pretty woman, and had passed on her beauty to her daughters, her face and figure becoming rounded with years. She looked upon Cecily with a cool neutrality, and Cecily did not know what to make of her appraisal.

She was certain that Adam had spent much of his youth complaining to this woman about his horrid mother, but she still wondered if Mrs Denham knew more. She couldn't have, though. Surely not.

"Claire, would you go and put on some tea?" Mrs Denham asked. "Please, won't you come in, Your Grace?" she invited, shuffling back away from the door.

Cecily offered a stiff smile as she turned back to her driver. "Wait," she instructed. "Please."

Cecily was led into a small kitchen. The ceiling was low and lined with dark oak beams. The home was kept quite neat and tidy, which Cecily attributed to Claire, and not Mrs Denham, as she was depending a great deal on the cane with which she walked. The kitchen was warm thanks to the stove, and Claire looked to be in the middle of dinner preparations with the ingredients on the bench. She stood at the stove with as she heated the water. Mrs Denham sat down at a small kitchen table.

"Please, sit down, Your Grace," Mrs Denham invited.

The table was covered in fabric, mending, it appeared to be, and Mrs Denham's sewing basket was open. The garment that she was attending to, however, looked to belong to a large man, so Cecily assumed she was mending for another. Mrs Denham quickly tidied the tabletop so that there was nothing in front of them, as Claire brought over teacups and a dish of biscuits.

"I am sorry I do not have much else to offer you, Your Grace," apologised Claire. "Jemmy, that's my brother, he's only twelve, and he eats as fast as I cook."

"That is quite alright," replied Cecily.

Claire appeared relieved as she returned with the teapot and strainer. As she was about to pour, Mrs Denham stopped her.

"I think we can manage, sweetheart," she uttered. "Why don't you wander down to the forge and visit with Kate?" she suggested.

"I only saw Kate this morning ..." frowned Claire, before her mother shot her a look. "Oh, alright." Claire nodded and untied the apron from around her waist. "Goodbye, Your Grace." She curtseyed again, a little smoother this time.

"Goodbye," said Cecily.

Claire was away a few moments later, and Cecily and Mrs Denham were left alone.

"Do you take sugar at all?" asked Mrs Denham as she held the strainer with one hand and poured the tea with the other.

"No," murmured Cecily. As Mrs Denham finished pouring, she uttered a thank you. She then poured her own cup.

Cecily felt the fluttering sensation in her stomach again, and hated that she felt nervous, of all things. When she didn't say anything, Mrs Denham did not hesitate to speak.

"Have you come to demand an end to Grace and Adam's courtship?" she asked bluntly, all formality gone. She was now a mother speaking to another mother. "Because I will not ask her to sacrifice her happiness. Grace deserves it."

Perhaps Cecily had been right in her initial judgement. Mrs Denham didn't know about her husband's past. "I suppose I was right to think that my son spent much of his childhood complaining about me," mused Cecily.

Mrs Denham didn't deny it.

Cecily sipped her tea. Ordinarily she would have taken it with sugar, only Claire had not provided any, and she did not think that Mrs Denham ought to be getting up and down with her cane. She could make do. She placed the cup back down on the saucer. "No, I have not come here to interfere with Grace's happiness, nor my son's. It may surprise you to learn that my son had the blessing of his parents to pursue Grace properly."

This certainly did surprise Mrs Denham. Her mouth dropped open for a moment though she had no words. When she finally found some, she remarked, "Well, I can honestly say that I did not expect that."

"Grace makes my son happy, and I hope that he will make her happy," continued Cecily.

"Forgive me ..." said Mrs Denham tentatively, "... but have you had a stroke, Your Grace?" she exclaimed. "My daughter spent much of her childhood terrified of you. You made her feel like an urchin, someone to be stepped on because she waspoor. You never approved of her friendship with Adam, that I know."

Cecily knew that she probably seemed like a mean, old witch to a young girl. She had scolded Grace terribly when she was a child, her and Adam both. And she had probably resented her for exactly the reasons that Mrs Denham had named, the prejudices that had been ingrained into her.

"Something like that," muttered Cecily. "An epiphany, of sorts, I would call it. My son forced me to reflect upon the choices, the sacrifices, that I have made through my life ... and it helped me to see that this choice is his. His choice is Grace, and I am going to accept it."

Mrs Denham leaned back into her chair as she stared across the table at Cecily. "Sacrifices," she repeated quietly, her tone changing to one that sent a shiver down Cecily spine, causing her to regret the word. "You are talking or Edward, are you not?"

Cecily felt herself pale as she saw the knowing in Mrs Denham's eyes. She did know. She knew everything. And it was senseless to lie. Edward was part of the reason why she had come to call on her. "Yes," confirmed Cecily, her voice quiet. "He told you?"

"Yes," confirmed Mrs Denham. Cecily watched as her lower lip shook for a moment before she controlled it. It greatly affected her as it did Cecily. "I was seventeen and living with my drunk of a father, miserable, and needing to be rescued. Edward came to me, completely unexpectedly, and told me that he had fallen in love with someone he couldn't have. We had always been good friends, and nothing more, but he asked me to marry him because he didn't want to suffer alone as she married someone else." Mrs Denham concentrated her focus on her index finger as it traced the rim of her teacup. "I didn't mind. He was taking me away from my father. I would have married anyone."

Cecily felt her eyes fill with tears as she heard those words. Cecily hated what her mother had done, and she knew now more than ever she had had to be better than her. It made her so upset to hear that Edward really had loved her.

"It was not difficult to deduce just whom Edward loved," continued Mrs Denham quietly. "He watched you every Sunday in church. You never looked at him, but he always watched you."

Cecily had forced herself to avert her eyes.

"I didn't think I minded in the beginning. We were friends, and we got on well. Edward had saved me." Mrs Denham took a deep breath. "But I did grow to love him, to love him terribly. And it hurt me considerably knowing that he pined for another. When you gave birth to Adam ... he was absolutely devastated." Mrs Denham's voice shook. "And it hurt me to know that he wished ..." but she couldn't finish her sentence. She took a sip of her tea and tried to collect her thoughts. "But things did get better. His pain lessened, and we grew closer. When Grace was born ... Edward was the proudest father, and his firstborn was his joy. Our marriage may not have begun with affection, but it did grow, and we did love each other deeply.

"I always thought ... I secretly believed ... I thought that you might have disapproved of Grace on another level, in knowing that she was Edward's daughter."

Cecily prayed that God would not allow her to cry in this moment. She was speaking to a man's widow, and she could not grieve as Mrs Denham did. "I disapproved of Grace because of the reasons you stated before. She was not of our rank, she was poor, and did not come from a family with connections or property." Cecily sighed. "But, in truth, I was resentful of Grace long before my son's infatuation had begun. For reasons that I am certain you can deduce.

"I am not heartless, Mrs Denham. I am a product of my upbringing. I believed that my son needed to marry as well as

I had, because that was what we are supposed to do. But in making the choices that I did, in listening to people who were unconcerned with my happiness, I became I person I do not like. My son is frighteningly like me when I was younger, and the last thing I want is for him to follow the same path that I did."

Mrs Denham finally brought her eyes up to look at Cecily, taking her attention away from the teacup. They were red and glassy. "If you could have chosen when you were in Adam's position, would you have married Edward?"

Cecily nodded. "Yes," she whispered, not wanting to lie.

Mrs Denham exhaled shakily, and she received Cecily's answer. "I struggle to picture it. You, a great lady, in this house."

Cecily had not thought of it like that. Perhaps, in another life, she might have lived in this house. "It is because of my choices that I want Adam to make his own," Cecily insisted. "He came to me, just as I went to my own mother once upon a time. My mother separated us, just as I separated Adam and Grace when they were younger. And what did I achieve but two people who seemed destined to return to each other? I won't repeat my mother's actions.

"Despite the way my mother's choice affected me, I do not regret my children," Cecily continued. "Adam, Jack and Susanna were meant to be on this earth. Just as your children were." She took a breath. "It does make me glad to know that Edward did find happiness with you, Mrs Denham." She did mean that sincerely. Perhaps, if she'd merely tried, she might have found the same happiness with Peregrine. "And perhaps it is God putting something right in your Grace and my Adam having found one another."

The notion brought a small smile to Mrs Denham's face. "You'll really allow it, won't you?" she queried, as though she had been sceptical up until that moment.

"I do admire Grace, Mrs Denham," complimented Cecily. "She is certainly a remarkable young woman, and a credit to you. Truth be told, I have not always made her time at Ashwood pleasant. But she has risen to every occasion, and I know she has the strength and gumption for what lay ahead of her."

"Thank you," replied Mrs Denham. "I know she is a wonderful girl. She would do anything for her family, and she would do anything for Adam."

"I know that Grace has been supporting you during your convalescence," Cecily noted, slightly awkwardly. Mrs Denham nodded while pursing her lips. "But, now that Grace has agreed to enter into a courtship with my son, her continued employment and residence at Ashwood House is impossible."

"Yes," agreed Mrs Denham. "Grace and I were only discussing the matter this morning." Worry was etched upon her face as her eyes flicked over the mending on the table, no doubt thinking about income.

Cecily reached into her pocket and felt for the folded document that she had found in Peregrine's study earlier. She pulled it out, unfolded it, and laid it on the table in front of Mrs Denham.

Mrs Denham peered at the document curiously, before looking up at Cecily with confusion. "What on earth is this?" she asked.

Cecily momentarily wondered if Mrs Denham could read. "It is a deed," she replied.

"I can see that," retorted Mrs Denham. "What I do not understand is why it is in front of me."

"The Ashwood Estate owns this house," said Cecily. "You pay a monthly rent to my husband, and that greatly swallows much of your income." Cecily stopped herself. This could not only be about income. "Mrs Denham, we are to know each other for many years to come. Our children will marry. We are to share grandchildren one day. Much had passed between us over the years without us ever knowing one another. I hope that by gifting you this, by giving you ownership of this house, it will signal a new beginning for me, my family, and for yours, too."

Chapter 27

Grace had not quite believed her mother when she was told that evening that the Duchess of Ashwood had called upon her. Not only that, but she had gifted Grace's mother the deed to their house. Grace had to look upon the document with her own eyes to believe it to be true.

Whatever doubts she had about the duchess' motives were seemingly gone, and she could believe that Cecily Beresford really would approve of her. The ownership of their home was such a gift and was such a significant burden off of Grace's shoulders.

While her mother would not go into details about what else was discussed between herself and the duchess, Grace could not have been more grateful.

Grace did not spend another night at Ashwood House as her things were transported out of her and Ruby's room, only after Grace had confessed everything to Ruby. Her friend had been shocked, as had everyone except for Mrs Hayes, but she was truly excited for Grace.

Grace and her possessions arrived back at her family home and she moved back into the bedroom she had always shared with Claire. When she thought back to how she had felt when she had spent her last night in this room, Grace could not quite believe what had happened, and how she had managed such luck as to have found Adam again.

"You look so happy," uttered Claire peacefully, as she looked upon Grace while they lay in their bed facing on another.

Grace smiled. "I am happy. I never thought that what happened today would come about. To think I was absolutely distraught this morning ..."

"Adam really loves you," mused Claire with a wistful, wishful smile, as she looked up towards the ceiling.

Grace knew where her younger sister's thoughts often went. "It will be your turn, Claire," she promised, "with a man far more deserving of you than Arthur Slickson."

Claire's eyes flicked back to Grace. "Oh, I know," she said with sad realisation. "I think my chance at Mr Slickson came and went at the assembly," she said regretfully. "Alas, I am certain there will be someone else who will catch my eye someday."

Grace would never voice it aloud, but she was so glad to hear Claire resigned to giving up all thoughts of Arthur Slickson. No level of handsomeness could outweigh the vices of vanity, conceit and selfishness. Claire would certainly find someone more suitable for her.

"I do wonder at Mama and the duchess' conversation today, though," said Claire. "You didn't see her, Grace, but the duchess looked so ... so ... well, I am just so used to seeing her with her nose in the air that I have never seen her appear so normal before. Why won't Mama tell, do you think?"

Grace could not deny her own curiosity, but she could certainly guess at the subject. Perhaps the duchess had voiced her last fears and concerns over the match to their mother, and Mrs Denham had defended Grace. She could certainly believe that. Grace had never before seen her mother converse with the duchess, so they certainly could have nothing else to discuss.

"If it were our business, Mama would have told us, Claire," murmured Grace. "Whatever happened, Adam and I are still going to enter into a courtship and the duchess consents.

Grace could not help but wake with Claire, as she was used to rising early and completing her chores. Claire was certainly grateful for the assistance and Grace enjoyed helping her with the cooking and the chores. It reminded her of when she used to help her mother when their father was still alive.

Before they all sat down to breakfast, there was a knock at the door. A footman from Ashwood had been sent with a note for Grace from the duchess.

Dear Miss Denham,

The duke expects you at ten o'clock to read to him as a standing appointment each day.

You will be invited to stay for luncheon thereafter.

Yours,

Cecily Beresford

Claire read the letter from over Grace's shoulder. "Luncheon at Ashwood?" she gasped. "Everyday?"

Grace had been reading The Divine Comedy to the duke, in which he spent much of the time asking her questions. Perhaps he had more. Whatever the purpose, of course she would oblige him. If she could bring a dying man comfort in any way, it was her Christian duty. She hoped, as well, that his father's comfort would ease Adam's mind as well.

"But you will come with me, won't you?" asked Grace. "As my chaperone?"

Claire smiled excitedly. "You will need a chaperone, yes." She grinned. "Oh, I would only be too happy to oblige."

"If you see Adam, which I am certain you shall, will you ask him to dinner on Saturday?" proposed Mrs Denham as she stirred her tea. "I will ask Kate and Jim, also. He has not had the opportunity to sit down with all of us yet ... and I think it best it happens sooner rather than later."

Grace understood her mother's meaning. "Yes," she confirmed. "I will ask."

It felt terribly wrong to approach the front door even though she was invited. Grace did not think she had ever used the front door of Ashwood House. Not even as a child. She had always entered through the kitchen.

She held onto Claire's arm as they climbed the steps up to the front door, which was opened pre-emptively by Mr Cole. How odd that was to be greeted by the butler as a guest, and not ordered about as a maid. Grace was quite at a loss of what to do.

"What an exciting twenty-four hours it has been for you, Miss Denham," remarked Mr Cole.

Grace was unsure if his comment was meant to be negative or positive. Mr Cole was a traditionalist, she believed, and it was certainly not traditional for a housemaid to be raised up as high as Grace was.

"Grace!"

Grace was saved from finding words for Mr Cole as Adam descended the stairs towards them. He was smiling, and it gave her such peace to see such an expression. As he drew closer, she noticed that the ends of his hair were damp, and they were curling a little more than usual.

Adam stopped himself from embracing Grace, and instead, bowed his head to her, before turning to Claire and offering her the same greeting. "Miss Denham, Miss Claire." His actions were formal, but his eyes were excited and intense.

"Good morning, milord," Grace and Claire said in unison as they curtseyed.

"May I take your coats, ladies?" asked Mr Cole.

Claire immediately went to her buttons, but Grace uttered, "I can put them away. We do not mean to trouble you."

"Please," urged Mr Cole, a small smile burgeoning. "Allow me." He took their coats and left with instructions from Adam for a two tea trays to be organised. One for Claire, and one for Grace up in the duke's bedroom.

"I feel so strange," whispered Grace when the three were alone in the foyer.

Adam smiled. "You had no qualms running rings around Cole when we were children," he reminded her.

"I had qualms!" she assured him. "You were the one with no qualms. I was always afraid that your mother would see me, or someone would tell on me!"

Adam chuckled quietly. "I cannot imagine how awkward and odd this must be for you to so suddenly be here as a guest. I can only hope that you will grow to feel comfortable ... as I do hope this will be your home one day."

Claire looked between them with a lovestruck expression on her face, and Grace immediately clamped her lips shut. She didn't much like having to have a chaperone as she felt her cheeks redden.

Adam seemed to read her hesitation immediately. "Claire, why don't I see you into the drawing room? My father expects Grace presently." He offered his arm to Claire. "I will come and collect you in a little while."

Grace climbed the stairs and took herself to the duke's bedroom, knowing the way perfectly. She knocked on the door quietly and opened the door when she heard him beck-on her softly.

Having only seen the duke the day before, Grace thought she would be accustomed to his appearance, but he seemed to grow paler each day. His face was looking a little gaunt, as his cheekbones became more pronounced. She remem-bered her own father struggling to stay nourished towards the end of his life and she felt a pang of sadness in her chest.

"Good morning, Your Grace," she greeted, curtseying in the threshold before she walked tentatively into the room.

The duke smiled from his bed, the skin around his eyes and mouth crinkling. "Ah, Grace, good morning. I am pleased

Cecily's note found you. I would like for you to read to me each day. Would that be alright?"

Before she could answer, Peregrine interjected.

"Of course, you would never deny a dying man his wish, would you?"

Grace's eyes widened.

Her reaction amused Peregrine and he chuckled. "I am sorry," he apologised. "I am beginning to have a rather gloomy sense of humour."

Grace sat down in the chair that she had occupied the day before, not before collecting The Divine Comedy from the duke's bedside table. "I am pleased to read to you, Your Grace," she promised him, "though I am certain you could find far better orators."

"There is something pleasing about your voice, Grace," complimented the duke calmly. "I think it is because you do not sound as though you have been educated to walk around with a book on top of your head, or to speak from the back of your throat."

Grace supposed her accent was as normal and as simple as any other Hertfordshire villager's. "I am pleased that something such as my voice can affect you so, Your Grace."

"My son seems in quite excellent spirits today," Peregrine commented. "Better than I have seen him ... ever."

Grace opened the book to the place she had left yesterday as she smiled to herself. "I suppose I am in good spirits as well," she replied.

"That is good." Peregrine's eyes flickered a little, and his voice strained for a moment as though he was growing tired. "Tell me, Grace. Are you a good girl?"

"Your Grace, you ought to rest," urged Grace. "Might I fetch someone?"

Peregrine frowned. "No," he mumbled. "Stay. Answer the question."

Grace nodded. "I try to be," she replied. "I ... I believe that one can always be better, but I strive to be as kind, compassionate, and selfless as I can. I think it is effort that makes us good. Trying makes you good. So, yes, to answer your question."

"Hmm," sighed Peregrine, sounding quite lethargic. "I believe you are good. Read, please."

Grace resumed from her place, and read for close to half an hour, looking up from her page every few lines to watch Peregrine. His eyes were closed, and his chest was moving up and down evenly. Soon, she was certain, he was asleep.

As silently as she could, Grace closed the book and returned it to the bedside table, before tiptoeing out of the bedroom and shutting the door behind her. Adam seemed to have had the same thought to come and collect her as he was nearing the duke's bedroom as Grace closed the door.

He was smiling once again, and Grace was still so pleased to see his happiness. It hurt to know how fleeting it would be when he had such pain so imminently near. How thankful she would be in years to come to have played a part in bringing him joy during this time.

"Your father is sleeping," she told him quietly as they met in the hall.

Now that they were alone, Adam brought Grace into his arms, holding her close to him. Grace settled into his embrace, resting her cheek against his chest.

"My mother has invited you to have dinner with my family on Saturday," she told him. "Will you come?"

"Now, I might have to think about it," Adam teased. At Grace's scoff, he laughed, and agreed. "We have a little time before luncheon. Susanna is downstairs with Claire. What do you say we sneak away for a little while?"

Chapter 28

Adam stole Grace away for a walk about the grounds. It was there that their courtship truly began, and continued, as these excursions became a daily habit after she had finished reading to his father each day.

Every day Peregrine grew wearier and wearier, and Adam's time with Grace became is single source of light in an ever-greying existence.

Adam felt the growing weight of what was rapidly approaching. His father's colour, energy, and life drained from him as quickly as they English skies turned dark for the winter. Everywhere he looked seemed a little duller as the prospect of mourning approached.

For what time he did not spend with Grace, Adam sat with his father. Each conversation he tried to make memorable, meaningful, for fear that it could be their last. Adam asked his father questions, too many really, as the reality of not having the answers was truly frightening.

And when Peregrine would sleep, Adam watched his father breathe, in and out, shallow at times, and staggered at others. Every day death drew nearer. It was something Adam had never seen before. He had never witnessed someone's death. He had had the fortune to never know someone suffer as his father suffered.

Adam had of course read of death before, and heard it described as peaceful, as though one was slipping away into a dreamless sleep. He now had first-hand experience in knowing that death was anything but peaceful. Death was painful, and his poor father took more and more laudanum each day to dull the pain. Peregrine felt pain all over. In his chest, in his belly, in his joints and bones. Adam felt entirely helpless.

"How long do you think he has?" Jack asked Adam quietly on Christmas Eve.

Adam knew his own brother was hanging on to his sanity by a single thread. Adam was well aware that Jack often felt as though he was the black sheep of their family, undesirable, troublesome, and hopeless. But Adam also knew that Jack did feel things keenly. He had an enormous heart, which was why he had the capacity to feel as he did.

Jack had been walking on shaking legs for several weeks. He hadn't run, though Adam knew he was getting ready to bolt. But he had spent several days of that time drunk, and it was only at Adam's begging that Jack had managed to pull himself together to spend what little time they did have with their father.

Peregrine was pale, and impossibly gaunt. He could not stomach food, which the doctor said could be attributed to possible tumours in his belly causing him pain. There was no way to nourish him, and Adam feared starvation would take him before the sickness did.

"I don't know," he told Jack honestly. "You can't leave, though, Jack," Adam requested quietly. "You can't leave me, Susanna, home ... Mother."

Jack remained quiet as his eyes were fixed on Peregrine's chest. After a few moments, he uttered, "He was on my side ... not all the time, but between him and Mother, he ... he at least liked me ..."

"He loves you," corrected Adam, "just as we do. And I'm going to need you, Jack. I won't be able to do this alone."

"You aren't alone. You have Grace," murmured Jack. "You are destined to be perfectly alright, Adam. Trust me."

At that moment, there was a quiet tap on the door, and Grace entered the bedroom quietly at her usual time. Her expression was soft with concern as she looked upon Peregrine with deep pity, a crease forming between her brows.

Her dress was plain, white, and suited her small frame well. Her hair, which Adam still longed to see unpinned, was fixed in a tidy knot, with two purposeful curls framing her heart-shaped face.

For a brief moment, when their eyes met, Adam felt at ease. Jack was right, he realised. There was going to be relief on the other side of this heartbreak. Grace would be Adam's salvation.

Christmas was a very dull affair indeed. Gifts had not been purchased, nor was an exorbitant meal prepared. The Beresfords elected to forgo church in order to sit beside Peregrine. Even Cecily, who had come to get on with her husband now more than ever before, looked quite forlorn as she watched over him.

As the grandfather clock in the corner chimed midnight, telling the family that the date had now ticked over to the twenty-sixth of December, Peregrine opened his eyes lethargically, rasping a little as he tried to crane his neck.

Susanna almost pounced upon him as she leapt to her feet. "Father, do you need some more laudanum to sleep?" she asked desperately.

"No, no," uttered Peregrine. "Not much good it will do now ..." he wheezed, before coughing, an act in itself which nearly took all the wind out of him. "Prop me up, Susanna, dear. I want to look at you ... at you all."

Susanna fetched a pillow from the other side of the bed, and gently placed it under their father's head, helping him to see his family. They instinctively drew nearer to him. Jack fell onto his knees from his chair, leaning on the side of the bed and holding Peregrine's thin, cool hand in his. Adam sat down on the side of the bed with a hand resting on his father's stomach, while Cecily stood at the end of the bed. Susanna had crawled into the bed beside him.

Dear God, it was time.

"My life will be but a fraction in time, of no real consequence nor significance. But I will know that I have created a legacy, three precious children, all of whom I am blessed to call my own.

"I want you to take care of each other," he said as forcefully as his strength could manage. "I want you to be happy. I want this house to be a happy place. This house was always a happy place, and it is meant to be thus." Peregrine's tired eyes found Adam.

Adam felt his stomach clench as he willed himself not to shed tears in this moment. He could not let his emotions cloud what his father would say. He wanted to remember. He couldn't allow himself to forget.

"It falls to you," he rasped. "You have grown into an exceptional young man who I am proud to call a son. You are decent, fair, and kind, and you will be an honourable duke. I want you to fill this house with happy children, I want you to honour your wife, to cherish her, cherish Grace, and to bring life back into these walls. You will take care of them all."

Adam swallowed his tears as he trembled, looking upon his father with utter scrutiny, trying to etch every moment into his brain. "I will, Father," he promised, his voice breaking unwillingly.

Peregrine's eyes dropped to Jack, who was kneeling beside him. "Jack ... my boy," he nearly choked.

Jack was trembling as well, almost uncontrollably, as he tried to keep himself still. "Father ..." he whispered.

"I know you have greatness in you ..." Peregrine uttered. "I know you need only find your purpose. You are more than what you allow yourself to be ..." He coughed again. "But above all, you deserve to be happy ... and I want nothing more than for you to find a young lady to make you feel as though you are deserving."

Jack shook as he bent his head down to kiss the back of Peregrine's hand. Tears had begun to stream down his face.

"My precious Susanna." It took all of Peregrine's strength to shift his head a little to look upon Susanna.

Like Jack, Susanna had silent tears running down her cheeks as she looked upon their father helplessly.

"I am so proud of the young woman you have become," Peregrine breathed. "You are clever and kind, spirited and witty, and you have a very beautiful heart. I pray that some-one will one day be deserving of you, for whomever he may be, he is certainly a fortunate man. You will look after your brothers, and your mother."

Susanna tearfully kissed Peregrine's cheek.

Peregrine's eyes at last flicked to Cecily, who, much to Adam's surprise, had tears in her eyes as well. She was holding onto one of the bedposts, using it for support as she looked upon the scene with much sadness.

"Cecily ..."

"Rest, Perry," urged Cecily. "You have certainly exhausted yourself."

"Cecily ... you are remarkable ... unmistakeable ... thank you ... for them." Peregrine coughed once more, the sound sickening, as though he would bring up his lungs.

"Perry ..." whispered Cecily, her lower lip trembling.

Peregrine said nothing more. His eyes fluttered closed and he breathed, shallow, and every so often, until at four min-utes past two that morning, he breathed for the last time.

All pain left Peregrine at his last exhale, and Adam watched as he truly did fall into a dreamless, peaceful slumber. He was stunned for a moment, before the pain quickly found him, breaking through his ribs and into his chest like an out of control horse.

Susanna let out an unholy noise as she sprawled herself across Peregrine's still chest, and Cecily collapsed into a fit of tears at the foot of the bed.

Adam cried out, every wretched, excruciating feeling exploding out of him at once as he realised that his father was gone. He was dead. He wasn't alive. He would never speak. He would never answer another question. He would never laugh or make a joke. He would never explain something. He would never be there for Adam again.

Adam felt cold, and utterly out of control as his sobs kept coming. But what brought him out of this nightmare for a mere moment was Jack rip himself away from the bed and storm out of the bedroom.

No, Jack couldn't leave.

Adam forced himself to his feet, making his legs run after his brother.

Jack thundered down the hallway, pulling the drapes from their pelmets, throwing pottery and vases from their pedestals and watching them shatter into thousands of pieces.

"Jack!" cried Adam.

Jack seized another vase and threw it wantonly. It immediately smashed through a window, letting in a bitter wind from outside. This made Jack stop momentarily, and it was enough for Adam to catch up and grab a hold of him.

The minute he was in Adam's arms, Jack turned around and buried his face in his brother's shoulder. Jack sobbed, just as violently as Adam had been only moments before. Adam held Jack tightly, and knew exactly the pain that he was suffering, the violence of the ache in his chest, as he was feeling it, too.

Chapter 29

It had just gone five in the morning, but Grace was awake. A force of habit that she had not been able to escape since leaving service. Claire usually awoke and began her chores at six o'clock, and so Grace used this time to start the bread.

What she had not been expecting was a knock on the door.

She knew immediately who it would be, and she knew immediately what this visit meant. Her heart was practically breaking as she opened the door, but upon seeing Adam's pain-stricken face, it broke entirely.

Adam was completely dishevelled, from his creased and crumpled attire, to his unkempt hair and reddened eyes. His eyes told her just what agony he was in, and Grace longed to take it away from him. But she knew she couldn't. She knew from experience just how terrible this was.

"He's gone," Adam whispered, and a flash of shock crossed his face, as though this was the first time that he had articulated his father's death.

Grace had only read to him the previous morning, just as she had been doing every morning since Peregrine had first summoned her. He had not looked long for this world for a little while, and Grace had known it was coming.

She said a silent prayer for Peregrine Beresford, and she truly hoped that he had found some peace now that he was free from pain.

Grace went to Adam, wrapping her arms firmly around his waist and resting her head against his chest. She could hear his erratic heartbeat. Adam reciprocated immediately, holding Grace as tightly as he could, as though his life depended on it. And he wept. He wept quietly, heartbreakingly, for his father.

And Grace cried, too. She cried for Peregrine, for the man she had come to know, respect, and admire as Adam's father. She cried for Adam and wished she could heal him in some way. And she cried for her own, dear Papa. He was never far from her thoughts, especially recently.

Grace and Adam held each other in the small entryway of her house, leaning against the closed front door. It was still very dark, and the house was quiet as her mother, sister, and brothers all slept. The only noise was both of their shaky sobs, which quietened after a little while.

Grace didn't know what to say. She had said so much since learning of Peregrine's illness, in an attempt to bring Adam some sense of understanding and compassion, but she knew now that nothing could heal him. He needed time to be sad, time to mourn.

Adam said nothing, either. Though as she heard the light footsteps of her sister moving about upstairs, Grace realised that Adam's breaths were even. Craning her neck up, she could see that his eyes were closed and that he had fallen asleep leaning up against the door.

For a brief moment, he was peaceful.

As Claire came downstairs, she stopped abruptly when she saw Grace and Adam together by the door. Her expression told Grace that she knew immediately why Adam had come. Her brows furrowed sadly as she sat down on the fourth step, facing Grace.

"Blessed are those who mourn, for they will be comforted," whispered Claire. Like Grace, Claire's eyes became glassy and a single tear fell down her cheek.

Cecily wouldn't have a viewing. She thought the idea far too macabre and insisted that Peregrine be given the dignity of being remembered as he was, and not the frail, thin, ill man he had been when he died. A funeral was planned and arranged in three days, and before the new year was celebrated, the Ashwood church was filled with mourners to hear the vicar speak fondly of the duke, whom he had christened some fifty years ago as a young man of the cloth.

Adam hadn't known that. He'd always thought the Ashwood vicar ancient, but this man had christened his father as an infant. It pleased him, even as he mourned, to learn something new about his father.

He, Cecily, Jack and Susanna all occupied the front pew of the church, dressed in their black, mourning attire. Cecily and Susanna both wore thick, black veils that concealed their faces.

In one hand, Susanna clutched a handkerchief. In the other, she held onto Adam's tightly. Adam was sitting in between his mother and sister, with Jack sitting on the other side of Susanna. Adam had allowed himself that morning with Grace to be miserable. Of course, he was still absolutely devastated. He was in shock, really, to be seated at his own father's funeral service. But it was his responsibility to look after his family know. Peregrine had said it himself. It was up to Adam now. And his chief concern was Jack.

Jack had been drunk for the best part of three days. He didn't know how to handle his own grief and regulating his emotions had been a struggle for him in his early adulthood. Jack seemed to Adam to be teetering on the edge of a cliff, and only a small gust of wind would push him over.

Were Adam sitting beside Jack, he was certain he would be able to smell the whiskey on his breath.

The vicar concluded his sermon, and the mourners were dismissed. Cecily, Adam, Jack and Susanna stood outside the church with the vicar as they politely accepted the sympathies of the Ashwood community.

Grace had been seated with her family. As much as Adam would have wanted her by his side, he knew it was not yet appropriate. Adam hadn't thought much about what life would be like after his father passed away. Of course, he had plans for the future, but he hadn't really wanted to envision what life would be like immediately after his father's death. It was far too morbid.

But now that he was here, in the thick of grief, Adam had no desire to wait. He had no desire to waste time. It was precious, after all, and could so easily be snuffed out by a wicked disease.

Grace was dressed entirely in black, as were most of the mourners, the only colour upon her was a rosy flush in her cheeks, and her bright, blue eyes, though they were soft and filled with concern as she looked upon him.

His father had bidden him cherish Grace, and cherish her, Adam would indeed.

Hang society. Hang anyone who had a negative word to say about it. He had just spent weeks watching his father suffer. Adam knew how cruel life could be. To waste life based upon unwritten laws seemed utterly ludicrous now. Adam had already lost so much time. Lord, had those years not been taken from him because of those stupid letters, he might have married Grace years ago.

He was in love with her. He always had been. He had known he had loved Grace long before he really understood what love was. Adam would go to her this afternoon, and if he had his way, they would be married before the new year.

Grace could not hug him. Not in public. She could not even hold his hand, and that was the straw that broke the camel's back. She could not but smile sympathetically at Adam, with a longing look in her eye, before she wrapped her arms around Susanna in comfort.

Adam was momentarily distracted by Grace as he saw Mrs Denham speaking to his mother. Adam did not think he'd ever seen the two converse before, and yet …

Cecily lifted her veil for a moment, long enough for both women to lean forward and kiss the other on the cheek. It was an act of friendship ... kinship ... respect. Adam had never seen such behaviour from his mother before, and he could not have been prouder in that moment to see her truly humble. Adam believed her to have forged this relationship for him, and he was grateful. As Mrs Denham moved on, Cecily pulled her veil back down and began to receive the rest of the mourners.

Mrs Denham smile sympathetically at Adam. "Your father would be so proud of you, Adam," she said quietly. "Don't you dare be a stranger, now."

Adam did not plan to be. "Thank you, Mrs Denham, sincerely. Might I call upon Grace later on?"

Mrs Denham appeared to understand Adam's intentions almost instantly, and Adam feared he lacked the ability to conceal his thoughts. "You have my blessing," she replied simply.

Peregrine Beresford was buried in the family's private tomb, a place that had brought Adam much indifference before this day. The names carved into the stone had been just that, names. People who had lived long before him, people that he had not known. But it was now Peregrine's place of eternal rest, and the vicar prayed for Peregrine and the family he left behind during this private burial.

When it came time to leave, the vicar, Cecily and Susanna walked on ahead, back towards through the estate and up to the house. Jack lingered behind, and Adam elected to stay with him.

Considering it was late December, it was an unusually sunny day. Though there was a chill in the air, the sun was just warm enough to melt the snow and leave a glistening dew across the expansive lawns.

Adam could see the anguish in his brother's face. Jack had been lost. He had been lost long before Peregrine had become ill, but now he was even more so. Once again, Adam could see his brother teetering on the edge of that cliff.

"Jack," he murmured, looking briefly over his shoulder to see his mother, sister, and the vicar disappearing into the distance.

Jack absently kicked the ground, his dark hair falling into his eyes. But he didn't say anything. His lips were pressed into a firm line.

"Jack," said Adam again, his voice firmer. "Please."

"I don't have anything, Adam," uttered Jack. "My life isn't worth anything. I was born to be insurance. And you've inherited now. I'm not needed. Nobody needs me." Jack kicked the grass again, more aggressively this time.

Adam wished that Cecily had put more time, more effort, into forging a relationship with Jack. Adam understood why Jack frustrated their mother. Their parents had paid a fortune for Jack's education, and as a second son, he had been meant for the church. With so little room to move, Jack had rebelled. He did get into trouble. He made trouble more often than not, especially when he was at school. Jack knew what he didn't want to do, but he had no idea what would make him happy.

And so, Cecily had fixated on Jack's mistakes whenever they had been together, and it was no wonder they did not have a very loving relationship. Now Adam wondered if it was too late.

With direction, with a purpose, with a partner, Adam hoped that Jack could finally know what it was to feel content and fulfilled.

"That is ridiculous, and you know it," retorted Adam. "You are needed here, and you are worth everything to me."

Jack looked up at Adam and shook his head. "No, I'm not," he replied firmly. "I know you want to look after me. I know you worry about me. But I also know I'm about two mistakes from you looking at me like she does."

"Mother has changed," insisted Adam. He wouldn't have believed it, but Cecily had changed. "And I have certainly never treated you ill." He resented that.

Jack conceded, nodding. "No, you are right. That was unfair," he allowed. "Perhaps I'm just afraid that you will look at me like that one day, and I don't want you to be disappointed in me, too."

Adam breathed shakily. "I will never be disappointed in you, Jack. You don't know what I hope for you."

Jack grimaced, as though he didn't have that hope for himself. He could not look at Adam any longer, and he looked back at the family tomb. He swallowed loudly. "I have to leave," he decided. "I can't stay, but you knew this was coming."

Adam felt his heart sink even deeper, a feat which seemed impossible after how he'd felt at the service. "Where will you go?"

"London," replied Jack quickly.

Adam realised that this had clearly been on his mind a while. "What will you do?"

Jack was quiet for a moment. "I don't know. All I know is that I need to get away from this place. You heard what Father said. I need to be more than what I am ..."

Adam knew he couldn't stop Jack. He had been watching Jack struggle for months, and their father was right. Maybe ... maybe it would be best for Jack to go out on his own for a while. "When will you leave?"

"Well, that depends," replied Jack, finally turning back around. "When are you planning on marrying Grace?"

Chapter 30

Upon returning from the church, Grace felt very hollow. She grieved Peregrine, having come to know him as a jovial man as he faced his maker. To be in such pain, but to find such spirit, Grace admired him deeply. She grieved for Adam, too. She despaired at his pain, and for knowing it exactly.

What bothered her further was that she was once again wearing her mourning dress, the one she had worn to her own father's funeral. She only owned one gown, after all, and it felt truly awful to be wearing such a garment again.

Claire place the teapot on the table, and Grace poured a cup for herself, her mother, and for her sister. Peter had not attended the funeral as he was at the forge, and Jem had already escaped with his friends.

"Well, I must say, I thought the service was very dignified," remarked Mrs Denham. "Very befitting. I think the duke would have approved."

In coming to know Peregrine, Grace wondered if he would have preferred a joke or two. He did have a good sense of humour, a characteristic often buried when he had previously been around his wife.

"Are you acquainted with the duchess, Mama?" asked Claire as she sat down. "We could not help but notice how she received you."

Claire had asked the question that Grace had wondered herself. The duchess had only received one mourner in such a familiar way, and it had been Mrs Denham.

"But, of course, the duchess and I have made an effort to become acquainted," murmured Mrs Denham. "How would it be for our children to court without the mothers getting along?" She tsked dismissively.

"Well, I thank you, Mama," said Grace sincerely, running her fingers over the handle of her teacup. "Quarrelling with his mother over her behaviour is the last thing Adam needs at the moment." Especially as he took control of the estate. "He has enough to worry about." It has not escaped her notice throughout the service that Adam's head kept turning to look at his brother. "He is deeply worried about Jack."

"Poor Jack did indeed seem extremely distraught," agreed Mrs Denham, her brows furrowed with concern.

"Of course, he is distraught, Mama," chided Claire. "His father has just died. I think you will find we all appeared quite the same at dear Papa's funeral. I am certain the last thing Lord Jack or any of them need is gossip."

Mrs Denham frowned. "Mind your tongue, Claire," she snapped, and Claire shut her mouth.

But Grace knew Adam's concern was for more than Jack's grief. Jack had long felt out of place, at the very least, in that house. She wondered if ... would it be appropriate before she was wed ... to extend the hand of friendship? He would certainly be welcome. Though her nearest brother in age was a little young, there was no reason why, chaperoned, she and Claire could not keep him company.

And, perhaps, that might eliminate one of Adam's burdens.

Later that day, Mrs Denham retired to her sewing, and Grace and Claire started on the preparations for supper. Claire hummed as she chopped, and Grace enjoyed the sweet tune. As she watched Claire move about the kitchen, she could not help but feel grateful and relieved that she had abandoned her hopes of Arthur Slickson. Surely there was someone better, someone kinder, for Claire. She would be eighteen next year. She had plenty of time.

The girls were surprised by a knock at the door, late in the afternoon. They had not been expecting anyone, but Grace quietly hoped it was Adam. It would not be appropriate to visit the house while they were in such early, full mourning. She would only be able to ensure Adam was alright by him visiting her.

Grace quickly untied her apron and draped it over one of the dining chairs and went to the door. Sure enough, Adam stood outside, looking tired, forlorn ... but hopeful. Hope was certainly never a look that she would tire of. His hazel eyes warmed as he saw her, and he smiled, despite everything that had happened today.

"Might I come in?" he asked softly.

Grace nodded immediately before opening the door wider. Adam passed through the threshold into the entryway. Grace immediately stood up on her toes to fix her arms around Adam's neck. He met her instantly, bending down to her height and securing his arms around her waist. He stood up straight, taking Grace with him, and her legs dangled beneath her.

"How can I fix you?" Grace whispered, her lips just above Adam's left ear.

His grip tightened. "You cannot know how dearly I wanted to hold you today," he whispered back in return. "That is how you fix me."

A few moments later, Adam placed Grace gently back on the ground, but remained holding her hand, and together they walked into the small sitting room and sat together on the settee. Behind her, Grace heard Claire quietly abandon her cooking before creeping up the stairs to give them privacy.

"How are you?" Grace asked, knowing it a foolish question. She was asked the same question many times when her father had passed away and had hated answering it. The asker only wanted to hear one thing.

I am well. I am sad, but I will be alright.

But it was a lie.

Though know her role was reversed, Grace fully understood wanting to hear such things. She desperately wanted those things for Adam. She couldn't bear his pain.

"I feel quite numb to be honest," Adam replied. "I am happy that he is free from pain. Watching him suffer like that ... it was inhumane. But the moment he passed, all pain vanished, and I felt relief for the briefest of moments. But my sadness is selfish. My sadness is for me, my family, and what we now lack."

"Sadness is not selfish," she promised him vehemently. "It is natural. You have a gaping hole in your life that had been filled for a quarter of a century. You have a right to be sad about that."

Adam nodded acceptingly. "It grieves me also that I allowed my own pride to get in the way of being here when you went through the same thing. I let you do this alone."

Grace's face softened. "You weren't to know," she assured him.

"But I could have known, had I gotten over my own pride and written to you, begged you for another chance ..." Adam shook his head. "It will be the last time I ever leave you, Grace."

She heard his tone change. There was determination in his voice, and she sat up a little straighter.

"My father spoke to each of us before he passed, he told us what he hoped for us, he found the strength ... he told me what I already knew," Adam murmured. "His vision for my future was what I wanted for myself.

"Grace, I watched my father's illness take a year from his life every day, until finally there was nothing left. It taught me that one is not promised a lifetime, and it would be criminal to waste the days you do have when it can all be taken away.

"The first time I saw you, your hand was in the air, desperate to answer a question in the schoolroom. You had a blue ribbon in your hair, which I thought was the prettiest colour until you turned around to look at me and I saw your eyes."

Grace instinctively met Adam's gaze.

"Beautiful," he uttered. "My father allowed my siblings and I to attend the village school and little did he know that such a decision would change my life. You were my friend, and you quickly became my favourite person in the world. You made me happy. You showed me what childhood ought to be. And it seemed the most logical thing in the world that one day I would marry you.

"I loved you. I loved you as much as a boy of that age could love a girl. I never wanted to be parted from you. And when it came time, I made you a promise.

"When I think about time, about it being wasted, it makes me furious these twelve years we have been apart. But in returning to you, I have had the honour of getting to know the woman you have become. You are kind, you are selfless, and there is nothing that you would not do for your family. You are diligent and passionate, and perhaps the only woman that has been able to change my mother's first opinion. You have been a true friend to Susanna, and you are the eldest sibling I can only hope to be.

"I see everything I loved about you amplified as an adult. You are my favourite person, Grace, and I have been, am, and always will be, yours. I am in love with you, and that will never change."

Grace was frozen still, not daring to move in case she would wake herself up. This could not be a cruel, teasing dream. But her head wouldn't allow it, and her worries bubbled to the surface. "Adam," she whispered, her voice barely audible. "I love you ... but –"

"But?" interjected Adam, dread flooding his face.

Grace could feel her insides contorted. "You needn't fear losing me ... needn't tell me these beautiful things before you are ready. I understand that you need time ..."

"Oh, my darling," Adam breathed. "I have had nothing but time," he assured her. "I don't want to wait. I do not want to watch the time I could have with you pass me by." Adam reached inside his coat and produced a golden ring. Grace immediately recognised it. She had kept this ring for the best part of Adam's ownership. Only ... it looked smaller than she remembered.

Grace realised what was happening, and her heart leapt into a nervous, rapid hum. Adam was right. They had had nothing but time. Time to miss one another. Time to hate one another. And time to see that the life that they could have together was within their grasp. They only need take it.

"I told you that I would replace this with a feminine ring ... but every time I look at this, I know it belongs to you. So, I had your brother-in-law, Mr Ellis, re-size it. It fits your sister, so I hope your finger is about the same as hers." Adam held the signet right out in front of him, looking deeply into Grace's eyes. "I made you a promise once, and I intend to keep it. But I will make you another," he declared. "We will live a beautiful life. You will not live one day by my side doubting how I feel about you. I will cherish, love, and honour you above all. Grace Denham, will you do me the honour of becoming my wife?"

Every sad thought vanished as a smile of pure elation spread across Grace's face as she allowed Adam to slip his signet ring onto her wedding finger. It fit perfectly. "Yes!" she exclaimed, happy tear swimming in her eyes.

Adam smiled, too. A glorious smile, one that reached his eyes, and her already rapid heartbeat increased as he leant forward towards her, lowering his gaze momentarily before he closed his eyes and pressed his lips against hers.

Epilogue

September 1809

"I do not think we will be fastening these laces for much longer, Grace," remarked Ruby as she struggled to tighten Grace's corset to its usual size.

Grace exhaled as she placed her hands on her hips, knowing that Ruby was right. "It is still early," she replied. "Adam is desperate to sing the news at the top of his lungs. I expect after the wine at dinner this evening he will be running his mouth." Grace smirked as she shook her head.

She was with child, as confirmed several weeks ago by the doctor. Only Ruby and Adam knew. Ruby, who had been Grace's friend and confidante, was the only logical choice for Grace's lady's maid. It had helped her to settle in initially, in what was such a drastic change in situation.

Grace knew Adam was anxious for a son. He would, of course, adore a new daughter, but a son, she knew, would make him so happy. Grace was about three months along, according to the doctor. He estimated that she would give birth in March.

No sooner had the idea crossed her mind, a wave of nausea hit her, and Grace abandoned Ruby for her chamber pot, emptying her stomach into it. "Oh," she complained. "I hate this part."

Grace felt Ruby's comforting hands on her back. "Get through today," she encouraged. "Then you can excuse yourself from everything for the next week and lie abed."

Grace chuckled even though she had a vile taste in her mouth. Ruby was right. Today was an important day for a multitude of reasons. She needed to get past the nausea in order to ensure that everything ran smoothly.

Becoming the Duchess of Ashwood had been a cruel learning curve. After becoming engaged shortly after Peregrine's funeral, Adam had not wanted to wait. Neither had Grace. They were wed on the first of January, privately, with only their families and the vicar in attendance. A small reception, once again, only for family, was given at Ashwood House, and Grace became the duchess. There was no ball as would not be appropriate. There were no public celebrations. The marriage was put into the papers, and Grace had naïvely thought that they might receive notes of congratulations.

Grace had never been the centre of gossip before. And for a time, her name seemed to be the one on everyone's lips. Who was this Grace Denham? How had she managed to secure one of the most eligible bachelors in England? What made things worse was that Lady Ashley seemed to be one of the gossip monger's fuelling the flames in London. Her daughter had been spurned for the help! Grace Denham was nought but a servant!

The opinion of every single society member had already been formed by the time that Grace had been introduced into society that June. And it would have been a complete disaster had it not been for Cecily. Despite their differences, and despite her efforts to separate them in the past, Cecily had well and truly taken Grace under her wing in her first year as the Duchess of Ashwood.

She taught Grace how to speak her mind without speaking it, how to operate within a ballroom, how to let a foe know that she had not won. She helped Grace to walk, talk, dance with confidence, to believe that she belonged in that room when everyone thought otherwise. If they couldn't affect you, couldn't control you, couldn't manipulate you, then their time was better spent elsewhere.

While Grace learned how to ignore the Lady Ashleys of society, she truly did settle in at home. Gossip could not change her nature, and her new position gave her such opportunities to engage with the people who relied upon the Ashwood Estate. These were the people who knew her and could think back to the days when Grace and Adam would run about as children. Grace quickly gained a reputation for being a doting and charitable duchess, and in knowing the people who mattered understood her, she could sleep well at night.

Despite her mother's vicious attempts to smear her name, Grace wrote to Sarah. She had wanted to apologise, to mend any residual ill will between them. Of course, Grace never thought poorly of Sarah, but there had been dishonesty. What became of that letter was friendly correspondence between the two ladies. Unlike her mother, Sarah did not resent Grace or Adam. While she had been initially heart-broken, or so she had thought, time had quickly healed those wounds, and she was ready to be romanced again. The following Season, she became engaged to a marquess, which had to please Lady Ashley. If it didn't, Sarah never alluded to it in her letters. As of her last letter, Sarah was nearing the end of her first pregnancy. Grace expected to hear of her child's birth the next time Sarah wrote.

Ruby finished helping Grace dress, and together, they left Grace's bedroom. The bedroom she and Adam shared had once been Cecily's. Adam couldn't live in the room where his father had passed away, and Grace completely understood that. Cecily had moved into the bedroom beside Susanna. While usually, a widow left the home of her husband, Adam wouldn't hear of it.

Grace and Ruby entered into the servant's staircase and descended down to the kitchen. It was a path she had once known well, and it still felt odd to have the people she had once dined with bow to her.

What was even stranger, and oddly frustrating, was that they would call her Your Grace, but not Grace. Mrs Hayes was the only one, aside from Ruby, to oblige Grace's request, and that was because Adam could talk his childhood nanny into anything.

The kitchen smelled divine, sweet, and of baking. The minute Grace was noticed, all preparations halted for polite, proper greetings and curtseys. In the centre of the kitchen bench was a three-tier cake, which looked perfect, completely covered in ornate flowers made of sugar.

"Mrs Reynolds!" exclaimed Grace, clapping her hands together and gasping. "Why, it looks beautiful!"

Mrs Reynolds smiled proudly. "I am pleased you like it, Your Grace," she replied. "But will Milady approve?"

Grace laughed knowingly. "You know Milady devours anything of your creating, Mrs Reynolds." Grace quickly inspected the other sweets, biscuits, puddings, and cakes, before she and Ruby quickly ascended up to the dining room.

Both Mrs Hayes and Mr Cole were in the dining room, ordering servants about as they set up for the party. Flowers were being arranged, furniture was being moved to accommodate gatherings, and refreshments were being organised. Grace and Ruby exchanged a smile as they observed that everything was under control.

Everyone knew how important today was.

"Pardon me, Your Grace," said one of the footmen from the doorway of the dining room. "Mr Cole, the Denhams are arriving."

Grace beamed as she raced out into the entry foyer ahead of Mr Cole, pulling open the front door to see her family's carriage approaching the house. The carriage had been a Christmas present the year before last. A necessity, really, as walking for extended periods of time was quite impossible for Mrs Denham. The break in her leg never seemed to heal properly, and so she relied on a cane.

Adam had offered rooms for Mrs Denham, Claire, Peter and Jem in Ashwood House once, but Mrs Denham had refused. She was not a prideful woman, only independent, and she preferred to live in the home that she had shared with her husband. The carriage was a thoughtful gift, and whenever she wanted to use it, Jim Ellis would always loan her the horses.

Ashwood footmen immediately went to the carriage to let the steps down. Peter quickly jumped out before assisting their mother. Grace saw Peter at least three times a week, and it never ceased to surprise her at how quickly he was becoming a man. He had recently turned eighteen and was very much a young man. He was strong, and he worked hard every day. Mrs Denham leant on her cane as fifteen-year-old Jem climbed out behind her. Jim, Kate, and their newborn son, James, completed the party.

Claire was nowhere to be seen. Grace frowned. Claire would certainly not miss today. Where was she?

Her family climbed the steps up to the front door, and Grace greeted every one of them with a hug and a kiss on the cheek.

'Thank you, thank you for coming," she told each of them. "But where is Claire?"

Mrs Denham huffed. "She will be along," she promised. "Something about the light ... she insisted we go on ahead."

Today? In the last few years, as the Denhams had gained some financial independence as Mrs Denham was not so heavily reliant on Claire as she could now afford a maid, Claire had taken to discovering pastimes that she had not previously been able to try. Painting, of all things, was what she enjoyed most. She often took herself off on nice days to capture a landscape.

"Well, so long as she is not late. The guests will be arriving soon," replied Grace. "Please, come in, come in." She ushered her family inside the house, where footmen were prepared to take their coats and hats.

Grace settled her family in the drawing room with refreshments, before taking her mother and Kate upstairs. As she ascended, Grace felt another wave of nausea, and had to stop, bracing herself by holding the banister, which immediately drew the concern of Mrs Denham and Kate.

"I am fine, really," she promised.

"Grace, you do look pale. Are you ill?" worried Mrs Denham.

Grace shook her head. "No, no. I just haven't eaten is all. I am a little lightheaded. Come on," she urged.

Grace could hear bickering before she even opened the door, and she tensed. She did not want fighting today. She did not want anyone in a bad mood today. Much time and effort had gone into their plans and a fight would not spoil it.

She quickly opened the door to the nursery, ready to intervene in whatever the argument was, when she was presented with a rather amusing scene.

"For goodness' sake, Adam," Cecily chided grumpily. "Blue!" she cried.

"Mother, I think I am quite capable of choosing a ribbon!" snapped Adam, comb and ribbon in his hand. "Pink!"

"Susanna, help me," Cecily demanded, motioning to Susanna, who was sitting in the rocking chair trying not to laugh. "For how many years did we hear about cornflower blue, and here I go to the effort of securing such ribbon to go with the darling dress and he wants pink."

Grace had discovered she was pregnant with her and Adam's first child two months after they had married. Both she and Adam had vehemently believed that she was having a son. Grace had felt it and was sure. She had been six months along during her first season in London which had only encouraged gossip about their reason for marrying, but both she and Adam knew that everything was done right.

The name they had chosen for their son seemed only right. Their son would be named for both of their beloved fathers. Peregrine Edward. The baby in her belly had been called Peregrine for months up until the birth. When their baby was born, and announced to be a girl, Grace had been shocked. She had felt so certain. Adam, however, was the proudest that Grace had ever seen him. Not for one moment did he feel disappointment in the sex of their child. Which was why she knew that if their next child was a girl, she would certainly be a lucky one.

When it came time to name their daughter, no other name seemed right after being called Peregrine Edward for so long. She was christened Peregrine Edwardia Beresford and was affectionately known as Perrie.

Perrie was seated on the small stool in front of her mirror, watching her father and grandmother bicker with an amused expression on her face. Perrie greatly favoured Grace, with large, beautiful blue eyes, and thick tufts of dark hair, though its curls could be attributed to her father.

Today was Perrie's second birthday, and a large party was being given. Ordinarily, Grace would have never gone to such a fuss. She would have much preferred a tea party, or a picnic outdoors with their family. However, they were expecting an addition to their party today.

Shortly after their wedding, Jack had left Ashwood. It was difficult for Adam, terribly so, to be so happy, and yet so hurt. They all understood Jack's need to go. He was lost, and need-ed direction and purpose, and he couldn't find those things at Ashwood. Owing to London being a thirty-mile journey, Adam did travel as often as he could to see his brother.

For a long while, Jack continued on with his bad habits. He drank. He spent time with women. He lost his temper. And he had no desire to return home. Jack spent his time reading when he wasn't in clubs, and his life had not changed much at all, according to Adam. This made him worry even more.

The change of scenery hadn't been the solution that Jack had hoped for.

But whatever his reluctance, Adam had managed to con-vince Jack to return to Ashwood for Perrie's second birthday, so that he might finally meet his niece. A grand party meant a lesser chance at interrogation, and Grace hoped that if all went well, Jack might be encouraged to stay.

"Oh, the blue will look darling on her!" exclaimed Mrs Den-ham as she made her way over to Perrie to place a kiss on top of her head.

"Thank you, Mrs Denham! At last, someone sees sense!" Cecily cried.

"What do you want, darling?" asked Adam of Perrie. "Blue," he said distastefully, picking up the blue ribbon from the dressing table, "or pink?" he encouraged.

"Pink!" cried Perrie, picking up on Adam's tone.

"There you have it," Adam declared, as he abandoned the blue ribbon and began to comb Perrie's hair back neatly.

Cecily scoffed and rolled her eyes. Grace almost wanted to give Cecily her way, but she hoped something as silly as a ribbon wouldn't spoil her mood.

Adam loved spending every bit of time he could with Perrie, particularly because his work kept him shut up for hours. He liked to take over the jobs usually reserved for servants, such as dressing and hair, and he and Perrie had started their own little routines because of it. Of course, Perrie's hair often looked a little lopsided, but Adam was definitely improving as her hair grew longer.

Watching them together often made Grace feel truly lucky, truly glad that what had transpired had brought them to this. Whatever time that they had been afraid of losing, or having lost, didn't matter anymore.

The bow Adam tied was actually quite neat, Grace thought proudly. Once Perrie was ready, the guests began to arrive, and the hum of noise throughout the house was busy. Perrie was disinterested in the conversation of adults and was instead occupied in the drawing room with several of the other village children.

"Adam," Grace whispered.

"What is it?" he replied, whispering back. They both smiled and nodded as they passed their guests.

"Adam, I am going to be sick!" A powerful wave of nausea hit Grace again, and she thought she might faint. Adam thought quickly, all but sweeping Grace inside the servant's staircase, and collecting a vase that had been displayed on a pedestal as he moved. As soon as they were behind the door, Grace threw up into the vase, not caring in that moment how much the piece of pottery was worth.

"I am so sorry," he uttered sympathetically.

Grace closed her eyes as she waited for the nausea to pass.

"I can make your excuses if you want to go up to bed," he offered.

Grace shook her head. "No," she breathed. "I want to be here when Jack arrives ..."

Thankfully, as with most of the nausea she felt, it passed, though it would be back. When she was certain it was gone, Grace looked up into Adam's eyes, and was met with an expression of guilty concern. "Don't worry about me," she urged.

"How can I not?" he countered. "I don't like to see you ill. Particularly when it is my fault."

Grace grinned. "Then you had better pray it is a son, for I shall not be this way again," she murmured jokingly, forcing Adam to smile.

He chuckled, before kissing Grace's forehead. "Selfishly, though, you know how excited I am. I think that adds to my guilt."

"I am excited, too," she promised. "Why ... why don't we tell everyone this evening?" she suggested. "After the guests go, when it is just our family. Hopefully the celebration will prevent your mother from saying anything ..."

"Good idea," agreed Adam, "though I have warned Mother already, but you know what she is like."

After cleaning the vase, Adam and Grace re-joined the party as though nothing had happened. It was not a party of aristocracy members, but friends, neighbours, and villagers, invited to celebrate Perrie. This was the sort of company that Grace was most comfortable in.

Grace was still a little lightheaded, as kept hold of Adam's arm for support, but she thankfully did not experience another wave of violent nausea for a while. As they spoke with the vicar, Grace could have sworn that she felt a fluttering of movement in her belly, no more than what she imagined butterflies to feel like. No sooner had a broad smile spread across her face, Grace noticed Claire entering into the dining room.

She tensed immediately, and Adam promptly responded to her rigidity.

"What is it?" he uttered. "Do you need to be sick?"

Grace shook her head. Claire was ashen. As pale as she had ever been, all blood gone from her face. She looked to be in complete shock. Grace nearly leapt over the dining table to reach her, latching onto Claire's arm as Adam hurried behind her.

"Claire!" she exclaimed. "What is it? What's wrong? You look like you have seen a ghost!"

Claire's wide, blue eyes were frightened, and her lips parted wordlessly.

At that moment, they heard an announcement from the
front foyer.

"Lord Jack Beresford has arrived!"